AUG   2006

Putting Lipstick on a Pig

Also by Michael Bowen
Screenscam
Unforced Error

Putting Lipstick on a Pig

Michael Bowen

Poisoned Pen Press

Poisoned Pen Press
6962 E. First Ave., Ste. 103
Scottsdale, AZ 85251
www.poisonedpenpress.com
info@poisonedpenpress.com

Printed in the United States of America

For JHB, with deep affection and, as always, high hopes.

Author's Note

In Vietnamese culture, a person's family name comes first and his or her given name second. Thus, if Mr. and Mrs. Duong have a son and name him Nguyen, he is known as Duong Nguyen. Vietnamese who emigrate to western countries adapt to the different naming conventions prevailing there in a variety of ways. Some simply retain their Vietnamese names without change: Xu Ky continues to be Xu Ky. Some (for themselves or their children) anglicize the Vietnamese name: Xu Ky becomes Sue Key. And some retain their Vietnamese given name as their family name and anglicize their Vietnamese family name: Duong Nguyen becomes Don Nguyen.

Chapter One

The instinct for justice is rooted so deeply in the human soul that even the finest law schools can't eradicate it entirely. Not quite two years after MacKenzie Stewart's phone call, Rep Pennyworth would find that noble truth highly inconvenient.

"Reppert, I'm calling with bad news," was how the call started. "Vance Hayes is dead."

"What's the bad news?"

This wasn't a joke and Stewart didn't laugh.

"He tabbed you for the eulogy," Stewart explained in his chiseled voice with patrician *gravitas*. "Last time we updated his estate plan, after the diabetes hit."

"That bastard," Rep muttered.

"*In re:* Hayes, 'bastard' has already been done. Try to come up with something a bit fresher for the eulogy. *In causa mortis* and all that."

In causa mortis—in contemplation of death. Requests made with the River Styx lapping at your wingtips and Charon's barge looming into view command special deference.

"They must have caught the diabetes very late," Rep said. "I didn't think it was terminal as long as you took care of it."

"The diabetes didn't kill him," Stewart said. "He took a small hours snowmobile ride over something called Lake Delton in Wisconsin Dells. Three sheets to the wind, left the snowmobile, hit a weak spot in the ice, and plunged through. It took them two full days just to fish his body out."

"I don't suppose you could say no?" Melissa Seton Pennyworth frowned when her husband gave her the news. "Considering that Hayes tried to destroy your legal career and everything?"

"Some Indiana lawyer has to give the eulogy, and Hayes did something nasty to every attorney who crossed his path."

"You're a saint," she said, kissing him on the forehead.

"Or a wimp."

"I exclude wimp *a priori*, without consideration of any evidence."

"Your dogmatism is charming."

"I know Ken Stewart has sent you some nice trademark work, but I'll bet a lot of lawyers would have refused anyway."

"Stewart is the one who saved my bacon on the complaint Hayes filed against me with the bar disciplinary committee. That was before Hayes took his trust and estate work to Stewart, so he didn't have to recuse himself."

"I didn't think it was that close a question," Melissa said. "All you did was take a deposition when Hayes didn't show up. It wasn't your fault that he didn't bother to open his mail and read the deposition notice."

"Hayes denied ever getting the notice, although our file said it was properly served," Rep said. "They could have spun it Hayes' way if they'd wanted to. The gentlemanly thing for me to do when Hayes didn't appear and didn't answer my phone call would have been to postpone the deposition. But law firms pay second-year associates for zeal, not manners."

"And Stewart was the one who precluded the unpleasantness and expense of a full-scale inquiry?"

"The way the story came to me, staff counsel summarized Hayes' complaint for the disciplinary committee. Everyone waited for Stewart's comment, because he was the senior member. His reaction was what the *New York Times* bashfully calls a 'barnyard obscenity.'"

"Two earthy syllables that combine rustic elegance with Midwestern resonance?" Melissa guessed.

"An ear-witness told me that Stewart said it with that genteel, old-money, Groton-Yale-Virginia Law School *éclat* that no one does better than MacKenzie (please call me Ken) Stewart. Sort of like the *Upstairs* half of a Masterpiece Theatre presentation. 'Bulllll*shit*,' with the voice going up a bit flippantly on the second syllable. Someone said, 'Second the motion,' and that was all she wrote."

"I see the impossibility of your position," Melissa said. "But can you come up with anything nicer than 'bullshit' to say about Hayes?"

"That will be a challenge. I've called Polly Allbright, the secretary who worked for Hayes for over thirty years."

"Devoted?"

"Hated his guts. I asked her if there was anything warm or human or decent he had done that I could talk about. She thought for about ten seconds, sighing audibly. Then she said, 'He let me smoke at my desk.'"

"Not terribly promising," Melissa said.

"On her thirty-fifth birthday he gave her a Piaget lighter, because he said he wanted her to be thinking of him sometime when she was happy."

"Well," Melissa sighed, "that's a start."

The game effort Rep made during the ten days it took to get Hayes' body back and finalize arrangements didn't improve very much on that lame beginning. Former Hayes clients whom he managed to track down described the deceased as a soulless legal machine. Hayes' closest living relative told Rep that she had spoken to Cousin Vance once in the past nineteen years. An attorney who had litigated against Hayes said that if he thought there was the slightest risk of meeting Hayes in hell, he'd step up his church attendance.

Hayes' brother had died in Vietnam, and Rep thought he might use that to soften the edges of the caricature. But hundreds of thousands of Americans had lost loved ones in the Vietnam War without turning into bastards. In a sense, Rep had lost his own mother to the conflict.

Nine days later Rep was still poring through three manila folders worth of Hayes files. His legal pad held only thirty-seven words, none of them promising. Rep leafed again through the top folder. A bullying letter to a local bookstore threatening a class action unless he were given the Loyal Patron Discount despite his paltry actual purchases. Pamphlets from anti-tax organizations. Travel agency billing records. Three pages of—

Whoa. He turned back to the billing records. In the last twenty-two months of his life Hayes had made seven trips to Singapore, Hong Kong, and Bangkok—not obvious off-season destinations for an Indianapolis attorney with a bread-and-butter litigation practice. A tiny gleam of hope briefly flickered. *Something interesting? A late-blooming fascination with Eastern religion? An unsuspected taste for Southeast Asian art?*

The phone rang and Rep grabbed it.

"Hank Llewyellen, returning your call," the voice said briskly.

"Thanks for calling back." Rep recognized the name of a lawyer who years before had managed to last eight months as Hayes' associate. "I'm looking for something decent I can say about Vance Hayes for his eulogy."

"Good luck. Can't help. Goodbye."

The next day, Rep fell flat on his face before the eighty members of the Indiana bar who bothered to appear in one of the courtrooms where Hayes had browbeaten scores of witnesses. After twelve minutes of thudding and leaden banalities he abandoned the lectern to damn-with-faint-praise applause, wondering if Hayes himself wouldn't have preferred that Rep offer instead several examples of the small-minded pettifoggery and mean-spirited malice that had studded his career.

"I'm surprised you didn't mention the *Leopold* order," Allbright said, to Rep's mystification, when she bumped into him on the way out. "But I guess you can't put lipstick on a pig."

Rep found little consolation in the well-meant (if baffling) comment, and still less in the reassurance Stewart offered him on the way to the cemetery.

"No one could have surpassed the presentation you gave," Stewart said as his Chrysler Imperial joined the funeral procession.

"That's the most elegant D-plus I've ever gotten."

"You have to play the cards you're dealt." Stewart shrugged. "Your task would have been challenging under any circumstances, but the existential absurdity of the way he died made it impossible. A plunge through thin ice during a midnight joy ride, with Jim Beam as accessory before the fact. It was as if Hitler had been run over by a bus. You were like a Greek chorus pushed on-stage during a French farce."

"You're right. He died in Nunn Bush dress shoes and a Brooks Brothers sport coat, with a shoehorn in one pocket and nine thousand soggy dollars in another. As accidents go, it was absurd."

"And suicides aren't terribly useful eulogy material."

"Suicide?" Rep asked in surprise. "Drowning yourself in icy water seems like a pretty complicated and unpleasant way to take your own life."

"Not conscious suicide, maybe," Stewart said. "Hayes hated the idea of living with diabetes while he played out his string. The police report computed his blood-alcohol level that night at point-oh-nine—legally drunk. In that condition he sometimes tended to pull off-the-wall stunts, death defying in the literal sense—challenging Death to come dance with him if it dared."

"The wrong guy gave this eulogy," Rep said. "That was better than anything I managed."

Rep didn't buy "legally drunk." He remembered Hayes at half-a-dozen Judges' Night receptions and State Bar Convention cocktail parties. Hulking, leather-skinned, owl-eyed, all but bald, two hundred thirty pounds of muscle, bluster, and bad manners, downing a Jack Daniels neat, immediately ordering another, and telling the bartender to have a "traveler" ready for when the chimes summoned everyone to dinner. In a Wisconsin police report, Vance Hayes with a point-oh-nine blood-alcohol level was legally drunk because a statute said so. But in real life Vance Hayes at point-oh-nine was stone cold sober and meaner than a New Orleans madam on the first Friday of Lent.

Twenty-five minutes later, Rep watched as Hayes' mortal remains were consigned to the dreamless dust. Watched junior ROTC cadets present arms and expertly fold the flag that had draped the coffin. Heard "Taps" played on a boombox, buglers being hard to come by these days. Watched the funeral party straggle uncertainly away.

Nagging at the back of his brain was a pesky whisper that something was wrong, some detail a bit off. But he brusquely expelled the notion from his disciplined mind. Not because the cold or the emotion of the day distracted him. He just didn't care. He'd failed and he wished he hadn't, but now it was over and he just didn't care.

October 2005
Milwaukee, Wisconsin

Chapter Two

"The thing is, I've never smoked a cigarette in my life," Sue Key told Rep, adding after a minute's pause, "You look skeptical."

"I'm a lawyer. I woke up this morning looking skeptical."

"Cross my heart," the young woman said, a grin splitting her almond face as she gave the pie-crust curls of her black hair a little shake. "Not even the experimental puffs in eighth grade that everyone supposedly has to see what it's like. I took a hit on a boyfriend's cigar once to be a good sport, but never a cigarette. Even when I tried pot I used a little pipe thingy."

Rep flipped back to the cover of the calendar that Key had brought him. *Pretty Girls Smoking Cigarettes* waltzed in friendly blue and white letters across the shiny, eleven-by-fourteen-inch sheet. Full-page, four-color photographs above each page of dates inside delivered twelve months of posed variations on that theme. Comely ski bunnies contentedly sharing menthols in front of a snow-frosted chalet window for January 2004. Sultry, pouting debutantes in evening gowns smoking languidly on the terrace of some generic country club for April. A radiant bride beaming as she and her bridesmaids relaxed with filter-tips for

June. Cute coeds puffing Ultra Light 100s amid their textbooks in a coffeehouse for September. All the way to smiling chums in Santa hats smoking under the mistletoe for December. People had apparently been willing to pay—what? Rep checked the back—nine-ninety-five for this.

He turned back to July. Three women who looked like they were in their early twenties sat at a weathered picnic table, implausibly ignoring a spectacular fireworks display bursting across the night sky behind them. Like most of the others, they shared the artless prettiness of youth, but with some un-model-like meat on their bones and makeup well short of perfect.

The blonde on the right side of the picture, a cigarette dangling insouciantly from the center of her lips, leaned across the table to offer a light to a chestnut-haired table-mate on the left side. Between them sat a woman whose jet black, piecrust-curled hair framed an almond-colored face with Asian features. Leaning back as she laughed at something, resting her right elbow on the table, she held a cigarette in her right hand, near her cheekbone.

"This certainly looks like you," Rep said to Key.

"It is. The picture was taken in broad daylight in Cathedral Square. They must have put the background in later."

"Do you know who took it?"

"I don't know the photographer's name." She handed him a twice-folded sheet of photocopier paper. "The check came from a company called Cold Coast Productions. This guy just came over and said he was doing pictures of Milwaukee scenes and that if it was published we'd get twenty-five dollars each. He asked us to fill out what he called a release with our names and addresses and then sign it."

"Did you?"

"Sure. It seemed like a lark. I mean I was thinking, like, *Milwaukee Magazine* or *North Shore Lifestyle* or something local like that."

"Okay," said Rep. "You knew the picture might be published, you gave written permission for it to be published, and you accepted payment for publication. What you didn't know was that they'd alter the picture to make it look like you were smoking."

"Exactly."

"And you object to that?"

"Well, sort of, I guess. It kind of bothers me."

"I can certainly understand it bothering you," Rep said, trying to draw Key out without actually coaching her. "Smoking is stigmatized as a loser habit these days."

"No, that isn't quite it." Another ingenuous smile. "I mean, I don't think like, Lindsay Lohan and Katie Holmes are losers. Or Wanda and Sharon, the two other women in the picture. To me it's just a personal preference type thing. But it's sort of like the gay episode that time on *Seinfeld*, you know, the 'not-that-there's-any-problem-with-that' one? I don't have any problem with smoking, but I don't happen to smoke. And then there's my mother."

"Ah. Childhood taboos."

Wrong again.

"My mother came here from Vietnam before I was born," Key said, shaking her head. "I visit her at home for tea almost every Sunday. She's an assistant liturgical director—you know?"

Rep shook his head.

"Someone who helps organize the services at a Catholic church. Conservative Catholics call them 'weapons of Mass destruction.' Anyway, she always has a cigarette, and if she thought I smoked she'd expect me to have one with her. So she'd be hurt that I don't."

At this point a resonant if not melodic baritone penetrated the wall separating Rep's office from the reception area:

> "*Will everyone here*
> *Kindly step to the rear*
> *And let a winner lead the way?*
> *Here's where we separate*
>   *the men from the boys,*
>   *the news from the noise,*
>   *the…the the the the….* Nuts."

Determined steps shook the floorboards, and three seconds later Rep's door opened. The head that burst through was male and thinly provided with gallant tufts of once blond and now graying hair.

"Counselor, what comes after 'news from the noise'?"

"'Rose from the poison ivy,'" Rep said.

"That's it!

> *Here's where we separate*
> *the men from the boys,*
> *the news from the noise,*
> *the rose from the poison ivy.*"

"The hearing went well, I take it?" Rep said.

"Motion granted in full. Costs to abide the event, but that's the way it is in the Milwaukee County Circuit Court. No one's rice bowl gets broken—not even insurance defense lawyers."

The singer came all the way into the office and extended his hand to Key.

"I'm Walt Kuchinski," he said, towering over the young woman who, at five-six, was only three inches shorter than Rep. "You'd be Sue Key, I'm guessing. Reppert here treating you right?"

Guessing? Rep thought. *You referred her to me, remember?*

Key confirmed her name and the high quality of Rep's services, although as far as Rep could see he had so far accomplished roughly nothing.

"Well, he's the man for this picture stuff you told me about on the phone. Anyone ever accuses me of knowing anything about intellectual property law, I'm gonna plead not guilty. 'Til I met Rep here I always thought IP lawyers were guys who wore bowties and drank Lite beer."

"Please imagine a little circle-r registered trademark symbol after 'Lite' in that last sentence," Rep said, adjusting his bowtie.

"But Reppert here can tell Leinenkugel from Miller Genuine Draft blindfolded, and he knows more obscure Broadway show tunes than any straight guy I've ever met. He'll get it done for you."

Exit Kuchinski, who waited until he'd closed the door behind him before he started singing, "*Weeee are the CHAMPions, my friend.*"

"Is he, like, your partner?" Key asked in a vaguely over-whelmed voice.

"More like my landlord," Rep said. "I'm with a law firm in Indianapolis. It's thinking about opening an office here in Milwaukee. Mr. Kuchinski has been kind enough to let me share office space with him while I look into it."

This was wholly true, but not the whole truth. The whole truth was that Melissa Seton Pennyworth, Ph.D., she of the green-flecked brown eyes with the minxish glint and the dogmatic attitude about her husband's sterling qualities, had secured a tenure-track assistant professorship at the University of Wisconsin-Milwaukee. (That is, *not* the Big Ten school in Madison but its blue-collar second cousin.) Rep had no inten-tion of being separated from Melissa for long by farther than he could conveniently drive a Mercury Sable. So he had pitched the management committee on the marketing *cachet* of having a branch office in Milwaukee—as if they'd have a better shot at Chicago business if they could come at it from two sides at once. His partners, who on the whole weren't stupid, had pointed out that this was perfectly insane. They didn't want to lose him, though, so they'd gamely allowed him to come up and test the waters on the cheap, hoping that he'd get this nonsense out of his system and come back to Indianapolis before he'd spent too much money.

Rep knew by now that he shouldn't even be thinking about taking Sue Key's case. He had to show his partners that he could find Wisconsin clients who'd pay six figures a year for trademark and copyright work. The only way billings to Sue Key would reach six figures would be if you counted on both sides of the decimal.

"If we were to go forward with this," he said to Key, "what would you want me to accomplish for you?"

"All I really want is for Cold Coast to admit that the picture is faked. And enough money to cover your fee, I guess."

Opening her purse, she took out a cylinder of currency with a rubber band around it. She slipped off the rubber band and began painstakingly spreading money out on Rep's desk: three hundred-dollar bills, four fifties, eight twenties, six tens and six fives.

"It's seven hundred fifty dollars," she said. "I know the retainer is usually a thousand, but I have most of the money I've saved tied up in six-month certificates of deposit. So I was kind of hoping you could sort of get started with just this."

Rep, in his mid-thirties and with three years of partnership behind him, had yet to accept a retainer of less than five thousand dollars. As Key laid the money out, though, he saw callouses on her fingertips. He'd deposed a witness or two when he was so young that litigators could tell him what to do, and he had a rough idea of how many keystrokes it took for this young woman to generate the modest collection of bills in front of him.

Unbidden, the creative side of his brain started to generate some respectable arguments. *Hey, this is a new office, looking for business. Court reporters know lawyers, and lawyers refer cases.*

"Where did you get Mr. Kuchinski's name when you were looking for a lawyer?"

"Actually," Key said, digging yet again in her purse, "I got it from my mother. I mentioned to her after I got the calendar that I thought I might want to talk to a lawyer about something, and she dug out this letter for me."

Dated December 3, 2003, the letter was addressed to Ms. Xu Ky:

Dear Ms. Ky:

   I have had occasion several times in the past to provide you with legal services on matters of concern to you. I do not know how much longer I will be able to do this. Accordingly, I thought it prudent to advise you of an alternative source of counsel in the event you found it impossible to reach me. I suggest that you call Walter Kuchinski, Esq., in Milwaukee, describe the problem (whatever it may be), and ask him to recommend an attorney to handle it.

Sincerely,
Vance Hayes

Chapter Three

When Pelham Dreyfus saw the Valkyrie pulling her turquoise Bic out at three minutes past four he figured the highlight of his day was coming up. The blond coed, pausing with a clutch of classmates on the south side of Wisconsin Avenue, bowed her head and cupped her left hand around the tip of a Marlboro to light it. When she took the cigarette from her mouth and blew a plume of smoke over her shoulder, she had an I'm-eighteen-and-I'm-gonna-live-forever grin on her face that it would've taken Dreyfus eighty shots to coax out of a professional model. Three hundred miles from Mom and Dad, just released from the last class on Friday in her freshman year at Marquette University, looking at a weekend in a city teeming with males who'd buy her a six-pack if she winked at them, her world at this moment was perfect.

Five-ten if she was an inch, lithe as a ballet dancer, and the only fat on her body exactly where it belonged. Young, cute, and *real*. Something you couldn't get from pros. Dreyfus caught it all at three digital frames per second from sixty feet away. With the ten-power optical zoom on his Sony DSC F828 digital camera he could have counted her nose hairs if he'd wanted to. He shook his head in silent wonder. Until he came to Milwaukee, he didn't even know God *made* blond Catholics.

If he really hustled he could make it out to Kopps Custard in Glendale for something younger and therefore even more appealing to the pathetic losers who religiously checked pretty-girlssmoking.com each day. Sophomore and junior coeds from Dominican and Nicolet High Schools would be smoking on the stone benches outside, showing boys the new trick they'd learned over the summer. Those could be mega-hits—something delicious about the shatteringly naïve poses, girl-women affecting blasé sophistication with Newports in one hand and chocolate malts in the other.

But he didn't have the nerve. The stiffs on the North Shore paid taxes with both hands. Cops in Glendale and Whitefish Bay didn't have much to worry about, and they'd be delighted to worry about Dreyfus if he gave them half a chance. Only one prior, but one was all it took if she was sixteen and you were twenty-three when it happened.

How did I come to this? he wondered in a flash of poignant self-pity. He should be on the coast right now, this very minute, shooting publicity stills for some R-rated feature. Or at Sundance, hustling indie producers on the way up and dodging groupies on the way down. Instead he was parked here at 16th and Wisconsin in Laverne-and-Shirley-land trying to pick up fresh web-site bait for guys so twisted they couldn't get off on regular, all-American porn.

◇◇◇

"At the risk of reinforcing gender stereotypes," Melissa said to Rep about two hours later, "does this make my fanny look too big?"

"Why don't you take that skirt off so I can make a fully informed judgment?"

"And make us late?"

"I'm just trying to avoid objectification of the female form."

"I know exactly what you're trying to do, tiger," Melissa said, pivoting athletically to plant a kiss on his ear, "but it's going to have to wait until we get back from this junior faculty wine and cheese reception. Faculty don't get any more junior than I am, so being late would be impolitic."

"We can't have that," Rep said. "It doesn't start until seven o'clock, though, and we're about ten minutes away. You'll have to spend another half-hour getting dressed to avoid being unfashionably early."

"As wound up as I am right now I could spend half-an-hour just picking out earrings."

"Are you too wound up for an off-the-wall question?"

"Actually," Melissa said, "an off-the-wall question would probably help."

"Would it bother you if someone faked a picture to show you smoking a cigarette?"

"You did say off-the-wall, didn't you?" Melissa flipped with practiced skill through a dozen earrings. "I guess it would depend. If someone caught me in a pose suggesting Virginia Woolf and then air-brushed in a cigarette for verisimilitude, I wouldn't mind that. Especially if it's the Hollywood version of Virginia Woolf, where she looks like Nicole Kidman."

"On the other hand," Rep prompted.

"On the other hand, if some smart-alec on the *UWM Post* used digital magic to make me look like I'm smoking in candid shots of tonight's event, that would lead to a short and unpleasant conversation."

"Because smoking just isn't done by junior faculty at events like that these days?"

"No, that's not really it." Melissa gave it a few moments' thought. She took one pair of earrings off, put the other on, and nodded slightly. "It's more that I just don't want someone else defining me."

"And you feel smoking habits are defining?"

"Absolutely," Melissa said. "When I was a teenager in the eighties, smoking was just a hint to boys that you might be a bit fast, without committing yourself to anything. For an adult today, though, my gut feeling is that it makes a very definite statement about yourself."

"I have the same gut feeling, but I'll need some footnotes if I'm going to do any good for my Sue Key." He told her about the case.

"You mean there's actually a market for calendars that just show women smoking, with all their clothes on and nothing naughty happening?" Melissa asked when he'd finished.

"Calendars, DVDs, videotapes, web sites. For twenty-nine-ninety-five you can buy a two-hour DVD of fifties and sixties cigarette commercials. For every guy who finds smoking repulsive, apparently there's one who finds it sultry and alluring."

"Maybe I should have tried harder to like it when I was sixteen," Melissa said. "Would you find it off-putting if I smoked cigarettes? Or would you find me sultry and alluring?"

"I wouldn't find you off-putting if you chewed tobacco, beloved. And nothing on earth could make you sultrier or more alluring than you already are."

"Wow. Was *that* ever a good answer."

"I need an answer that good for Cold Coast Productions. I've gotten their attention, but their basic position is that unless Sue Key is an OB/gyn or a member of a Southern Baptist church choir, it's no-harm/no-foul."

"Time to call in the litigators?"

"I can't afford to put any litigator in the firm on this case," Rep said, "including the kid we hired last week. But we'd better get going."

As they walked from the bedroom to the front door of the generic, single-bedroom, Maryland Avenue apartment that represented their first Milwaukee residence, Melissa glanced at the improvised card-table furnishings and half-open cardboard boxes that cluttered the living room/dining area. Rep had left a comfortable house in Indianapolis and a partner's office at an established firm to try wildcat lawyering in a new city. He was doing this for her, doing it so that she could take a shot at a solid academic position instead of becoming one of the credentialed serfs who haul their Ph.D.s from one second-rate fill-in lectureship to another, without time for serious research or any shot at tenure.

If Sue Key's case was Rep's problem, then it was her problem too.

When Pelham Dreyfus checked the new hits on prettygirlssmoking.com, he saw that the Valkyrie had come through already. Six hundred fifteen more visitors just since seven o'clock. Each of them would have seen pop-up ads for calendars and DVDs and photosets, and if experience were any guide at least eight percent of them would buy something. And any of the six hundred fifteen email addresses that weren't repeaters would go on lists that he could sell to other E-tailers for fifteen cents a hundred. The real money, though, lay in the credit card numbers he'd collect. Send the card-holders bogus emails supposedly coming from Ebay or their banks, fishing for their security codes and SSNs. Two or three out of every hundred would bite. Dreyfus would check them over to guard against cop-stings and then out-source the identity theft to someone he could trust to share the proceeds equitably.

Hey, he thought with a shrug, *it's a living.*

◇◇◇

"I actually learned something at this thing tonight," Melissa said to Rep as he showed her back into the apartment around ten-fifteen that night. "One of my colleagues is emailing me a presentation of his that might help Sue Key."

Twelve minutes later Rep and Melissa leaned over Melissa's laptop, looking at Burt Reynolds and Sally Fields in a scene from an early seventies movie called *Smokey and the Bandit.* "You smoke much?" Reynolds asked Fields. "I just started," she answered as she puffed haplessly on a Marlboro.

"I get it," Rep said. "Burt Reynolds as the Bandit is driving his super stock Trans-Am like a lunatic, and Sally Fields as the love interest is saying his maniacal driving is making her so nervous that she's taken up smoking on the spur of the moment to calm herself down. Not a bad little joke, but I'm not sure how it helps Sue Key."

"Subtext, munchkin mine. The nervous wreck isn't Sally Fields, it's Sally Fields' character. On the screen, though, we're seeing Sally Fields herself, not just her character."

"Right," Rep said. "Ten on a scale of ten. But so what?"

"Sally Fields spent the sixties on television, playing squeaky-clean, cute-as-a-button, all-American teenagers in shows called *Gidget* and *The Flying Nun*. In *Smokey and the Bandit* she didn't smoke just to set up a lame joke. It was a way of saying, 'I'm not a kid anymore.' Same thing with Melissa Gilbert when she moved on to adult roles."

"Melissa Gilbert smokes?" Rep demanded in anguished distress. "That sweet thing from *Little House on the Prairie*?"

"Sad but true."

"My last illusion is gone."

"You'll get over it."

"Okay," Rep said thoughtfully. "And so when Meg Ryan sort of halfway smoked in *Proof of Life*, looking like she could just barely stand it, she didn't do it just because her character was on edge about her husband being kidnapped. She was saying that, even after all those chick-flicks she starred in, she was nobody's sweetheart anymore."

"*Very* good," Melissa said. "Not quite be Ph.D. material, but you've definitely qualified for the senior honors seminar."

"In other words, we have solid empirical evidence to back up your intuition. Cigarettes have become character-defining. Smoking puts you in certain categories—not necessarily bad categories, but not categories you should be in against your will, either. Thank you, Doctor Pennyworth."

"Do I get to be an expert witness?"

"That depends. Let's get to the bedroom and discuss your qualifications."

Chapter Four

Nothing Rep had seen in walking through Cold Coast Productions' south Milwaukee facility prepared him for the conference room. Rep and Sue Key had entered the down-at-the-heels, red-brick building through a heavy metal door with mustard-colored paint chipping off of it. They had walked behind a crew-cut guy in a short-sleeved white shirt across a bleakly lit shop floor where an ancient web press commanded the attention of five older men—men whose faces immediately told Rep that he was on the wrong side of one of those us/them lines that guys in suits can't cross. Through another metal door, this one with a frosted glass window, up five flights of echoing metal stairs, through one more metal door, like the first two except for a pebbled steel surface and a fresher paint job. Past a warren of empty cubicles, over threadbare industrial gray carpeting to the conference room's double doors—wood, finally.

"In there," the guy said. "I'll let Mr. Levitan know you're here."

Past the doorway lay a different world, as if the rust-belt exterior were a reverse Potemkin Village. Rich odors of wax and old leather replaced the lubricant and burned metal smells permeating the floor below. Three tiers of bookshelves lined two of the walls. A polished mahogany table and leather chairs sat on parquet flooring.

The spine of a book a yard or so from Rep's face said *The Story of the Malakand Field Force*, by Winston Churchill. Next book: *The River War*, by Winston Churchill. Hmm. His eyes ranged one shelf over. *World Crisis* in four volumes, by Winston Churchill. *Marlborough, His Life and Times*, by Winston Churchill. *The Second World War* in six volumes, by Winston Churchill. *History of the English Speaking Peoples* in four volumes, by Winston Churchill. *The Last Lion*, by William Manchester, about Winston Churchill. Pelham's biography of Winston Churchill. Severance's biography of Winston Churchill. The eight-volume biography of Winston Churchill by Martin Gilbert and Randolph Churchill. *Churchill on the Home Front, 1900-1955*, by Paul Addison. *The Young Churchill*, by Celia Sandys. *Forged in War: Roosevelt, Churchill, and the Second World War*, by Warren Kimball.

"Miss Key, Mr. Pennyworth?" a gravelly baritone boomed from the doorway. "I'm Max Levitan. Welcome to Cold Coast Productions."

Levitan looked to Rep like he was just under six feet tall, and he had to be sixty years old. He wore a blue poplin work shirt, a pair of khaki slacks, and a baseball cap—blue with a red bill and a plain block M on the front—that Rep didn't recognize at first. After three or four seconds, it clicked. Braves. Not Atlanta. The Milwaukee Braves. A cap from some forty years in the past.

Levitan's handshake wasn't quite a bone-crusher, but Rep would still remember it when he went to bed that night. He felt odd lumps of scar tissue here and there, and at least one bone that he suspected had knit in a rough-and-ready way after a break.

They sat down. The moment Rep had been dreading approached. The great client let-down.

Melissa's pop-culture jetsam and professorial deconstruction had produced a settlement of Sue Key's claim. Rep needed only two business days to put a little lawyerly spin on the stuff, shine it up a bit, and make a deal. He thought he could have bluffed Cold Coast out of a bit more money, but clients get the last word on those decisions. When he'd told Key that Cold Coast's offer included a personal, face-to-face apology from the CEO himself, her thrilled squeal had signaled the end of negotiations.

Now she was about to hear a hollow, *pro forma* recitation of suit-speak that would never measure up to her stratospheric emotional expectations.

Levitan took off the Braves cap and cleared his throat.

"First of all, Miss Key, on behalf of Cold Coast Productions and myself personally, I want to express my deepest apology for this error in judgment." His eyes held hers and his head leaned in her direction as his expression appealed for understanding. "It should *not* have happened, and it *will not* happen again. To you or to anybody else. I give you my promise on that. I have had an unambiguous discussion with the person who doctored that photograph, and believe you me, there is *no* room for any future misunderstanding on this point."

"Thank you," Key said, bowing her head and fiddling with the top button on her pink sweater.

"As chief executive officer of Cold Coast Productions, I accept personal responsibility for this foul-up," Levitan continued. Rep sensed that he'd changed "screw-up" to "foul-up" at the last second to avoid offending Key. "I want to be sure the corrective measures we have taken meet with your complete satisfaction."

Opening a maroon leather portfolio that he'd carried into the room, he took out a compact disk and an eleven-by-fourteen inch white envelope and handed them to Key.

"The disk contains the original picture and all of the alterations that were made. In the envelope you'll find the print-proofs of the calendar page where your picture appears, and all the tear-sheets we could trace. I have no reason to believe that there are any more copies of that photograph anywhere in my company's files."

"Thank you," Key said again, her voice now church-pew quiet.

Levitan now took out six sheets of bond, stapled in the upper left-hand corner, and a letter-sized envelope. He turned toward Rep.

"This is the agreement that you sent over, which I have signed," he said, "including my written apology, and the certification that we have pulped all copies of the calendar that we could retrieve."

"Good," Rep said.

"And, of course, the check."

"Right." Five thousand dollars. Not exactly King of Torts money, but enough to cover the charges he'd booked plus a modest write-up, keep the bean-counters back in Indianapolis quiet, and bulk up Sue Key's savings account. Rep got the precious documents securely in his mitts.

"I very much appreciate your coming by so that we could bring appropriate closure to this unfortunate situation," Levitan said. "If you have half an hour or so, I'd be happy to show you around our facilities here."

"That would be wonderful," Key said, "but there's a transcript I need to get out by tomorrow morning."

"In that case," he said, rising, "I hope that we meet again soon under happier circumstances. I'll show you out."

"The library in that conference room is very impressive," Rep said when they were back on the metal steps. "It must have two hundred fifty volumes."

"Three hundred five," Levitan said.

"Are all of them by or about Winston Churchill?" Rep asked.

"Yes, but with a footnote. All but one are by or about Sir Winston Leonard Spencer Churchill, the British statesman. There's one Civil War story in there by an American novelist who also happened to be named Winston Churchill. I bought it by mistake, and it was such a laugh I decided to keep it."

"That's pretty single-minded," Rep said.

"Winston Churchill was the greatest man to live in the twentieth century," Levitan said. "He was the last English-speaking politician who was remotely interesting for anything he did outside of politics. Once I really knew Churchill's life, I couldn't work up much interest in anybody else's. Would you call that pathologically obsessive?"

"Not unless I were paid to," Rep said.

"Now, there's a guy I know has over a thousand books about Adolf Hitler. *That's* obsession. I mean, Hitler *lost*."

They had reached the bottom of the stairs. Rep noticed that, despite the speech, Levitan wasn't panting. They went back across the shop floor fringe, drawing the same wary/disgusted glances from the men working there. Levitan propped the door open with his shoulder as Rep and Key stepped outside. Instead of going back inside immediately he just stood there, as if reluctant to give up the Edenic lake breeze gently ruffling tufts of steel wool colored hair that showed under the edge of his baseball cap.

"You're new to Milwaukee, aren't you?" he said to Rep.

"Been here less than two months."

"This is a blue-collar town with blue-collar memories. Those guys in there used to be heroes. They're not anymore, but it's not their fault. They held up their end of the deal. They didn't turn the mightiest industrial machine on Earth into the rust belt. That was done by guys in suits."

Levitan stepped back inside and with metallic finality the door snapped shut behind him.

"Where's your car?" Rep asked his client.

"I took the bus over."

"Can I give you a ride back to your office?"

"Actually, could you take me to my flat over on College? I do most of my proofing and corrections there."

"How do I get there?" Rep asked as they slid into his Sable.

"Start by going west on KK." She caught Rep's blank look and grinned. "That's right, you just said you haven't been here long. KK is Kinnikinnick. Just turn left at the stop sign and we'll take it from there."

The trip took almost fifteen minutes, as they rolled past bungalows with life-size statutes of the Blessed Virgin in front, squat, six-unit apartment buildings, and postcard-sized lawns being worked by septuagenarians sweating through white tee-shirts and placidly puffing fat cigars. It seemed shorter to Rep because Key spent most of the quarter-hour telling him what a fabulous lawyer he was and how thrilled she felt and how if she *ever* had to put a legal dream-team together, he'd definitely be the captain.

She finally directed him to the curb in front of an upper/lower duplex whose covered-porch design screamed pre-World War II. It was trim and neat, though, with its wood frame freshly painted and a pale yellow stone foundation that Rep would remember when he later heard the term "Cream City Brick."

He didn't have long to savor these reveries. Before he had the ignition off, the unmistakably stentorian roar of a Harley Sportster motorcycle split the languid air. The cycle had just rounded the corner ahead of them. It growled down the block, skimmed elegantly across the street, and squealed to a stop fender to fender with Rep's Sable. The helmetless rider shook longish, coal-black hair away from his face, disclosing Asian features and almond-colored skin. Frowning in puzzled concentration, he stared through Rep's windshield for several seconds before his dark eyes flashed with recognition.

"Sis," the biker yelled then, "we got a problem."

Safe bet, Rep thought; for strapped to the storage compartment lid behind the bike's saddle he saw a calf-brown scabbard with a rifle butt sticking out of it.

Chapter Five

"Your apartment alarm went off," the biker panted as he pulled out the rifle. "Home-Protex couldn't reach you and called me."

"Why isn't it still going?" Key asked.

"They turn it off after ten minutes. It's taken me at least twice that to get over here."

"Skip the cannon," she told him. "I heard a siren."

"The siren was a toy on my Harley," the biker said, pulling a clip from the calf-pocket on his cargo pants and snapping it into the weapon. "Trying to scare them off. We won't see cops before lunch. You two stay here."

"I don't *think* so," Key responded jovially, falling into step behind the biker. "I can't lose face in front of my lawyer."

"Hasn't the alarm company called the police?" Rep asked Key.

"The police won't come until someone actually sees broken glass or something," Key explained. "They say less than five percent of home alarms come from actual break-ins. The only point of having one is to scare off juvies and maybe alert a neighbor."

"That's your brother with the rifle?"

"Half-brother. His name is Duong Van Nguyen. He goes by Don, but pronounce it carefully. Some guys think it's funny to call him 'Dong' but I don't know anyone who's done it more than once."

Nguyen by now had scampered up a stairway at the side of the duplex and reached the entrance to the upper unit. The screen door that Rep and Key could see from the bottom of the stairs looked intact, but the wooden door behind it gaped open and the glass in its upper half was shattered. As they hustled up the steps to follow Nguyen into the flat, Rep saw what looked like blood smears on the door frame.

"The bad guy is long gone," Nguyen called to them a minute later after he'd rattled through the upper floor with his rifle at port arms. "He made a mess, but I'm not sure he took anything."

The first room Key and Rep reached looked to Rep like the circle of hell a particularly vengeful deity obsessed with insider trading might have reserved for Martha Stewart. Hide-a-Bed, unhidden and unmade. Several days' worth of unsorted mail towering precariously atop a pinewood chest of drawers. X-Box Game Cube beside a tiny TV, Gateway laptop sitting open on the bed, multiple copies of *Sports Illustrated* and *Maxim* competing for floor space with empty pizza cartons, crushed beer cans, and sweat socks. A guy lived here.

"Your room?" Rep asked Nguyen, who shook his head.

"A slacker named Travis uses that one," Key said over her shoulder as she hurried down the hall. "I sublet it to him for half the rent."

As soon as she reached the doorway of the second room her piercingly indignant shriek split the flat.

"The mess the burglar made?" Rep asked Nguyen.

"Yeah."

Fearing the worst, Rep hustled to his client's side. Surprise and relief came as he spotted her stenographic recording machine and a Mac computer in a hot pink, translucent case sitting unmolested on Key's desk. When his gaze dropped, though, he saw what had provoked the shriek.

Reams of narrow stenographic paper, each piece two inches wide and six inches long, joined end to end in yards-long, awkward, snaking strips, littered the floor from the bed to the opposite wall. Testimony from what looked like a dozen hearings and depositions, recorded in the arcane purple symbols of the court reporter's trade, strewed the carpet with forensic litter.

On the far side of the room Rep saw a six-foot-high green metal cabinet with its doors flung open. The top two shelves were empty, but the two below them held steno paper just like that strewn over the floor, except that these were stacked in neat, rectangular blocks, boldly dated in felt-tip at their ends and with the names of witnesses on their top sheets.

Key snapped open her cell phone.

"Don't bother," Nguyen said. "I don't see anything missing. He must have set off the alarm when he came in, looked in the cabinet for jewels or something, and then lost his nerve and split."

Key impatiently shook her head and strode down the hall with the phone pressed to her ear.

After he saw the guy's room, Rep wondered, *why would he turn his nose up at easy snatch-and-run stuff and hit Key's room instead? And after he did that, why would he ignore clearly valuable swag and loot a cabinet full of paper?*

"You don't look like you buy my brilliant theory either," Nguyen said.

"I'm less interested in why he left than in why he came," Rep said.

"I don't think it was a stack of funny-looking paper."

"Hard sell, all right," Rep agreed.

"If Sue wants cops she can have cops. Back to work for me." Nguyen popped the clip from his rifle and opened the bolt. "My buds tell me that doing this makes it legal to carry this baby around. They right about that?"

"I don't have the faintest idea."

"I thought Sue said you were a lawyer."

"Ask me a question about palming off under the Lanham Act. Is that an M-16, by the way?"

"M-14. I wouldn't have an M-16 if you gave it to me."

A uniformed police officer, at least eight years younger than Rep's thirty-four, reached the flat within two minutes after Nguyen roared away. He asked world-weary questions, filled out a one-page form in neat block letters, and gave Key a copy.

"Can you think of anything the perp could have been look-ing for?"

"Nope," Key said. "Nothing in there but paper and ink."

"Do you think anyone—say, someone you know, maybe—could have gotten the idea that there might be medications or…something in there?"

"Like pot?" Key asked, a bemused lilt lifting her voice as she deciphered the bashful circumlocution.

"Well, yeah," the cop said. "Like pot."

"No way. My bong's in the shop." She waited half-a-beat to watch his eyebrows go up before adding, "Just kidding about the bong."

A delicious nanosecond of tension intervened before the cop grinned. He walked back toward the outside door, with Rep and Key in his wake.

"Did you have a motion detector on the glass?" he asked.

"The landlord was too cheap to spring for that system," Key said. "We just got the basic contact thingy on the door."

The cop gestured at the apparent bloodstains on the door-frame.

"One theory might be that he got in without triggering the alarm by breaking the glass and climbing through," the cop said. "Then when he tried to leave the same way he got careless and cut himself. That honked him off, so he impatiently jerked the door open and set the alarm off."

"That's why you asked me about the pot," Key said. "Because if the alarm wasn't wailing while he was going through the flat, there'd be no reason for him to leave before he found whatever he was looking for."

"If something does turn up missing," the cop said, "call the number on the form. Unless the guy comes back and trips on his shoelaces, there's probably not much we can do."

"Right," Key said. "Thanks."

Key, frowning and deflated, took a deep breath, squared her shoulders, and expelled air from her lungs in a long, weary exhalation. With the brutal violation of her home, her morning of triumph had spiraled downward into ashen anticlimax.

"Okay," she said in a stiff-upper-lip voice. "Let's get your bill settled up so I can get to work on this dump."

Rep knew that this was exactly what he should do. He wasn't a workaholic like many of his colleagues, but he was a partner in a corporate law firm. *Ergo*, having no more billable time in prospect on Sue Key's modest case, he should wrap things up with Key as fast as he decently could and head back to the office to log some time for some other client.

But he hesitated. He hesitated partly because he didn't want the morning to end on a sour note. Intellectual property lawyers don't get to be heroes very often, and he'd kind of enjoyed it.

Beyond ego trips, though, the shards of broken glass on the aqua floorboards gave him pause. For no reason he could have articulated, they made him think of shattered ice over still, deep, and suddenly fatal water. Of Vance Hayes plunging to an ugly death a few weeks after writing a letter to Sue Key's mother touting a lawyer named Walter Kuchinski—who happened to be one of maybe half-a-dozen people who knew for certain that Sue Key wouldn't be typing up a transcript at her flat this morning. He didn't know what light another forty minutes with Key could shed on that Byzantine spider web of weird coincidence, but he didn't feel comfortable just turning his back on it.

"You have renter's insurance?" Rep asked.

"Sure," Key said. "American Family. Like everyone else in Milwaukee."

"Tell you what. While you start cleaning up, why don't I chat with someone at American Family about whether they know a glazier who can beat a one-hundred thirty-five-dollar estimate on fixing the glass in your door. Then we'll worry about my bill."

"But I don't have any estimate yet," Key protested.

"Sure you do. For a hundred-thirty-five I'd do it myself."

"You've got yourself a deal, counselor," she said, the delighted squeal back in her voice. "I've heard of full-service lawyers, but this is over the top."

Twenty-eight minutes later—rounded up, that's five-tenths of a non-billable hour—Rep looked with satisfaction at aqua floorboards on which he could have walked barefoot and at a neatly rolled brown paper bag with BROKEN GLASS written on it in black Magic Marker. The cardboard he'd duct-taped to the window frame looked amateurish, but he'd just dictated a letter confirming American Family's promise that someone who knew what he was doing would be out forthwith to improve on that effort.

"This looks wonderful," Key said, beaming, as she strode down the hallway from her bedroom, where she had been straightening up. "But you weren't supposed to be doing any clean-up yourself."

"Oh, I don't know," Rep said. "In one sense cleaning up is about ninety percent of what lawyers do. Anyway, I had to do something to occupy myself while I waited for American Family's adjuster to call back."

"You're a peach," Key said. She pecked him on the cheek. "Now we take care of your bill. I insist."

"Good idea," Rep said.

She led him past the flat's cramped kitchen, back to her bedroom, which now looked ready for a *Better Homes and Gardens* photo op.

"Has anything turned up missing?" Rep asked.

"That's a funny thing," Key said. "Nothing valuable is gone, but he took one of my bricks."

"You mean the notes for a deposition you covered?" Rep asked, recognizing the professional jargon. "How in the world can you be sure that one of those is gone?"

"You're talking to Xu Ky's daughter," Key said. "If mom had been in charge of the Normandy invasion we would have captured St. Lo at H-Hour plus six. I got every one of those genes. I keep the notes for every deposition for two years, because once in a blue moon a lawyer squeaks about a supposed transcription error. I store them in chronological order. And between my Palm

Pilot and my Daybook I can give you date, time, and office address for every gig I've had in the last thirty-six months."

"I see," said Rep, who now understood why the cleansers in the kitchen utility closet had been arranged alphabetically—Ajax next to Bon Ami, followed by Formula 409 and, finally, Mister Clean. "So which notes were stolen?"

"Guy named Roger Leopold," she said. "Dep taken on November 10, 2003, in a case called *Murphy Alpha Numerics v. Orlofsky Publications.*"

Roger Leopold, as in "the Leopold order"? Rep wondered, thinking of Polly Allbright's enigmatic allusion after Rep's eulogy. He inhaled sharply as an invisible little fist punched his diaphragm.

"Can you dig up a copy of the transcript itself?" he asked.

"I can try. I'll call the office about it this afternoon. If they don't have one, Walt Kuchinski might. He was local counsel in the case."

"Kuchinski?" Rep muttered. "That's an interesting coincidence."

"Not really. He gets a lot of local counsel stuff in Milwaukee because he knows every judge in five counties. You want coincidence, I can do better than that. The lawyer who actually took Leopold's deposition was Vance Hayes."

"You're right," Rep said, a bit weakly. "You win."

"Now, you've done a great job for me, and everyone in the Milwaukee County Courthouse is going to hear about it, so I want you to give me your bill and we'll settle up."

"Right," Rep said absently. "Thanks for reminding me."

Chapter Six

Ninety percent of life is just showing up. Rep couldn't remember who'd said that, but the longer MacKenzie Stewart talked the truer it seemed.

All Rep had done was observe a basic professional courtesy. While driving back to the office he had left a voice-mail for Stewart about the weirdly intersecting coincidences tying Vance Hayes to Sue Key's offbeat case. Just being polite. And now a new client was about to drop into his lap.

"What in the world are you doing in Milwaukee, Reppert?" Stewart asked when he called Rep back about five minutes after Rep's return.

"Following the woman I love."

"Well, then, it looks like she's a lucky charm for both of us."

"We're in complete agreement," Rep said judiciously. "But what are you talking about?"

"You've met my wife, Gael, haven't you?"

"She and I shook hands a couple of times at bar functions when she was still general counsel for Pritzger Medical."

That is, Rep thought but didn't say, before an assiduous, painstaking, years-long campaign by her husband turned Gael Cunningham-Stewart last year into the newest judge on the obscure but prestigious United States Court of Appeals for the Federal Circuit, which handles patent and trademark cases.

"Right," Stewart said. "Well, during a recent spell of corporate absent-mindedness Pritzger managed to acquire a Wisconsin company called Precision Micro something-or-other. Pritzger's hot-shot deal-makers have now discovered to their consternation that no one still at Precision Micro knows exactly how many registered trademarks the company holds or what countries they're registered in or which of them are being licensed."

"They need an IP audit," Rep said—figuratively reaching for his handkerchief, for drooling is an intellectual property lawyer's Pavlovian response to the magic words "IP audit."

"Gael's very term. Her replacement at Pritzger is still the new kid on the block, so he's asked her to recommend outside counsel. My firm has an IP department, of course, but there's the whole nepotism angle. Not that I have delusions of grandeur, but Caesar's wife and all that."

"Just be careful on the ides of March."

"Quite. Anyhow, I told Gael that you could walk and chew gum at the same time and didn't pad your bills. If you'll fly to D.C. early next week so she can size you up for herself, I think she'll be inclined to pass your name along."

"Just tell me when and where," Rep said. "I'll be there with bells on."

"If you have bells on they might not let you into the Yale Club. Best go for business non-casual. Say six-thirty or so on Tuesday?"

"Done. Ken, I really appreciate this. Thank you very much."

"Not at all. And thank you for passing on the news about Hayes. Oddest client I've ever had. He baffles me even in death."

Not as much as he baffles me, Rep thought, hanging up and scribbling the appointment on a Post-It.

He knew the next thing he should do was chat with Kuchinski about the testimony Roger Leopold had given in this very office almost two years before. But he found himself doing other things instead. Shuffling through his message slips. Checking for new emails. Thinking that, you know, when you get right down to it, if you really sort through all this Vance Hayes stuff—so what? Some eerie spasm of ancient history playing itself out in a broken window and some purloined paper—who cares? What could anyone today do about it except fix the window and call the insurance company?

Yeah, I know: a rationalization, and a lame one at that. Rep just wanted Vance Hayes to rot politely in his grave without any more bother to anyone—especially Rep. The only thing worse than confronting Hayes in life was confronting him in death, and Rep didn't like confrontation. Confrontation was for litigators, who came to work with their ankles taped and were always yelling into their phones, as if they weren't clear on the basic concept of telephonic technology. It wasn't for guys who'd been fifteen months old when their mothers were arrested.

No one in Rep's young life had *ever* talked about the arrest, or what came after. Not his father, who tried to raise him. Or his aunt, who did. Or anyone else. He hadn't found out what had happened until he tracked it down himself in college. Only when he reached his thirties had Rep confirmed that his mother was still alive. Only then had he talked to her for the first time in his life—learning, in the process, that she made a living taking money from grown-ups to scold them and paddle them and stand them in the corner and turn them over her knee.

Rep resignedly watched his tidy little *so-what* excuse evaporate under the searing heat of traumatic memories. He remembered pelting down streets at the age of six or eight in small-town Indiana after strange women baffled to hear him yell, "Mommy! There's Mommy!" No good trying to blow off the past. Not for him.

Squaring his shoulders, Rep marched across the reception area to Kuchinski's drafty, capacious file- and paper-strewn office. Kuchinski was leaning far back in his swivel chair, feet parked on his credenza, ankles crossed, hands clasped behind his head. Approaching the open door, Rep heard Kuchinski's voice booming in the general direction of his speaker phone.

"Can't do it then, judge. Deer camp. They just had their second hard frost up north, and it isn't mid-October yet."

"Oh," came over the phone, as if "deer camp" automatically trumped speedy justice and efficient use of scarce judicial resources. "How about the week of February third, then?"

Kuchinski flipped through a calendar, studied one page for half-a-second, then sent it spinning across the office like a rectangular Frisbee.

"Can do," he said. After similar syllables crackled over the speaker, presumably from his opposing counsel, he added, "Shall I draft the order, your Honor?...Will do. Thank you."

"Which brings us," Rep said, "to Vance Hayes and Roger Leopold."

Kuchinski swiveled in his chair and looked blankly at Rep.

"How does it bring us there?"

"Well, it doesn't, actually, but I couldn't think of a segue. Do you remember Vance Hayes deposing a witness named Roger Leopold here in '03?"

"Very vaguely. Couldn't tell you anything about it from memory."

"What are the chances of you still having a copy of the transcript?"

"Let's check the file room," Kuchinski said, springing to his feet. "Remember the name of the case?"

Astonished at the notion of Kuchinski's highly improvisational office having anything as uptight as a formal file room, Rep shouted the case name while he scurried to catch up with the older lawyer. Kuchinski led him to an oversized walk-in closet. He pulled a chain to turn on a naked overhead bulb. The scant light disclosed banker's boxes stacked six high and two deep all the way around the room.

"I've been thinking of revising my document retention policy for about ten years," Kuchinski said apologetically, "but I've never actually gotten around to it."

"Ten years should be just about what it would take us to find the case-file in here," Rep said.

"Us, maybe," Kuchinski said, "but not Paris Hilton out there." Pivoting and sticking his head through the doorway, he bellowed, "Hey! Princess Anastasia! Back here, on the double!"

After seventy-five seconds of silence Kristina Mueller, Kuchinski's red-headed receptionist/secretary/administrative assistant/office manager, strolled up to them at a sedate and unhurried pace.

"You lose your key to the men's room again?" she asked.

Kuchinski gave her the case name and the datum that it had been active in 2003. She went instantly to the far corner, pulled three boxes down from the last stack of the front row and, resting one knee on the top remaining box in that row, began pulling a box from the middle of the rear row.

"I thought the rear on that side was supposed to be for 1999 and earlier," Kuchinski said.

"You run the American legal system," she snapped over her shoulder. "I'll run the office."

Five seconds later a hefty banker's box sailed toward them, landing neatly at Kuchinski's feet and scattering sneeze-inducing dust in every direction. Kuchinski dug into it and promptly emerged with a fat brown file folder filled with thin, brown file jackets, each neatly labeled with the case name. He pawed through it impatiently.

"No deposition transcripts," he said in a puzzled tone.

He pulled out the correspondence file and flicked through the pages. Pausing at the third letter from the top, he examined it intently.

"I remember this now!" he said then. "Damnedest thing. Hayes takes the deposition, and the very next day I get a call that the case has been settled. Call the court reporter and cancel the transcript. Return the exhibits. Draft a stipulation."

"Do you remember anything about the deposition?" Rep asked.

"I was just local counsel," Kuchinski said, shaking his head. "I gave Hayes a place to sit and all the coffee he could drink and then went back to my office to do my own work."

"It sounds like there must have been a bombshell buried somewhere in Mr. Leopold's testimony."

Rep then gave Kuchinski a brisk run-through, starting with Hayes' death not long after the Leopold deposition and ending with someone stealing the Leopold deposition notes from Sue

Key's apartment a couple of hours before. He added the Leopold order (whatever that was) to the mix at the end.

The story had its intriguing aspects, and Rep wasn't surprised that it held Kuchinski's interest. He wasn't prepared, however, for the urgent intensity of Kuchinski's reaction.

"So the wild-card here," Kuchinski said, "is the cat who took Sue Key's picture and put it in that calendar."

"He does seem kind of hard to ignore," Rep agreed. "But we don't have any idea who he is."

"Not yet we don't."

Kuchinski tramped out of the file room and back down the hall.

"Did you clean up the mess?" Mueller asked, without looking up from her keyboard.

"It'll wait. Martha Stewart won't be coming by today. Emergency meeting of the Brady Street Ski Club. Seven o'clock tonight, Art's Performing Center. Send out an email, stat."

Rep retreated to his office. He often felt the need to catch his breath after a close encounter with Kuchinski, but this was different. One minute Kuchinski was lounging behind his desk, blowing off a trial date so he wouldn't miss the start of deer season, and the next he was diving head first into a minor puzzle with the barest wisp of a tangential relationship to him.

Either Walt had way too much caffeine this morning, or there's something going on here that I don't understand.

Rep called his Indianapolis office and left a message instructing his secretary there to FedEx him the bundle of material he'd used to prepare his ill-starred eulogy of Vance Hayes—and while she was at it, to have someone dig up the probate report on Hayes' estate.

Chapter Seven

The Marcus Center for the Performing Arts sits in sleekly marbled elegance between Kilbourn Avenue and State Street in downtown Milwaukee, eminently convenient to Kuchinski's suite in the Germania Building. The Brady Street Ski Club, however, met that evening not at the Performing Arts Center but two blocks north, at Art's Performing Center. That establishment was neither sleek nor elegant but offered the advantage of permitting adults to smoke on the premises. (It would have permitted non-adults to do so as well if they were allowed in—which, however, they were not.)

"Doctor and Mr. Pennyworth Esquire," Kuchinski said shortly after seven o'clock, "it is my high honor and distinct privilege to introduce you to the Permanent Standing Committee of the Brady Street Ski Club, to-wit: myself; Rudy 'Speedbump' Markowski; Splinters Marcinski; Vince 'Topper' Topolewski; and our honorary member, Harry Skupnievich."

"Don't call me 'Splinters,'" Marcinski said from beneath a toupee of expensively woven silver-gray hair. "My mother calls me Leonard, and that should be good enough for anybody else."

"Splinters represents the only failure in my long career of getting colleagues elevated to the bench," Kuchinski explained. "Through a mischance of malignant fate he was caught on videotape during the election campaign purloining his opponent's yard signs—hence his nickname and his sensitivity about it. The *Milwaukee Journal-Sentinel* solemnly opined that these harmless shenanigans reflected poorly on his fitness to wield a gavel, and that proved to be a handicap that even my genius couldn't overcome."

"Bastards," Marcinski muttered.

"Begging your pardon for the off-color language, Doctor Pennyworth," Markowski said gallantly. "Splinters, watch your goddamn mouth."

"I've heard the term before," Melissa said.

"And now to work," Kuchinski said. He launched into a succinct exposition of what he dubbed the Sue Key Calendar Problem. He had reached what Rep took to be the penultimate sentence and gotten as far as "… guy who took" when a healthy young lass who apparently could only afford halter tops one size too small appeared with a tray holding two pitchers of beer and a heaping platter of chicken wings. Kuchinski stopped speaking as his tablemates received the serving with sacramental reverence.

"My compliments to the chef," Skupnievich said, having already polished off one of the wings. "This is a lot better than the slop at the place you picked last time, Markowski."

"Bull," Markowski protested. "Those ribs were done to a turn."

"True," Skupnievich said. "They were done to the clubhouse turn at Hialeah. That was horsemeat, and I speak as someone whose great-grandfather served in the Polish cavalry."

"We need to find the guy who took the picture," Kuchinski said, at last completing the sentence. "So how do we do that?"

"He figures to be a free-lancer, right?" Topolewski said.

"Someone who works at one of the studios, you think?" Markowski asked. "One of those outfits that does mostly weddings, with a little portrait business on the side?"

This speculation provoked a comprehensive and highly analytical discussion of the professional photography business in Milwaukee, some of whose practitioners had had run-ins with the consumer protection authorities of what Marcinski called "the People's Republic of Wisconsin." Others focused (so to speak) on commercial art.

"We're not narrowing this down much," Kuchinski said.

"We're going at it backwards," Markowski said. "We should be thinking about the people in front of the camera instead of the guy behind it."

"So where's that get us?" Topolewski asked.

"Reppert said most of the calendar shots looked like candids with generic backdrops digitized in, but one or two were probably pros. Who would you look for if you wanted a model who wouldn't pout about smoking?"

"Leaners," Marcinski said.

"Leaners," Topolewski said.

"Leaners," Skupnievich said.

"What's a leaner?" Melissa asked.

"A leaner," Topolewski explained, in a tone suggesting that he was about to dissect the intricacies of the Rule Against Perpetuities, "is an attractive young woman who gets paid to spend time in bars trying to interest young men in brands of cigarettes that they otherwise wouldn't have on the end of a stick."

"Buck Bradley's," Kuchinski said, jabbing an index finger at Marcinski. "Major Goolsby's," with a finger-jab at Skupnievich. "Judge Jason Downer's," pointing at Markowski. "And Topper, you cover Brady Street."

"Move to adjourn," Topolewski said as he stood up.

"Second," Marcinski said.

"Carries by acclamation," Markowski said.

Thirty seconds later Rep, Melissa, and Kuchinski were alone at the table.

"What a remarkable group," Melissa said.

"We met at the armed forces induction center at 6th and Wisconsin on June 26, 1968," Kuchinski said. "A few months after the Tet offensive in 'Nam, draft going full bore. Pious ladies passed out rosaries to us as we went in. We're all standing there inside, maybe forty of us, waiting to take one step forward and go into the Army. Then a gunnery sergeant with red stripes on olive drab instead of green on khaki comes out and gives us a pitch about joining the Marines instead of being drafted into the Army. *Halls of Montezuma, Sands of Iwo Jima*, all that stuff."

"In the era of Da Nang and the DMZ?" Rep asked. "Good luck."

"No one moved a muscle," Kuchinski said, nodding. "The gunny goes away. Five minutes later he comes back out with a list in his hand: 'The following inductees have the honor of entering the United States Marine Corps: Kuchinski; Topolewski; Marcinski; Markowski; and Skupnievich.' Ended up doing fourteen months in-country together."

"During one of the roughest parts of the war, too," Rep said. "That would've been, what, late sixty-eight to early 'seventy by the time you got through basic and advanced infantry training? Had fragging started by then? Enlisted men killing their own officers if they were too aggressive?"

"There was some of that. We had one blowhard in our unit who told everyone he was gonna take care of Captain Titleman before Titleman got us all killed winning himself a medal. One night in a pleasure house near Da Nang, this guy's blowing off in the bar and Titleman walks in. Instant silence. Now, you have to understand, no one has a weapon. There is no stricter gun control on the planet than at a U.S. military base. Officers may be dumb, but they ain't crazy. So Titleman walks in and he has this little Cong pistol, things that were about a dime a dozen and untraceable."

"What happened?" Melissa couldn't help asking.

"Titleman takes a nice, long, slow look around. Then he says in this cracker accent right out of William Faulkner, 'I've heard some scuttlebutt about threats to my physical well being. I don't wanna seem yellow, but I am partial to my physical well being, so I don't fancy walking back to base alone in the dark. I need someone to watch my back.' Then he takes out the Cong pistol, hands it to the blowhard, and says, 'Private, you walk ten feet behind me back to base, make sure I don't encounter any inconveniences.' He turns around and walks out, unarmed, with this pistol-packing bad-ass wannabe right behind him. And that was the end of *that* talk. I've never seen guts like that in my life, before or since."

"You all came back and went to law school?" Melissa asked.

"Not all. Skupnievich sells insurance. He probably makes more than the rest of us put together. Topolewski and Markowski started out as prosecutors after Marquette, and Marcinski just hung out his shingle. I wasted three years at a mega-firm before I got the sense to go out on my own."

"Corporate law just didn't take?" Rep guessed.

"It was a personality problem," Kuchinski said. "I had a personality, and they had a problem with it. They were always going, 'Don't wear brown shoes with a blue suit. Don't wear a short-sleeved shirt with a vest. Don't run barefoot through the law library.' I mean, it was eight o'clock *at night*. It wasn't like there were any *partners* there."

"I'll bet if the guys running that firm had known about these buddies you have they'd have cut you some slack on the dress code," said Melissa, who was blissfully unfamiliar with the mentalities at work in corporate law firms.

"You might be onto something there." Kuchinski saluted Melissa with a beer mug. "Our group may be a little rough around the edges, but if you need people who'll jump into something with both feet you definitely want our business cards."

"That raises an interesting point," Rep said. "For sheer strangeness, stealing notes of Roger Leopold's deposition from Sue Key's flat was off the charts. My idea of being galvanized into action was to track down the transcript and read it. But you made me feel like I was standing in cement. One good look at the file and you dropped everything, mobilized a SWAT team, and turned this little side-show into your top priority. That suggests more than casual curiosity."

"You got yourself a smart husband here, Doctor Pennyworth," Kuchinski said.

"He proved that the day he proposed."

Kuchinski fished a tin of small cigars and a lighter from his inside coat pocket. Opening the tin, he tendered it to Rep, who smilingly shook his head. Kuchinski swung the tin in Melissa's direction.

"Thanks, but I'd better say no," Melissa said. "My experience with cigars is neither extensive nor discriminating, and I'm afraid the superb tobacco you're offering would be wasted on my uneducated palate."

Kuchinski whistled quietly as he extracted a cigar for himself.

"I'm in love, Reppert," he said. "Don't leave me alone with this woman."

"Point taken," Rep said.

Kuchinski bit off one end of the cigar, lit the stogie in leisurely fashion, and settled back contentedly.

"Here's the deal," he said. "If you practice law you're gonna see some weird things, but when Rep told me about the burglary the weirdness here seemed to be spinning out of control. The case where Vance Hayes used me as local counsel wasn't the kind of thing you'd get on a plane for. Only way it made sense at all was for him to handle it locally on the cheap."

"But Hayes flew to Milwaukee to take Leopold's deposition," Rep pointed out. "And then the case settled in record time."

"Which made things more strange, not less," Kuchinski said. "And Hayes taking his last bath in Lake Delton didn't make me feel any better. But I couldn't bill anybody for thinking about it, so I didn't bother."

"Until Sue Key called you almost two years later out of a clear blue sky because Hayes bird-dogged you to her mother."

"Right," Kuchinski said. "I dumped her nameless dog of a case on you and the next thing I know you've bluffed your way to a good result and our client has had her window broken."

"Conclusion," Melissa offered. "Something's going on."

"That's the way it looks to me. I live here. People in the Courthouse and the Safety Building know me. Not all of them like me or trust me, but I'm a known quantity. That's what turns the lights on in suite nine-oh-nine of the Germania Building every morning—well, every morning my hangover isn't too bad. If something funny is going on and it has my fingerprints on it, I finally got it through my thick Polish skull that I'd better find out what it is."

The first three bars of Chopin's "Valse Polonaise" punctuated this comment. Kuchinski took a cell phone from a clip on his belt, raised his eyebrows in mute apology, and brought the phone to his ear. After listening for five seconds he mumbled, "Right." He looked up at Rep and Melissa.

"Live one at Buck Bradley's," he said.

Chapter Eight

"She's good," Melissa said. "This is the first time since I was sixteen years old that I've wanted a cigarette."

The she in question stood winsomely at Buck Bradley's polished oak bar, now and then rippling auburn curls coiffed to make her look about nineteen—though Melissa felt sure she'd never see twenty-five again. She sipped sparingly from something clear with a lime twist. Each time she took a drink she returned the tumbler to a spot beside a dark blue, flip-top cigarette pack.

An extra little hair flick suggested that the woman sensed scrutiny. She picked up the pack with her right hand and drew a cigarette from it with the first two fingers of her left. She did this with the luxuriant languor of someone who wasn't feeding a habit but anticipating a sophisticated, multi-textured pleasure so intense that she wanted to savor every morsel of the experience. Shifted the cigarette to her right hand. Rested her right arm on the bar, holding the unlit cigarette prominently, while with her left hand she rummaged in leisurely fashion through her purse. Searching for a lighter, presumably, but this inference would remain forever unverified. A young male with straw-colored hair in a surfer cut shuffled up to her and bashfully offered a light.

She accepted, with a smile that outshone his by a megawatt or so. She raised the cigarette to her mouth, bowed her head slightly as she bent with hooded eyes toward the flame from his Ronson, and used her left hand to steady his right until between them they'd managed to ignite the tobacco. Still brushing his

Ronson-hand with her left, she pulled the cigarette from her mouth in a sweeping motion of her right arm. She turned her head away from the guy long enough to blow a ladylike ribbon of smoke politely over her right shoulder, then immediately swiveled back to offer him a high-beam thank-you. As she did this she rested her right elbow on the bar, managing to draw attention simultaneously to the cigarette and her ample breasts.

Kuchinski signaled unobtrusively to a waitress. Rep watched the conversation at the bar tread water for ninety seconds or so. The surfer agreed to try a cigarette from the leaner's pack. He liked it, or at least pretended to. She fished a mini-pack from her purse and gave it to him. He seemed to realize that he'd been had, but he took the sample pack, smiled gamely, and went back to tell his buddies about the new brand in town.

"What's up, Walt?" the waitress asked.

"Same again for everyone here," Kuchinski said, "and tell Christina Ricci over there that if she'll come talk to my friends when she's ready for a break I'll buy her a real drink."

"She's ready about now, I'm guessing," the waitress said.

"Better get your butt over there then, hey?"

"When was the last time you had beer spilled in your lap, cowboy?"

"When was the last time you ate breakfast standing up?" Kuchinski asked just as jovially, but Melissa thought she saw a momentary glimmer of real fear in the waitress' eyes as she scurried to relay Kuchinski's message. Two minutes later the leaner strolled over to their table.

"Debbie Cantwell," she said, tossing mini-packs to each of them.

"You're pitching to the wrong demographic here," Kuchinski told her.

"I could tell that from the bar. If my supervisor walks in, though, you're gonna have to fake it or this will be a short conversation."

"What're you drinking?" Kuchinski asked.

"Pinch, since you're paying," Cantwell said, sitting down. "It's already on the way. What's on your mind?"

"We're looking for a photographer," Kuchinski said. "Guy who's into women smoking, or at least makes pictures for people who are."

"Oh, God," Cantwell said, pressing the heels of her hands to her temples. "You have no idea the memories that brings back."

"I wouldn't think a photo shoot could be that bad," Rep said.

"Mine was a video," Cantwell said. "They had me sit at a cocktail table in an evening gown and smoke. They had these extra-long cigarettes, and I had to light a new one anytime the one I was smoking burned down too far. By the time I got through I was a walking surgeon general's report. Splitting headache, raw throat, sick to my stomach—I swore I'd never smoke again."

"You've sure gotten over that," Kuchinski said.

"Only when I'm getting paid. Or drinking. Or sometimes after a rich meal. Or, you know, when—"

"Right, got it," Kuchinski said. "Who was the cat doing the video?"

"That was actually some flatlander, believe it or not."

"Chicagoan," Kuchinski explained, noticing Rep's baffled expression.

"A Chicago studio had to come to Milwaukee to find pretty girls smoking cigarettes?" Rep asked incredulously.

"They were going for a certain look," Cantwell explained. "Fresh scrubbed, girl-next-door, nonthreatening—you know, Erin from *Happy Days* being naughty instead of Madonna relaxing after a three-way."

"I'm guessing you didn't take a gig like that on spec," Kuchinski said. "How did they get your name?"

Plunging her hand into her purse, Cantwell pulled out a Palm Pilot whose stylus and thumb-wheel she began energetically using. After well over a minute she paused, frowned thoughtfully, then gestured for a pen.

"I've narrowed it down to three," she said, as Kuchinski handed her an efficient-looking Parker. "One of these guys called me for a clothes-on calendar shoot with a smoking theme that I couldn't do. I gave him a couple of referrals that worked out, so he tipped the video to me to say thanks."

Rep offered her a business card to write on, but she waved it off in favor of a cocktail napkin.

"This may be a yuppie bar, but it's still a bar, and I'm old school."

She passed the napkin to Kuchinski and, in almost the same motion, downed the rest of the scotch in one impressive swallow.

"Thanks for the drink," she said, rising. "Back to work."

"Well," Kuchinski said as with painstaking concentration he studied her return to the bar, "we've got ourselves a start."

Chapter Nine

When the first tool-using homo sapiens finished sharpening the flint on his first spear and went out with his buddies to find a woolly mammoth to bring home for dinner, Melissa thought with some asperity as the Germania Building's elevator carried her creakingly upward, *his mate undoubtedly had to come running out of the cave after him grunting, "Honey, you forgot something!"*

"Hi," she panted to Kristina Mueller as she reached the reception area for Kuchinski's office. "Is my husband here?"

"No," the receptionist said. "He and the world's greatest trial lawyer are out playing Paul Drake."

"Nuts," Melissa said. "He has to drive to Wausau this afternoon to meet with a potential client tomorrow. The only shirt he packed has French cuffs, and he forgot his cufflinks."

"There's the elevator," Mueller said, cocking her ear toward the door. "Five to three that's the two of them returning now."

Rep and Kuchinski strolled in a mere three minutes later.

"These might come in handy," Melissa said, handing a palm-sized velveteen box to her husband.

"Oops," Rep said.

"Productive morning?" Melissa asked then, in the exaggeratedly patient, men-will-be-boys tone that wives learn early in successful marriages.

"In an addition-by-subtraction sense," Rep said, handing her his notes from last night's napkin with two names and addresses crossed out.

"How did you eliminate these two?"

"Well," Kuchinski said, "one is sixty-five years old and works in a wheelchair. The other weighs about three hundred fifty pounds. I can't see either of them burglarizing Sue Key's flat."

"Suppose one of the guys you saw had been twenty-four and in peak physical condition?" Melissa asked. "What would that have proven?"

"Nothing," Rep admitted. "It would have focused follow-up inquiries."

"Which I hope you'll be entrusting to professionals," Melissa said.

"Pros like facts, and right now we don't have many," Kuchinski said. "Before we can delegate chores to anyone we need to come up with a couple."

"You're right, I shouldn't be flippant," Melissa said, turning toward Rep. "The Sable is parked at a meter outside. Would you like me to just take a cab back to the apartment so that you can get on your way?"

"That would actually be quite wonderful, if you really don't mind. This morning's little excursion took longer than I expected, and I'd like to reach Wausau before it gets too dark."

The phone rang. Mueller answered it and almost immediately handed it to Kuchinski. After a quick and agitated phone conversation he spun around and headed for the door.

"Judge Pastor's court, maybe for twenty minutes and maybe for the rest of the day," he said to Mueller. "Some outta-town lawyer is trying to ambush my only corporate client with an *ex parte* restraining order motion, and Judge Pastor apparently needs some help kicking his butt."

"Wait," Rep called. "My bag is still in your trunk."

After a quick kiss he hustled after Kuchinski. They had disappeared before Melissa noticed that she was still holding the note he'd shown her.

"The great thing about being male in America," Mueller said, shaking her head, "is that you never really have to grow up."

"Mmm," Melissa said ambiguously.

Two minutes before, she had been squirming to get on her way. Now, though, she lingered in the reception area, gazing thoughtfully at the door. Rep definitely had his boyish side. He could sit playing chess against the computer until fifteen minutes before it was time to leave for a party, then jump up, shave at the same time he was knotting his tie, and not see anything wrong with it. He could sink to the couch at eleven p.m. when *True Grit* or *McClintock!* was starting on TCM, knowing that he had to be up at seven the next morning, swearing that he was just going to watch the opening scenes, and then crawl into bed at one-thirty.

But Rep didn't go off on mindless frolics the day before a major client-hunting expedition. If he'd spent this crisp, sunny morning riding around a city he barely knew looking for potentially unpleasant people, it was because Kuchinski was right. They'd have to produce some hard data before they could expect the cops to take the invasion of Key's apartment seriously.

Melissa opened her purse to stash the note. Her eyes fell on the three sample packs of cigarettes that Cantwell had distributed last night. Melissa had kept them to save for a colleague at UWM. She thought she detected a complicit glint winking at her from their cellophane wraps. Impulsively, she grabbed one. Fumbling with unpracticed fingers, she slit the cellophane, opened the flip-top, and extracted a cigarette. Without being asked, Mueller tossed her a Bic.

Melissa had to fuss with the lighter for half a minute before she could coax a flame from it. She raised the cigarette tentatively to her lips and awkwardly lit it. Thought she was going to cough but didn't. Backed up and shook her head, as if to help the wisp of smoke she'd inhaled dribble out. Strolled a few steps away from the desk, tried another mini-puff, and felt dizzy for a second or two. Then her head cleared.

"You don't look like you're enjoying that very much," Mueller said.

"I never really did," Melissa said.

"How long ago did you quit?"

"I barely even started. I smoked for about two months my junior year in high school, and I don't think I got through five packs. That was it."

"My sister was the same way. Smoking turned her off right away."

"It didn't turn me off, exactly," Melissa said around a third half-hearted puff. "At first, in fact, the sheer depravity of such wicked decadence was thrilling all by itself. And even after the forbidden fruit stuff wore off, I didn't find smoking disgusting or repulsive. One day I just realized, 'You know, I'm not *getting* this. I know it's supposed to be really fun, but it's just not doing all that much for me.' So I stopped."

"You're a lucky young woman," Mueller said in a tone of maternal admonition. "Anyone who dodges the smoking bullet at sixteen and then takes it up in her thirties ought to have someone go upside her head."

"I'm definitely *not* taking it up," Melissa said. She raised the cigarette again and this time managed a serious drag, followed by a reasonably competent exhalation.

"What are you doing, then?"

Melissa glanced again at the note Rep had left.

"Practicing," she said.

She was still practicing when a uniformed Milwaukee police officer turned away from a guard at the security desk in the building's lobby and strode toward Rep and Kuchinski. Rep noticed that the guard was pointing in their direction.

"You been letting your parking tickets pile up, boy?" Kuchinski asked.

"I don't think that's it," Rep said.

It wasn't.

"Do either of you know whose card this is?" the officer asked, showing them a somewhat dog-eared business card.

"Mine," Rep said.

"I'd appreciate it if you'd come with me right away, sir," the officer said. "It's very important."

Chapter Ten

It simply isn't true that Brady Street, north of downtown on Milwaukee's east side, is all bars except for an occasional coffee shop. Its several closely packed blocks have boasted at various times a socialist bookstore, head shops, the occasional gas station, and a body-piercing parlor. Mostly, though, it's bars, with an occasional coffee shop.

The Ground Rules Café, for example, where Melissa seated herself at a white metal sidewalk table about twenty minutes after the cop had politely accosted Rep. She set a tall, cardboard cup of black coffee on the table in front of her, next to an earnest essay by a student deconstructing a Jane Austen novel that his first sentence referred to as *Scents and Sensibility*.

Next to the cup she placed the sample cigarette pack. She positioned it with some care, in a spot where it could be seen by someone from the second floor window of a frame building across the street whose address matched the one not crossed out on Rep's note. The guy she glimpsed now and then through the window should be a photographer named Pelham Dreyfus.

Melissa reminded herself firmly that she wasn't going to do anything silly. She was going to sit at the table; sip some coffee; read the essay; smoke one cigarette, without inhaling any more than she had to; and keep her eye discreetly on the window. If Pelham Dreyfus took a picture through the window, she'd see him and she'd have learned something useful. If he didn't, she would have wasted some time.

After a fortifying drink of coffee, she picked up the pack. She took her time about it, as Cantwell had, teasing Dreyfus (if he chanced to be watching) and giving him plenty of time to react. Flipping up the top of the pack, she stole a sly glance at the window. Nothing. She paused and looked down the street, as if something had distracted her for a moment. She slowly took the second cigarette from the pack, gripping it with as much finesse as she could manage between the tips of the first two fingers of her left hand. She settled back, tossing the pack on the table with her right hand while she cocked her left elbow and rested it on the arm of her chair. She sat that way for five or six seconds, flaunting the unlit cigarette like a small flag.

She checked the window again. Nothing.

Again she glanced away. She toyed distractedly with the cigarette, as if she were thinking of something else. Twenty seconds of this, maybe, and she opened her purse. She quickly found the cheap Bic lighter she'd bought at an Osco drugstore up the block, but she went on pretending to look for it.

Another sidelong glance at the window. Nothing.

Well, she thought, *here goes nothing.*

She took the lighter out. She flicked it twice, with no result. Oops. She tried again. Nada. *I should have sprung for a Zippo,* she thought.

"Can I offer you a light?" a masculine voice behind her said.

Startled, she glanced around. The man who stood there wore a cream and mesh equipment vest and had two cameras with lenses of different lengths hanging around his neck. His elegant Calibri lighter worked on the first try.

"Thanks," Melissa said.

She brought the cigarette to her lips and leaned toward him to accept the light. This was still an unfamiliar experience, and she concentrated on not blowing it. She almost did blow it, though, because as she inhaled a lungful of smoke and rocked gently back, she opened her eyes. When she did that she noticed a heavy, gauze-and-tape dressing running from the base of the man's right hand to halfway up his little finger.

Take it easy, she told herself as she stifled a gasp. *We're talking about an incompetent burglar who almost blew a two-bit B&E, not a serial killer. This is still basically a lark.*

On May 2, 1886, a small army of workers striking for an eight-hour day marched to the North Chicago Rolling Mills Plant on the south side of Milwaukee, intent on shutting it down. They met three companies of Wisconsin militia, intent on keeping it open. The strikers insisted, the militia opened fire, and all but six of the strikers ran away. The six who didn't were dead.

Rep learned about this local tragedy, shortly before Melissa noticed Pelham Dreyfus' bandage, by reading a historical marker at the site where the slain workers had fallen. He found himself within reading distance because that's where his escort told him to wait until he was summoned into the Cold Coast Production building a few hundred feet away. Yellow crime-scene tape and swarming investigators kept them from getting any closer at the moment. Ninety minutes ago Cold Coast's general manager had found Max Levitan's body, shot through the heart at close range, in the conference room filled with Churchill books. Levitan had had Rep's business card in his pocket.

The summons finally came. A uniformed officer escorted Rep to the building's second floor and pointed to an African-American plainclothesman at one of the desks. After Detective Lieutenant Latrobe Washington introduced himself, he and Rep ran through a *pro forma* exchange of apologies and "no problems." Rep explained how Levitan had come to have his card.

Occasional comments from Kuchinski had hinted that Milwaukee detectives favor a rough-and-ready business casual approach to on-the-job attire, but Washington apparently hadn't gotten the memo. He wore a dark, two-piece suit, white shirt, and blue tie knotted right up to the throat. Rep had to look up slightly to meet the gaze of out of his well-seamed black face.

"Can you think of any reason anyone would want to kill him?"

"Nope. I talked to him for less than half an hour, but he impressed me a great deal."

Washington showed him a letter in a glassine paper protector. The letterhead read:

UNITED STATES SENATE
COMMITTEE ON THE JUDICIARY
COMMITTEE STAFF

The letter thanked Levitan for his recent inquiry and said that, as it implicated potentially confidential information, it had been referred to staff counsel for review. Rep noticed that the letter was dated nine days after the demand letter he'd sent to Cold Coast Productions on behalf of Sue Key. He knew a couple of people on the committee staff, but not the one who'd signed this letter.

"This was in a personal file Levitan had apparently started on Ms. Key's claim," Washington said. "Do you have any idea why he'd be contacting politicians in connection with that case?"

"No," Rep shrugged. "The Judiciary Committee handles trademark and copyright stuff, but it wouldn't get involved in a particular case."

"Did anyone from this committee get in touch with you, maybe hint you should back off?"

"No."

"I take it you'll want to help in any way that you can," Washington said. Just a hint of a tease colored his tone.

"Yes, as a matter of fact I would."

"In that case, could you sit down for about forty-five minutes with that notebook-toting officer over there and run through this calendar/legal claim/burglary stuff in more detail?"

"Absolutely," Rep said.

Any prospect of reaching Wausau with the sun still shining had just disappeared, but this wasn't negotiable. Penny-ante burglary is one thing. Cold-blooded murder is something else. Whatever Sue Key's case might have been up to now, it wasn't a silly-season lark for adventurous amateurs anymore.

Chapter Eleven

Okay, this is a little weird.

Would she mind if he took her picture? Dreyfus had asked that before he had his lighter back in his pocket. Melissa had sketched a "go ahead" shrug to accompany her murmured assent, trying for minimal politeness without encouragement. Dreyfus' overture gave her all the information she figured to get this afternoon, so there was no reason to prolong her little charade. She had assumed he'd take a couple of shots, and then she could put the cigarette out and go back to being a grown-up.

Now, though, Dreyfus was burning film at what sounded like three snaps a second, jumping back and forth, squatting, popping up, dropping one camera and grabbing the other, shooting one-handed, asking her to take a long puff.

"Not exactly the first time you've ever done this, is it?" Dreyfus asked.

"No, I've smoked before."

"Burn!" Dreyfus said, grinning gamely at what he apparently regarded as world-class repartée. "I mean this isn't the first time you've ever had your picture taken by a professional photographer."

Ah, Melissa thought, spotting the fraternity row pick-up line. *"You must be a model."*

Melissa drew on the cigarette to stall for a second or two while she decided how to respond. Was Dreyfus' question a possible lead-in to something that might produce more information after all?

Or was it just his idea of snappy patter? As she expelled a generous burst of smoke toward the sky she decided on a guarded answer.

"I've had my picture taken before too," she said. "Always with my clothes on, if that's what you're getting at."

Dreyfus lowered the camera and gave Melissa a steady, thoughtful look.

"If you know the drill," he said, "I'll cut to the chase. Twenty-five bucks if one of these runs. I'm doing this on spec, so no guarantee. But my studio is right across the street. If you're up for a costume change, you can walk out of there in forty-five minutes with a benjamin."

Just how stupid do you think I am? Klaxons went off in Melissa's head. This was as NO WAY as any decision could be. What she'd picked up already seemed to pin Dreyfus as the photographer for Sue Key's calendar-girl shot and the guy who'd broken into her flat. Melissa, right now, this very second, should mutter something about thanks-for-the-offer and take a hike.

And yet. And yet. Would her memory of the bandage and Dreyfus' banter even interest a cop, much less pry a search warrant out of a judge? And if it didn't, where would that leave them? Rep and Kuchinski playing guys-will-be-guys again, teaming up on some more-guts-than-brains scheme to talk their way into Dreyfus' studio?

Melissa spent two more seconds studying Dreyfus. She didn't see a lot of muscle on the pear-shaped torso under his equipment vest. He looked young—with a little more hair he'd seem almost boyish—but not especially fit. A stern little common-sense Melissa in her head scolded that she was rationalizing a foolhardy impulse. The pest had a point, but she decided to go ahead anyway.

If Rep pulled something like I'm about to do, I'd make him watch chick flicks for a week as penance.

"Sure," she told Dreyfus. "I can spare just about forty-five minutes."

◇◇◇

Rep asked the younger detective with the notebook if he could call Melissa before they started, just to bring her up to speed.

With no great enthusiasm but a show of patient understanding, the detective told him to go ahead.

Rep did, but got no answer. This struck him as odd, because generally the only time Melissa left her phone off during the day was when she was driving—and she couldn't be driving now, because Rep had their car. But he shrugged and figured he'd just have to touch base with her later.

This is no longer weird. It just officially became creepy.

The outfit that hung from the shower curtain rod in the bathroom of Dreyfus' studio consisted of a plaid skirt, white blouse, and gold blazer, all to be complemented by the white socks and penny loafers on the floor. "Like Erin from *Happy Days* being naughty" suddenly seemed a bit more sinister than it had sounded when Cantwell said it last night.

What was I thinking? had throbbed through Melissa's brain throughout the three minutes or so she had spent so far examining these vestments. She had stolen every look she could in every direction on her way from the hallway door to here, and she hadn't seen anything that seemed likely to shed much more light on what Dreyfus had to do with Sue Key, Vance Hayes, or anyone else. She had spotted an elaborate computer setup and desk, but it didn't tell her anything more. She saw the usual "men's interest" magazines lying around—*Maxim, Penthouse*, and so forth—and several issues of one she'd never heard of called *Soldier for Hire*. But she hadn't learned anything that could remotely justify the risk she'd taken, and she didn't think she was going to.

Which doesn't make any difference, Melissa thought as she took a final, disgusted look at the convent school uniform, *because this is over the line.*

"How's it coming?" Dreyfus asked through the door.

Melissa grabbed her purse and yanked the bathroom door open.

"You know what," she said, "this isn't working. I'm taking off."

She tried to brush past Dreyfus but bumped into him instead. He didn't back up. And he didn't feel very soft.

"What's the problem all of a sudden?"

"The last time I got carded was years ago," Melissa said. "If you want pictures of a kid, you'd better find someone else."

"Hey, no probs." Dreyfus retreated eight inches and held his hands up, palms out, in a placatory gesture. "Just leave that to me. I won't be using film on this shoot, like I was outside. Put that uniform on, give me some digital snaps and an hour with that computer, and I'll have you looking as fresh-faced and dewy-eyed as you were the night of your junior prom."

"You must really be good with that computer," Melissa gushed.

"The best," Dreyfus said in an aw-shucks tone that didn't match the chilly eyes that he kept fixed on her.

"Good." Melissa shuffled to her left to go around him. "Then do the whole thing on the computer and leave me out of it."

Dreyfus' right hand snapped out and grabbed her left forearm. Nothing soft about his grip, either. Lancing pain shot through to her shoulder. Her left hand went numb and she reached over with her right hand to grab her purse.

"Look," he said, his tone still soothing, "we're both reasonable, intelligent adults here, right?"

"We're both carbon-based life-forms," Melissa said. "That's as far as I'll go. Let go of me right now!"

"Uh *huh*. You hustle your way in here with some dime-store diva routine and then all of a sudden you're too delicate to pose in a blazer? What game do you think you're playing?"

"I don't do kiddie porn, all right? And I didn't hustle my way into anything. Coming up here was *your* idea, remember? Now *let me go*."

"Answers first," Dreyfus said, tightening his grip. "Who sent you after me? What are you looking for?"

"A benjamin. One hundred dollars."

"Then what's with the last-minute choke? For all you knew I was asking you up here to put on a g-string or a studded leather bustier. Sorry, I'm not buying cold feet over a schoolgirl costume. I want to know who you really are and what you really do."

Melissa straightened, gritting her teeth against the pain in her arm. Sometimes there's nothing quite like the unvarnished truth.

"My name is Melissa Seton Pennyworth. I'm an assistant professor of English at the University of Wisconsin—Milwaukee."

Dreyfus grinned sardonically, and wagged his head from side to side.

"You expect me to believe that?"

"Believe what you like," Melissa shrugged. "It happens to be true."

"English, huh?"

"That's right."

"Okay, 'professor.' Who wrote *Silas Marner?*"

"George Eliot," Melissa said. "Actually Marian Evans, using George Eliot as a pen name because critics wouldn't take a woman novelist seriously."

"Ooh, *primo* bluff," Dreyfus said, sarcasm dripping richly from each syllable. "But no sale. It so happens *I* was an English major at Florida State University. Samuel Butler wrote *Silas Marner.*"

"No, he didn't," Melissa said, "but he did write *Hudibras*—which ironically includes some advice that's particularly helpful here:

> Love is a boy by poets styled;
> 'Then spare the rod and spoil the child.'

She swung her purse as hard as she could at the bandage on Dreyfus' right hand. Her car keys, dimpling the purse's leather skin, caught the dressing squarely. Cursing with vehement eloquence, his face paling in agonized rage, Dreyfus dropped her arm and staggered backward.

Melissa darted past him and headed for the door. Or thought she did. Instead of the hallway door, though, she found herself looking at the front of a classroom: teacher's desk backed by a blackboard with DETENTION printed boldly on it. It took her three seconds of panicky turns in all directions to figure out that the schoolroom was a life-sized backdrop that Dreyfus had put in place so that he could pose a properly costumed Melissa in front of it. That looked like three seconds more than she had to spare, because Dreyfus was now coming after her with a full head of steam.

She ran straight for the backdrop. She had almost reached it when she barked her right shin on something and pitched head-long to the floor. She heard Dreyfus' waffle-stompers pounding heavily toward her. Rolling over, she reached for the metal waste basket that had tripped her. She grabbed it by the rim with both hands and raised its bottom toward the charging Dreyfus.

"No more Mister Nice Guy," he panted. "You're getting bitch-smacked."

He was almost on her. Lacking any better ideas, she threw the waste basket directly at his face, as if she were making a two-handed set shot in a 1950s girls' basketball game.

She caught him on the nose—one part of his body that, it turned out, *was* soft, and had apparently received previous attention from people more pugilistically gifted than she. Newton's laws operated with their usual predictability, and she found much of the contents of the waste basket scattered over her hair, face, and sweater. She nevertheless came out of the encounter in better shape than Dreyfus, who recoiled once again to clear blood and tears from his face.

Melissa rolled under the easel propping up the backdrop. She bruised her shoulder on it as she scrambled to her feet, knocking it over. She found the door, found the knob, twisted it.

Nothing happened. Locked. She heard Dreyfus scrambling again. Fingertips slick with sweat, she fumbled for a latch, came on a button, pushed it. It popped out. She turned the knob. She felt Dreyfus' breath on her neck as she pulled the door open and squeezed into the hallway.

She began running for the stairway ten yards away. She could hear Dreyfus breathing in ragged grunts just behind her, and she had a sick feeling that she'd run out of miracles.

He caught her just as she reached the top of the stairs. His left hand clamped the back of her neck and stopped her cold, pulling her back so hard that her feet almost flew out from under her.

"I don't think you've ever been properly slapped," he muttered.

"You've just insulted my mother and two congregants of the Sisters of St. Joseph," Melissa said indignantly.

He jerked her backward, flung her violently to the floor, and pinned her belly with his knee.

"I'll show you what an insult *is*," he hissed.

"I'll scream," Melissa warned him in a desperation-tinctured voice that was much smaller than she wanted it to be.

"Scream all you want. Coming from here, anyone who hears you will think it's sexual ecstasy. Which cheek shall I start with?"

The best answer Melissa could think of involved a suggestion that Dreyfus perform an anatomically impossible sex act. Before these unladylike words could cross her lips, however, another voice intervened.

"That'll do, junior."

Dreyfus rose slightly, flew two or three feet to Melissa's left, and landed heavily on his side. The hand that he had raised in preparation for slapping Melissa now gripped his diaphragm, attempting to rub away the aftereffects of a wing-tipped toe that Walt Kuchinski had just artistically planted there.

"Who in hell are you?" Dreyfus moaned.

"Someone who picks on people his own size," Kuchinski said. "Although in your case I'll make an exception."

"She was burglarizing my studio under false pretenses," Dreyfus whined. "You're aiding and abetting."

"The only times I've ever been in prison have been to see clients, which puts me well up on you. So if I were you I'd leave the legal conclusions to me."

"Technically, I've never actually been in prison," Dreyfus insisted. "Work release at the county jail doesn't count."

"I'll keep that nuance in mind," Kuchinski said.

"Unless you want me to call the police, what you'll do is get the hell out of here so I can teach this bitch a lesson."

In no haste whatever, Kuchinski helped Melissa to her feet and planted her protectively behind him. Then he leaned over Dreyfus. He kept his arms down, as if pleading with Dreyfus to take a swing at him.

"You say one more stinking word, short eyes," Kuchinski whispered, "and you are going to piss off the wrong polack."

Dreyfus seemed to deflate, apparently cowed even more by the epithet "short eyes" than by Kuchinski's looming physical presence. He lay in sullen docility as Kuchinski and Melissa retreated down the stairs and out the door.

"Thanks," Melissa said.

"I just don't hold with hitting women on the face," Kuchinski said.

"How did you know I was here?"

"As soon as I got back from court, Her Serene Highness described your exit performance this morning. No one in town is auditioning people for *Private Lives*, so I figured you were smoking to get ready for an appearance over here."

"Well, I'm glad you guessed right. I feel pretty silly right now, but getting the stuffing smacked out of me would have been excessive atonement."

"Did you learn anything?"

"He's definitely the guy," Melissa said, and told Kuchinski about the bandage and the smoking shots. "Why did you call him 'short eyes'?"

"I had the Duchess of Devonshire back at the office run a computer check on him while I was on my way back from court. He has a prior for sex with a sixteen-year-old when he was twenty-three. Not exactly cradle-robbing, but it is underage in civilized jurisdictions."

"Probably a career-limiting move for him."

"Doubt it. I make him for a loser from the get-go. What you cleverly dug up just now reinforces that view."

"I wish I'd been clever enough to quit while I was ahead," Melissa said. "I didn't learn one useful thing by grandstanding my way into his studio."

"Maybe not, but after Rep gets through chewing you out he'll be proud of you. And it looks like you have a souvenir."

With that, Kuchinski plucked a scrap of cardboard from Melissa's hair and handed it to her. It was a business card. Melissa glanced at it, then did a double-take and examined it at greater length.

"Isn't that interesting?" she said, showing Kuchinski the card.

Karen Wilkinson
Certified Shorthand Reporter

Chapter Twelve

As soon as Melissa slipped into Kuchinski's 1968 Buick Riviera she caught herself pushing an imaginary accelerator, desperate to get them on their way. Kuchinski, though, seemed in no particular hurry. He unlocked the Club anti-theft device from the steering wheel, stowed it carefully behind the front seat, and checked traffic with the elaborate care of a driver's ed teacher before he pulled out.

"I'm careful with the Club," he said. "One time I didn't lock it properly, came back for the car eight hours later, and it was gone."

"Someone stole your car?" Melissa asked sympathetically.

"No, stole the Club. Got the thing off the steering wheel and walked off with it. And *left the car*. I have never felt so *disrespected*."

"If you're kidding me to help me get over the trauma, I appreciate it," Melissa said. "If you're serious, then I'm blown away."

"I'll take that as a compliment either way. Home or—hold on."

Kuchinski made a sharp right turn, roaring up a residential street with less than a yard of clearance from the cars parked along both curbs. Another sharp right onto a street that seemed to curl back the way they had come. Over the next seventy-five seconds or so street signs flew past Melissa with dizzying incoherence as her breakfast made an encore appearance in her throat. Cambridge-Warren-Albion-Farwell-SomethingElse-Prospect-

Royall, Farwell again, Brady again, then blurs until North. Only at that point did Kuchinski stop the *Dukes of Hazzard* routine and begin driving sedately toward the upper east side.

"Home or school?" he asked at that point.

"Home. I'll go back for my stomach later."

"I thought I spotted someone following us," Kuchinski explained. "Pulled out the same time we did, kept a car in between him and us, burned through a red light to stay with us. Red sedan, looked like some kinda rice-burner, but I didn't get make or model."

"You lost him, though?"

"Oh, I lost him all right. Right now he's probably trying to find his way out of DiBrito's Car Wash."

"What's a rice-burner, by the way?"

"Japanese car," Kuchinski said, winking broadly at her.

"Any chance the guy following us was Pelham Dreyfus?"

"No way. As soon as he finishes puking, that little wuss is gonna be curled up in bed with a bottle of aspirin for two days."

Melissa, who had deliberately left her cell phone off during her escapade, pulled it out now and turned it on.

"I've got to talk to Rep," she explained. After four unanswered rings she got a voice-mail prompt and said, "Honey, please call as soon as you can. This Sue Key mess just got a lot more serious."

◇◇◇

"You don't know the half of it," Rep said to her when she answered the phone in their apartment two hours later. "Max Levitan was murdered, apparently during the small hours this morning."

"Murdered," Melissa repeated numbly.

"I'm afraid so. Sue Key's case is connected to Levitan and may be linked to his murder. Therefore, it has now officially dropped off my job description. Detective Lieutenant Latrobe Washington and the Milwaukee Police Department can track down Roger Leopold's deposition and figure out what it means."

"Uh, well, actually," Melissa stammered, "they won't strictly speaking have to track the deposition down."

"Why not?"

"Because I've sort of indirectly stumbled over a copy of it. Dreyfus did steal Sue Key's notes, and then had the transcript typed up by a court reporter in Chicago. Sue called her and the transcript is probably sitting in my email right now."

"'Sort of indirectly stumbled over a copy of it' is provocative diction, *carisime*. How did you manage that little trick?"

Sounding fairly contrite, for her, she told him. Then she sighed and said, "Okay, let me turn off NPR so you can chew me out."

"'Lucy, you got some 'splainin' to do!', that kind of thing?"

"Yes. Plus a caustic observation about behaving with remarkable stupidity for someone holding three university degrees."

She braced herself.

"Well," Rep said then, "this is as close as I'm going to come to chewing you out. Quit beating yourself up. You spotted the danger. You decided to go ahead because you underestimated Dreyfus. You miscalculated a calculated risk. That's not stupidity, it's an error."

"An unforced error."

"But not an error of sloppiness or laziness. An error of enthusiasm."

"You say that almost like it's something admirable," Melissa said.

"It is. I'm proud of you."

Rep had every intention of leaving things right there. After Melissa got the Leopold transcript to Detective Washington, the only place they'd get further information about Max Levitan or Pelham Dreyfus would be the *Milwaukee Journal-Sentinel*. Adulterating the purity of these good intentions, however, was a worry that germinated in Rep's mind as he reviewed what Melissa had told him. It grew while he drove through the night to Wausau, and blossomed just before he found his way to a Hampton Inn near Exit 191.

Melissa had said that Dreyfus asked who'd sent her. So Dreyfus thought someone else was interested in something he had, whether it was the Leopold deposition notes or something else. And Dreyfus was apparently right, because someone had followed Kuchinski and Melissa—someone who had to have been keeping an eye on Dreyfus' studio while Melissa put on her act. Now this unknown character presumably suspected that Melissa might somehow have extracted the valuable information from Dreyfus, and he might come after her for it. By the time Rep finished unpacking in his room, this worry hadn't gone away.

Pretty Girls Smoking Cigarettes itself wasn't pornographic, but Dreyfus had clearly wanted Melissa to pose for something that crossed that line. Dabbling in porn risked involvement with organized crime. The mob doesn't control all production and distribution of pornography, just like it doesn't control all commercial trash hauling in New Jersey, but if you don't see it there at all you're not looking.

Rep had one source that Detective Lieutenant Washington didn't—and never would, if Rep could help it. He had to check his Palm Pilot for the number because it had recently changed— something it did with regularity. He thought for a moment about getting a fistful of quarters from the front desk and blundering out into the night in search of a pay phone. Then he realized that such thriller-novel precautions were unnecessary. Most of the calls to this number probably came from hotel rooms like this one, from lonely men away from home.

He used the room phone to dial 556-685-4968. Four rings, followed by the answering machine. After the insinuating introduction—"Have you been naughty?" and so forth—the beep finally came.

"This is Spoiled Sibling," he said, because events a generation ago kept him from using his name when he talked to his own mother. "I—"

"Hello," a voice he recognized interrupted.

"Hi." Rep checked his watch and subtracted two hours for California time. "I thought you'd be with a client right now."

"He left early. He wanted to test limits. The limits passed. In fact, you might say they aced the exam. What's on your mind?"

"I need to know about some people on the fringe of the industry. Max Levitan, Pelham Dreyfus, and I guess Roger Leopold."

"Hold it, let me get a pen....Okay, how far out on the fringe?"

"The final knot at the end of the last tassel on the far edge of the rug would be my guess," Rep said. "But I don't know."

"Well, I can't tell you anything right now. I'll ask around."

"Thanks. I appreciate it."

"You may not appreciate it right now, young man, but you will. Believe me, you will."

The words sounded familiar and well practiced. Rep wondered how many men in the last couple of weeks had felt a delicious *frisson* of fear and excitement tremble through their bodies when they heard that carefully cadenced phrase.

Well, it could be worse, he thought. *She could be an insurance defense lawyer.*

Chapter Thirteen

The warming trays in Helmsing Corporation's board room the next morning told Rep he was wasting his time. Danish, juice, and bagels were the stuff of a working breakfast. Scrambled eggs and sausage were a sin offering: *Sorry about the wild goose chase. Eat hearty.*

Rep surmised that Helmsing's vice-president of risk management had agreed to Rep's presentation only to extract lower rates and a more acute sense of urgency from the local lawyer the company already had. By ten-twenty Rep had finished a professional but brisk run-through and gotten back on the road, determined to drive straight through to Milwaukee and salvage a fraction of the day. By twelve-forty-five this firm resolve was evaporating rapidly. It disappeared altogether at twelve-forty-seven, when he saw the words FOOD NEXT EXIT on a freeway sign.

That promise proved less than candid, for the nearest restaurant lay more than a mile from the freeway and its appearance did nothing for his appetite. Rather than turn back he foraged a bit further. He was on the verge of giving up when he saw a weathered billboard announcing that Sally's Lake Delton Bar and Grill lay just around the next bend.

Either God has a sense of humor or the lords of coincidence are working overtime, and I'm too hungry to care which it is.

Nothing in Rep's southern Indiana boyhood prepared him for Lake Delton. Aside from the Great Lakes, which are basically freshwater inland seas, Rep's idea of a lake was a self-contained body of water that you could see across on a clear day. Lake Delton's deep blue, sailboat-dotted water started about three hundred feet from Sally's parking lot and with heart-stopping majesty stretched to the horizon in every direction. The idea that in two months this expanse would be a vast slab of ice thick enough to drive on—or not, as Vance Hayes had found out—took his breath away.

He entered the bar and grill under a sign that promised FISH FRY EVERY FRIDAY. He saw only six other patrons on this weekday afternoon, and none of them looked like they'd worn a tie outside of church in a long time. He heard the first flatlander joke before he had his menu open. Something about cannibals and stabbing yourself repeatedly with a fork. The risible possibilities struck Rep as limited, but the punch line drew guffaws. He assumed that the joke was for his benefit, and that telling the three guys at the table ten feet away that he was not, in fact, a flatlander would just spoil the fun.

Though he wasn't sure how, Rep could tell that the solidly built blonde in her mid-forties who came to take his order was the owner rather than just a hired waitress. She gave him a good-sport half-smile when she approached him at the bar with her pad. Rep studied the menu for an extra five seconds, wondering what "lutefisk" was.

Well, as long as I'm here anyway, how am I going to get these taciturn locals to open their mouths for me?

"Cheeseburger and a Leinenkugel," he said. "And some lutefisk."

Her eyebrows rose at the last word, but then she nodded and walked away, returning promptly with an open bottle of Leine's.

Twelve-by-eighteen photographs above the bar depicted Lake Delton's four seasons: fishing and swimming in spring, boating and water skiing in summer, canoeing and fishing again in fall, and ice-skaters and hockey players sharing the ice with scattered wooden huts and—Rep blinked, but there it was—pickup trucks in winter. Instead of being charmed by the bucolic idyll, the lawyer in Rep saw torts waiting to happen. Looking at the photographs, it was easy to imagine lots of ways to die under the water. Or the ice.

The next flatlander joke echoed through the room with considerable volume, but as with the first one Rep caught only the punchline: "So the ref says to the flatlander, 'On further review, the Bears still suck.'"

Rep swiveled in his chair and raised the Leine's.

"We feel the same way in Milwaukee," he said. "Go, Pack." He figured the Indianapolis Colts could take care of themselves.

Predictable murmurs of approval gave way to expectant silence as the lutefisk arrived. It looked like brownish-white Jell-O. When Rep dug in he found that it tasted like boiled cod that had been air-dried, soaked in lye, and then skinned and boned before cooking. This wasn't surprising, because that's what it was. By choking down four bites, Rep had apparently won the grudging tolerance of the other patrons. And of Sally, if that's who she was, who delivered the cheeseburger.

"I saw some kids ice-skating on the way in," Rep said to her. "I'm surprised that it's started already."

"We had a good, hard freeze last week," she said, as if a good, hard freeze was just the thing any sensible person would want. "Even so, those kids today are just on skating ponds with water two or three feet deep. I don't let mine go out on any lake until after December first, and not even then if we've had too many days above freezing. They say three inches for skating, four inches for snowmobiling, and six inches for trucks and cars, but I'm not taking any chances."

Rep worked a bit harder on a healthy bite of his burger while he tried to think of some clever follow-up that would keep Sally talking. No need. She resumed speaking before he could swallow, much less say anything himself.

"The big resorts, they actually drill cores out of the ice to see how thick it is," she said. "Their insurance companies make them, that's why they do it. They have to. It's right in their policies."

"Seems wise," Rep managed while Sally caught her breath.

"You can't go by that, though. No sir."

She rested both elbows on the bar and leaned toward Rep, reverential seriousness on her face and lutefisk on her breath.

"A lake is a living thing," she said with insistent intensity. "Especially spring-fed. The real heat isn't above the ice, it's below. That water is coming up from underneath the earth's crust, and it's not the same all over the lake. No sir. There are currents and eddies and flows that no one can see. There might be places where the ice is a foot thick, and places three hundred yards away where it's only a couple of inches. You can't tell. You just can't."

"No sir," Rep agreed. "Er, ma'am."

"They can have their rules of thumb, but I play it safe."

"Yeah. Actually, I thought I read a while back that someone at one of the big resorts on Lake Delton had gone through the ice and died."

"I know exactly what happened there," Sally said, with an emphatic forward head-snap. "Like I saw it myself. Guy got a snootful. Well, that happens. You know?"

"Yes," Rep said.

"And he goes out on the snowmobile. Happens all the time."

"Right."

"Now, this is in December, and I'll bet the cores they drilled that morning showed half a foot of ice if they showed an inch. But this guy who's three sheets to the wind, he zooms his Ski-Doo out there, you see?"

"Sure," Rep said.

"I know this is the way it happened. Had to. He gets out there four hundred, five hundred yards from shore." Sally's voice suddenly grew very quiet. "And guess what happens?"

Rep had no idea and was about to say so, but Sally didn't wait. She leaned forward and spoke slowly, giving deadly emphasis to each word.

"He hears the ice begin to crack."

Rep's belly dropped and he felt himself pale a bit at the sinister image.

"He panics," Sally said, speaking quickly now. "If he'd just turned the Ski-Doo around and headed back to shore, he'd have been all right. The hole they found wasn't all that big. But he panics, gets off the snowmobile and starts running in dress shoes across the ice. Slipping and falling down. Getting up. Getting more and more scared. That's when he went through. I'll betcha anything. That's when he went through."

"I may not be too smart," Rep said, panting a bit, "but I'm not dumb enough to bet against you."

Sally smiled at this gallant compliment. The local comedian rose from his table and bellied up to the bar next to Rep.

"You're smooth, boy," he said. "You Scandihoovian?"

"I don't have that honor," Rep said.

"'Don't have that honor.' You're all right."

"Thank you."

"You ever hear the one about the three flatlanders who wanted to go ice-fishing? You and Sally talking about the ice reminded me."

"Can't say I have." Rep began to wonder if these loquacious locals were ever going to shut up. And he suddenly realized what the huts in the winter scene were all about.

"Okay, there's these three flatlanders, see, and they decide they wanna come up to Wisconsin and give ice-fishing a try. So they drive up and go to Charlie's Bait and Tackle to get their kit. Course, Charlie tells 'em they'll need a saw to cut through the ice, so they buy one."

"Makes sense," Rep said.

"An hour later they're back. They've worn the saw down and the hole isn't big enough. Charlie says he can't understand that, but he sells them three more saws. Three hours later they're back again, and this time they're mad. They say, 'What's goin' on here? We've worn out four saws and we still can't get that boat in the water."

"That's good," Rep said, laughing. "I'll give you credit when I tell that one back in Milwaukee."

"Remember Charlie's Bait and Tackle," the guy said.

"Will do."

Rep put a ten on the bar and gestured to Sally to keep the change.

"Hello, beloved," Rep said to Melissa about five hours later, when he finally got back to their apartment. "Anything new?"

"Well, I got the deposition transcript to Detective Washington," Melissa said. "I hope he finds it more enlightening than I have. I've never waded through anything more tedious in my life."

"Yeah, as a general rule we have to pay people to read them."

"Well, I doubt that you pay them enough."

"Anything at all in there?" Rep asked.

"Nothing that I'd break a window for. Roger Leopold worked in Wisconsin for Orlofsky Publications, which had offices in Ohio."

"What was the lawsuit about?"

"Something boring about computers," Melissa said. "Specialized file maintenance software wasn't working properly, so the buyer was cross with the seller. The buyer wasn't paying, so the seller was cross with the buyer. That seemed to be the gist."

"Did either the buyer or the seller have anything to do with Cold Coast Productions?"

"Orlofsky and Cold Coast are owned by the same company, and they each used the other's employees now and then."

"So, much ado about money, as usual, but no smoking gun?"

"Not that I could see. One part wasn't just tedious but very odd. Maybe you can make more sense out of it. Fifth Post-It note."

Melissa tossed a hard copy of the emailed transcript to Rep, who flipped to the indicated page and began reading.

CONTINUED EXAMINATION BY MR. HAYES

Q: Showing you the document the reporter has marked exhibit seven for this deposition, do you recognize it?

A: Looks like a print-out of an email.

Q: Dated August 14, 2003, less than three months ago, is that correct?

A: That's what it says.

Q: Addressed to rleopold, is that you?

A: Yes.

Q: From someone called cincyfileuser. Who's that?

A: That was just the staff desktop computer at headquarters. Anyone who was there that day and knew the password could have sent the message.

Q: Do you have any recollection of receiving it?

A: Nope.

Q: Can you read the text of this email?

A: No. What's on this page is gibberish.

Q: Can you just read what's there into the record?

MR. SMITH: Objection. That's going to take all day. It speaks for itself. Just have the reporter type it out.

MR. HAYES: As long as she does it right now.

[TEXT OF EMAIL DEP EX 7]

Okat tge .gaek card uf tiy wabtm byt keave ne iyt if ut, /abd bever asj ne fir abttgubg agaub,

MR. HAYES:

Q: And your testimony under oath, Mr. Leopold, is that you have no idea what this message was intended to communicate?

A: No idea.

Q: And no recollection of getting this very odd message?

A: I assume this was picked up by my spam filter. I got a dozen of these a day, at least, talking about cheap pills and horny housewives and all that stuff. A lot of times they stuck garbage like this in to try to fool the spam filter and get you to click on a link.

Q: That's your story and you're sticking to it, huh?

MR. SMITH: Objection. Asked and answered and argumentative. You're harassing the witness now. Move to another topic or this deposition is over.

"Mean anything?" Melissa asked when Rep glanced up.

"Well, attorney Smith had a point about having a witness read a printed document into a deposition record. You don't do that unless you've got a very specific reason."

"So Hayes was up to something?"

"Yes, but he was apparently a better lawyer than I am because I can't tell you what it was."

"And now that Vance Hayes is dead," Melissa said reflectively, "Neither can he."

Chapter Fourteen

"The pun has to be intentional, don't you think?" MacKenzie Stewart said, nodding at the title of an oil painting in the foyer of the Yale Club in Washington, D.C.

Rep dutifully examined the canvas. It depicted a charming lass, sixteen or seventeen years old, in nineteenth-century country dress, carrying a basket brimming with peaches. Her ample straw hat emphasized candid and ingenuous features that, however, a slyly knowing look in her eyes and a rakish cock of her eyebrows subtly contradicted.

"*Filette aux Peches,*" Rep said, reading the title. "'Young woman with peaches,' I think, although my French is so rusty I'm getting that mostly from the painting itself. I'm afraid the pun eludes me."

"They've left the diacritical marks out," Stewart said. "Put a circumflex accent over the first *e*, making it *pêches,* and the title is indeed 'Young woman with peaches.' With an acute accent over both *e*'s, though, the word is *péchés* and the title becomes, 'Young woman with sins.' Too good to be accidental. Doesn't that gleam in her eye suggest that she might have had a little romp in the orchard while she was filling her basket?"

"She might be on her way to confession, at that," Rep agreed.

They entered the dining room to find Gael Cunningham-Stewart behind a glass of chardonnay in the far corner. The rich, French blue wallpaper might have been chosen expressly to set off generous silver strands that delicately filigreed her otherwise brown hair. She looked up from what Rep guessed was a bench memo, used a fingertip to scoot half-moon glasses from the tip to the bridge of her nose, and then smiled broadly and waved to them.

With the wave and the smile a glow of pure adoration lit Ken Stewart's face. His own hair matched his crisp, light gray mustache. Parted near the middle and combined with the puckish twinkle that normally lit his blue eyes, the gray paradoxically underscored a youthful élan. Female heads turned as he strode with effortlessly athletic grace through the room. His eyes, though, never left Gael, and his smile broadened as he and Rep approached. Rep hung back while Ken and Gael embraced. He noticed a happy flush on Ken's face when they broke the clinch.

"How is life as Your Honor?" Rep asked after they had seated themselves and ordered wine and appetizers.

"Better than life as 'shysterette,' which is how the last group vice-president I worked with referred to me when I was out of earshot."

"In this day and age? I thought male chauvinism that blatant went out around the time *Dynasty* was cancelled."

"It wasn't *male* chauvinism," Gael said. "The group v-p was a she who'd come up through marketing. In her view, there are three separate and unequal classes in corporate life: sales; engineering; and scum."

"Lawyers fall into the third group, in case you're wondering," Ken said.

"I've been putting up with that kind of attitude since 1978," Gael said. "Inside counsel have to swallow it at a lot of companies—especially the kind you can work your way up to with degrees from third-tier universities. There weren't any Wall Street firms pestering me for my resumé during my last year at Drake. You can imagine the appeal of a judgeship—even though Pritzger Medical paid me a lot more than the taxpayers are."

"Well, naturally," Ken said. "If you don't have to take a pay cut to be a judge, you're not qualified for the job."

"It took a solid ten years of Ken's life to make that judicial nomination happen," Gael said, brushing her knuckles tenderly against her husband's hand. "Sitting through party meetings, laughing at national committeemen's jokes, hustling tickets to thousand-dollar-a-plate fund-raisers. It was more than heroic—it was chivalric."

"Oh, it was tons of fun, really," Ken said with a dismissive finger-wave. "The year I was elected congressional district party chair, our fiercely leftist oldest son emailed me, 'Congratulations on becoming *Obergruppenfuhrer*.' I thanked him but suggested that it was illiberal of him to omit the umlaut over the final *u* in *Obergruppenführer*. That was worth the aggravation all by itself."

"Goodness, dear," Gael said in a mildly joshing tone, "how many foreign languages *do* you speak?"

"I'm not fluent in any," Ken said, "but I can be pretentious in three or four."

"Sometimes," Rep said, "I think it's incredible that any qualified candidate would be willing to go after a judicial position, given the pitiless scrutiny you have to endure."

"You got that exactly right," Ken said, with rare vehemence. "The interrogations seemed endless. Had we been paying nannies or pool men off the books? Hiring maids without green cards? Exceeding limits on campaign contributions? Buying laptops over the Internet without paying Indiana use tax? Belonging to private clubs that didn't have the requisite quota of lesbian midgets? They put our entire lives under a microscope."

"In a funny way," Gael said, "the most embarrassing question was whether I'd ever smoked marijuana. The handlers told me it was okay to just say 'of course' to that one, because everyone did some pot in college in the seventies. But I hadn't. I was too much of a grade-grubbing little nerd, scrambling after my chemical engineering major and then the law degree. You should have seen the fresh-faced young FBI agent's expression. He was like, *This is incredible—even I̲M̲ hipper than you are!*"

"All kidding aside," Ken added, "it was a very challenging experience psychologically. The partisan bitterness was bottomless. The staffers on the other side would have seized on any pretext they could find to shoot Gael down, just so they could get some face-time for their bosses on CNN and score a point against the White House."

Rep raised his glass.

"Here's to votes that come out the right way," he said.

"Here, here," Ken said, grinning jovially.

A waiter came over and they ordered. Rep felt that the pitch was going rather well. The easiest way to be charming is to let other people talk about themselves, and he was managing that just fine. Even so, more than a few butterflies fluttered in his stomach. A big Wisconsin company generating regular billings could by itself justify a real Milwaukee office with his firm's own name on the door and his own secretary working there. He decided to go for a little more charm.

"I know the judicial selection process is intensely political, but I hope your substantive qualifications helped a bit. I have your book on Trademark Office procedure on my shelf. That has to be one more book than most politicians have written."

"That's one more book than most politicians have *read*," Ken said. "Bruce, that scapegrace offspring I mentioned earlier eventually got a job on a senatorial staff. His first assignment was to compile a list of books his boss could mention when reporters asked him if he'd read anything recently."

"I never heard about that," Gael said. "What books did he suggest?"

"He came up with a couple of *really* short ones: *Better Luck Next Time, Sergei: Great Soviet Defense Attorneys;* and *Twice a Week in Summer: Case Studies in British Nymphomania.* He claims the guy never caught on."

When the entrées arrived, Rep figured that the time had come to move from polite charm to actual marketing. Ken Stewart helpfully made the transition for him. He casually mentioned solid IP work Rep had done for clients Ken had referred to him, and asked Rep about some of his other cases. This drew intrigued nods from Gael, who asked Rep for the new business card that showed contact information for both the Indianapolis office and the improvised space in Milwaukee.

Without warning, however, just about the time the three of them asked for coffee instead of dessert, Rep's meeting turned from a pitch into a beauty contest—that is, two lawyers going after the same client at the same time. Effecting this metamorphosis was a sixtyish man in a tuxedo (like Ken) instead of a suit (like Rep). Booming "Ken—what a stroke of luck!" from across the room, he bounded toward the table with the kind of confidence that comes from not being told no very often.

"I had no idea you were in D.C.," he said to Ken as he reached the table. "I'll steal a minute of your time to save a game of phone-tag tomorrow."

"Don't be rude, Jeremy," Ken said. "People will think you went to Harvard."

"I did go to Harvard," Jeremy said in a puzzled voice. "Oh, that's your point. Good one."

"Thank you."

"One word," he said then, holding up his left index finger as visual reinforcement of the promise. "Matt Cavendish told me you have a line on a potential new IP client, and asked me to remind you that the firm has a very good IP department itself. I told him you knew that, of course—"

"I know that we have an IP department."

"Now, Ken, Matt's work is first rate. He knows the field thoroughly."

"In that case his work should speak for itself and he'll need no marketing help from me."

Jeremy frowned. A glimmer of disappointment spoiled his heretofore sunny smile.

"Are you still upset over that silly remark he made years ago about you being the, uh, the—whatever it was?"

"'The decaying remnant of the shopworn WASP ascendancy,'" Ken said. "No, I was never upset about that, although the acronym is fifty percent inaccurate in my case."

Ken paused and sipped coffee to see if the bafflement on Jeremy's face would clear. It didn't.

"Scots-Irish, not Anglo-Saxon," Ken explained then. "We beat Anglo-Saxons up on the playground."

"Well, then," Jeremy said, "if Matt has been guilty of some other indiscretion—"

"Trying to steal billing credit for a client I brought into the firm isn't an indiscretion. It's a capital offense."

Jeremy leaned forward in an effort to introduce a man-to-man element into the conversation.

"Ken, I'm the managing partner of the second biggest office in the firm. I have the entire firm's welfare to think about—not just the egos of two partners. What would you do in my position?"

"I'd bother some partner who has less than a million a year in billings," Ken said. "Have a pleasant evening. And by all means, give my best to Matt."

It took Jeremy a full second to realize that he'd just been told to go to hell. It didn't take Rep that long to be *very* glad that he'd given the Hayes eulogy Stewart had asked for, and to make a mental note never to cross Stewart the longest day he lived.

Half an hour later Rep and Ken were standing on the sidewalk outside the Yale Club, waiting for Gael to rejoin them and for a valet to bring Ken's Lincoln Navigator around. They moved a few feet down Connecticut Avenue to distance themselves from a patron just out of the Blue Note Jazz Club whose inability to flag a cab was producing increasingly audible frustration.

"Don't count your chickens yet," Ken said to Rep, "but I think you're in. You made the right noises at the right times. Five-to-one Gael is making a phone call from the cloak room."

"I can't tell you how much I appreciate it, Ken."

Gael came out and strolled in their direction. Rep noticed that she was re-stowing a cell phone in her purse.

"Hey!" the jazz patron yelled, flapping his right arm as a cab whizzed by.

"Not to show off," Ken said, "but I can't take this anymore."

Putting both pinkies into his mouth, he strode into the middle of Connecticut Avenue. A shrill, piercing screech blasted from his mouth. Two cabs going in opposite directions screeched to a halt a few feet from each other.

"Thanks," the patron blurted. Then, eyeing Ken's tuxedo, he tendered two crisp dollars to him on his way to the nearer cab. With a smile and a mock forelock tug, Ken accepted the money.

"Are you going to keep that?" Gael asked as the Navigator pulled up.

"I'm not only going to keep it," Ken said, "I'm going to include it on our tax return—or, as I like to call it, our opening offer to the government."

"I talked with Eddie Muser and he'd like to meet you," Gael said to Rep as they climbed into the massive vehicle. "He tends to blow with the latest breeze, though. You might want to get in there as fast as you can."

"My flight tomorrow is at eleven and I pick up an hour flying west," Rep said. "I'll call him from the airport and see if I can set something up for late afternoon."

"I'll go you one better than that," Ken said. "I'm flying to Wisconsin on the Gulfstream at the crack of dawn to track down a client who's up in Door County to fish. He has to sign some new trust instruments before his next quarterly estimated taxes are due. I'd back-date them but I'm already over my felony quota for this fiscal year. I can drop you off in Milwaukee on the way, and with any luck you can be chatting face to face with Mr. Muser before noon."

"What can I say?" Rep asked, grinning and shaking his head in wonder at his luck. "Let me know if there's someone you need to have killed."

"Careful," Ken said with a gentle laugh. "If Jeremy leans on me too hard, I might call that chit in someday."

Chapter Fifteen

"Bruce calls that my ego wall."

Rep glanced politely at the eight-by-ten and eleven-by-fourteen color photographs covering the Gulfstream's port bulkhead: Stewart hammering a piton into rock on El Capitan; Stewart in a crash helmet behind the wheel of a Formula One race car; Stewart in dripping scuba gear on the stern of a cabin cruiser; Stewart on a snowboard catching air off a mogul; Stewart surfing into a curl off Malibu; Stewart hang-gliding; Stewart airborne on water skis; Stewart in chest-waders and knee-deep in rushing water, a fly rod describing an unmistakable casting arc over his head; Stewart rafting through boiling white rapids; Stewart sailboarding; a much younger Stewart in olive drab with an M-16 in his right hand, silver bars on his shoulders, and rice paddies behind him; Stewart with a Browning over-and-under double-barreled shotgun cradled in his left arm.

"'Ego wall' seems harsh."

"He's exactly wrong," Stewart said. "It's an insecurity wall. An insistent shout that I'm not just a member of the lucky sperm club."

"Well, I'd say you've laid that to rest, whatever it is."

"The phrase comes from Mathew Thomas McCann—the 'Matt' who came up during my encounter with Jeremy at the club last night. I opened my firm's Indianapolis office when I was a fourth-year associate."

"I'm surprised your firm needed an Indianapolis office," Rep said.

"The management committee was surprised too. I forced the issue, and they wanted to hang onto me. Always was a pushy little sonofabitch. Anyway, I came home to Indy, set up shop, played golf and tennis at the country club, passed out business cards, and sat at my desk waiting for the phone to ring."

"It must have rung quite a bit."

"It rang all right. In two years I had a comfortable little white shoe practice going. I was at a firm retreat, getting patted on the head and offered early partnership, when I overheard the lucky sperm club line from Matt."

"Envy is the defining sin of the mediocre," Rep said.

"So it is. Notwithstanding which, he was absolutely right. My family has had real money since before the Civil War. I went to prep school with rich people, college with rich people, and law school with rich people. They didn't call the lawyers whose dads had been truck drivers or shop stewards because they'd never met them or heard of them. They called me."

"So you—what? Overcompensated?"

"As a means to an end. I decided to get clients who didn't already have me on their Christmas card lists. I found comfortable, affluent residential streets in Indianapolis, with BMWs or Corollas in the driveways. I figured that in one or two houses on each block I'd find people with two million dollars in the bank instead of eighty thousand. They needed sophisticated estate plans and *inter vivos* trusts as much as the swells in the gated mansions—*but they had no idea that they needed them.* I went after those people—and I got them."

"By mountain climbing and fly-fishing and duck hunting?"

"Bingo. They lapped it up. It's skeet-shooting in that last picture, by the way, not duck hunting. Hunting was one part of the testosterone pool where I refused to swim. I still remember Joseph Wood Crutch's line from the fifties: 'Destroy something man made and they call you a vandal; destroy something God made and they call you a sportsman.'"

"Well, I hope Bruce gets his issues worked out," Rep said.

"He will," Stewart answered confidently. "He's only twenty-four. Gael says he's knocking the felt off his antlers—looking for his own way to show he's not just a member of the lucky sperm club."

I could take all the name-calling in the world if it went along with trappings like this. Rep settled back luxuriantly against a soft, leather headrest and idly swirled fresh orange juice in a real glass tumbler. No waiting in the security line at Reagan National Airport or Dulles. No taking his shoes off before the metal detector, or struggling to put them back on after it. He took out his Palm Pilot to check the name and telephone number of the guy he was supposed to call as early as he decently could.

"Wait a minute," Rep said suddenly. *No taking his shoes off.* "I just thought of something about Vance Hayes."

"What's that?" Stewart asked, stabbing a paragraph on the sixth page of the *Wall Street Journal* with his index finger as he looked up.

"The police report on the recovery of Hayes' body said he had a shoehorn in the right-hand pocket of his sport coat. I just figured out why."

"I'll bite. Why?"

"He was planning on flying somewhere. It's a savvy traveler kind of thing. If you fly commercially and you're wearing dress shoes, it's smart to carry your own shoehorn along with you so you can put your shoes back on properly after you've cleared security."

"I'm not very familiar with the airports in central Wisconsin," Stewart said, "but I don't know of any he'd have been going to at that time of night on a snowmobile and without any luggage."

"You've got me there."

"Senior moment, maybe. All the time he spent with his good friends Jack and Daniel had to have destroyed some brain cells. And the diabetes depressed him. His doctor said if he didn't change his drinking habits he'd die, and he said, 'Never drinking is a lot like being dead.'"

"I can see his point," Rep said.

"Why did the Hayes file suddenly spring to mind, by the way? Are you still re-writing that eulogy that you've tormented yourself about so much?"

"Not exactly. It's that odd series of coincidences I mentioned to you earlier. Instead of going quietly into the archives, my new client's case keeps ramifying in unexpected ways." Rep then brought Stewart up to date on developments since their phone call a couple of days before.

"Extra effort is always a plus, but revisiting Vance Hayes seems above and beyond, even for a new client," Stewart said.

"I tend to obsess a bit over the past."

"Excessively rigorous toilet training, or is there a less prosaic reason?"

Rep hesitated. He'd never told anyone but Melissa about this. In this warm, male-bonding milieu, though, especially after Stewart's comments about his son and with the Gulfstream's throbbing engines providing a soothing background drone, Rep felt a current of complicity running between himself and the older man.

"My mother was arrested for murder when I was fifteen months old," Rep said then. "During Vietnam she'd hooked up with a loser who planned on selling weapons grade fulminate of mercury to anti-war radicals. It turned out to be a sting. The dissidents were really Oklahoma highway patrolmen."

"Not a promising scenario."

"No. Gunfight in a rural parking lot, followed by a tire-squealing getaway leaving a dead cop behind. Texas Rangers gunned the loser down a couple of days later. By then he'd abandoned Mom for her own good. She hitched a ride with Dad during her escape, came back to Indiana with him, and had me while she was hiding in plain sight for two years. Arrest, imprisonment, and escape after eight years. That's where the record stops."

"And you never saw her while she was in prison?"

"The entire time I was growing up, no one told me about her," Rep said. "I mean not one single thing—not even her name. It was as if she'd just been erased from history, like one of those guys purged in the Soviet Union. I had no memory of her, no record of her except an old photograph."

"My God. What a thing to grow up with."

"I didn't find out what had happened until I tracked it down myself while I was in college. Even then, I wasn't even sure whether she'd really escaped or just been killed by a guard who covered it up."

Rep stopped talking. If a Greek chorus had been present it would have been chanting, "And then? And then?" But the Gulfstream was short on Greek choruses, and Stewart was too savvy to ask such clumsy questions. If his mother had died, Rep would have said so. If he still didn't know what had happened, he would have said that. Since he wasn't saying, he must know. Which was why he'd just shut up. Friends don't give friends guilty knowledge.

Neither of them spoke for several seconds. The silence began to hang a bit heavy, and Rep cast about for something innocuous to fill it.

"Speaking of coincidences, do you know what Hayes was working on only a couple of months before he died? Some collection-slash-commercial fraud case involving a defendant called Orlofsky Publications—which turns out to be a sister company of Cold Coast Productions. He took one deposition and the case settled the next day."

"I'm not surprised," Stewart snorted. "Ohio company, right?"

"Right."

"I set up the spendthrift trust for the little twit who ended up as chief operating officer of that outfit. Sammy Baldwin. He's a broken twig on the end of the shortest branch of the Baldwin family tree. They wouldn't let him anywhere near the family business, so he clipped a few coupons and bought himself a job at Orlofsky. If his lawyer called and said Hayes looked mean during the dep and Sammy was next on the witness list, Sammy probably told him to settle up so he wouldn't miss his flight to Gstaad."

"Why don't my clients ever get to sue companies like that?"

"Hayes was a good client," Stewart said. "He paid his bills on time, and I wish he were still alive and paying them. As long as he had to die, though, I just wish he'd roast comfortably in hell instead of sneaking back to complicate lives here in the temporal realm."

"Amen," Rep said as he set the Palm Pilot down. "I think I'll use the restroom."

"Please," Stewart joshed, "on a plane this expensive it's the head."

◇◇◇

"The idea of having a female hard-boiled private eye is provocative," Melissa said to the multiply-pierced, ringlet-haired young man across the desk from her, "but it isn't strictly speaking new."

"No sh— I mean, really?" the sophomore creative writing aspirant said, his eyes widening in disappointment. "Man. I'm thinking, like, *man*, Mike Hammer in drag, right? I'm like, *no one* has *ever* done that before, am I right?"

"N is for Not Exactly." Melissa stole a glance to see if he'd caught the allusion. He hadn't. "Sue Grafton. You might also want to check out Sara Paretsky. Those two will do for a start."

The phone rang.

"Oh," the student said.

"Why don't you run this through the word processor again and see what happens?" she suggested gently as she answered the phone.

"Hello," Rep said, shouting a bit to be heard over engine noise in the background. "Is this a bad time?"

"No, I've just finished a conference." Melissa sketched a quick bye-bye wave in the student's direction to emphasize the hint.

"I need a favor," Rep said. "Could you look up the number of whatever the biggest cab company in Milwaukee is? I'm going to be landing in a private plane at a secondary airport called Timmerman Field in a little over an hour, and I don't think there'll be a cab-stand there."

"Let's see," Melissa said. "This is the part where I say, 'No darling, don't be silly. I'll just drop what I'm doing here at the university so that I can run out and pick you up myself.' Right?"

"Almost. I'm kind of hoping that you'll also offer to bring a couple of Sausage McMuffins with you."

"That was dangerously close to flippant, dear."

"Well, I just left the airspace of Virginia, the Cavalier State."

"I'll do it because I owe you for not chewing me out over Pelham Dreyfus," she said. "But I want you to know that you're not fooling anyone—and you'll be getting yogurt instead of McSausages."

Chapter Sixteen

"Have you heard anything about Detective Washington getting a search warrant for Dreyfus' studio, based on your adventure there?" Rep asked Melissa about ninety minutes later as she drove the Sable away from Timmerman Field, toward the sun and downtown Milwaukee.

"Walt says that they're still trying to get a statement from the court reporter in Chicago to verify that Dreyfus sent her the notes stolen from Sue Key's apartment. Without that, he doesn't think there's enough of a link to Levitan's murder for a warrant. I've been wondering if I should talk directly to Detective Washington about it myself."

"*That's* a thought-provoking comment." Rep shot an appraising look at his wife. "Why do you say that?"

Melissa found this question awkward. She generally bet against coincidence, and Kuchinski-coincidences were piling up at a dizzying pace. She didn't feel comfortable sharing this opinion with Rep quite yet, though. It seemed harsh to imply that his best friend in Milwaukee—and the guy who'd rescued her from Dreyfus—might have his own unlovely agenda. She'd feel guilty about prevaricating, but she figured she could handle that.

"Well, it just doesn't seem fair to dump so much of the burden on Walt in a case where he's already done so much even though his real involvement is pretty tangential."

"Done things like coming to the aid of a damsel in distress."

"Things like that, yes," Melissa said. "Although I think it's 'domina in distress' if the rescuee no longer has her maidenhead."

"That's why your cumulative SATs beat mine by twelve points."

"Only ten, dear."

"Thank you."

That was WAY too easy.

They had by now reached Capitol Drive, which would take them through what the *Milwaukee Journal-Sentinel* bashfully calls "the near north side" of Milwaukee to the upper east side, where Rep could drop Melissa at UWM. The speed limit had dropped from forty-five to thirty and they had passed two Kentucky Fried Chickens and one Popeye's before Rep spoke again.

"Suppose one of your colleagues was putting a conference together and he asked you who the leading Trollope scholar in the Midwest was. What would you say?"

"Harry Simpson at Washington University in St. Louis. Ask me a tough one."

"Suppose this same colleague called an assistant professor in the English Department at, say, the University of Minnesota and asked the same question. What would that prof say?"

"Barring incompetence or professional jealousy I expect he'd say the same thing. It's not a particularly close question."

"Picking local counsel for an out-of-town case is like that," Rep said. "You want someone who really knows all the judges and the clerks and the nooks and crannies of the system. So if I call one of my law school classmates in Milwaukee and ask for a recommendation, and Vance Hayes calls a completely different Milwaukee contact a few years later and asks for a recommendation, you wouldn't be shocked to the soles of your shoes if they recommend the same guy."

"Walt Kuchinski, for example."

"Yes, Walt would be a highly pertinent example."

"I take your point."

"Right. It isn't necessarily an unlikely and highly suspicious coincidence that Hayes and I independently stumbled over

Walt. It doesn't mean that Walt exploded into this case because he has his own secrets hidden somewhere in the murky depths of Hayes' unsavory past."

"I did mention that I got your point."

"You did at that. Sorry."

"You're absolutely right," Melissa said.

"Happens every once in awhile."

"So when you said okay about ten minutes ago you realized that it was actually the coincidences that were bothering me—right?"

"Guilty," Rep said. "They've been bothering me, too—and since your cumulative SATs were ten points higher than mine, you must have spotted the issue at least as soon as I did."

"I don't mean to be cross," Melissa said as she smacked the dashboard in irritation, "but you could have just said that you'd seen through me. You didn't have to trap me in a Socratic dialogue, like a law student who hadn't thought the problem through."

"No, I didn't have to, exactly. It was entirely voluntary."

Melissa double-parked outside Curtin Hall at UWM.

"One trip on a private jet and you're verging on insufferable," she said, raising a reproachful index finger. "Although perhaps I lost my temper a little quickly over it."

"You piqued too soon, so to speak. To quote the smartest person I know, I just didn't want you to think you were fooling anybody."

"I had that one coming. See you sixish. Good luck with the prospective client."

Chapter Seventeen

"How did the client meeting go?" Melissa asked, her words on Rep's cell phone muffled by the roar of traffic on I-43 South.

"I won ugly. The new general counsel and I didn't click, but he figures he won't get fired for listening to Gael Cunningham-Stewart. The engagement letter will go out first thing tomorrow morning."

"Honey, that's wonderful. Congratulations."

"Thanks. How was your day?"

"Outstanding, actually," Melissa said. "I had a student this afternoon who not only had tumbled to the fact that Napoleon Bonaparte lived at the same time as Jane Austen but wondered whether that curious fact might have had some impact on her writing."

"Curiosity awakened. A pedagogical triumph."

"Of the first order," Melissa said, adding casually, "I did have a chat with Detective Washington. They're talking to a judge about a warrant."

"Just in case Walt was putting the wrong spin on things."

"That's one way to put it. Upset?"

"Nope. I married a clever girl and I knew what I was getting into. I should still make it by six, even with a stop at the office. I just crossed the Milwaukee County line."

"'Til then, beloved."

Rep disconnected and put the phone in the cup-holder. He sighed with contented relief. *Pros are on the job. God's in His heaven and all's right with the world.* Practicing law was a lot more fun than playing cops-and-robbers with Kuchinski, and he suspected it was a lot healthier as well.

That's when his phone beeped.

"Reppert," MacKenzie Stewart's voice said after Rep answered, "I feel like a perfect ninny."

"Where are you?"

"At a strip mall coffee shop about a quarter-mile from the east gate to Timmerman Field. I had to caffeinate myself and walk off some frustration before my head exploded."

"What happened?"

"My hideously expensive airplane got temperamental on the return trip from Door County, to start with," Stewart said. "I decided not to risk flying all the way back to Indianapolis, so I had the pilot land here to look things over. We seem to have thrown a rod."

"That doesn't sound good."

"It's quite bad, and it gets worse. My pilot thought he had a line on a replacement part somewhere in a place called Waukesha. He just called to say it's the wrong part. My Gulfstream will be stuck here for a couple of days."

"So you'll be flying commercial back to Indianapolis?"

"I will if I can get to Milwaukee's main airport within the next hour or so. Unfortunately, Veterans Taxi has promised me a cab within ten minutes three times in the last half-hour and hasn't delivered. I'm losing confidence in it."

"Tell you what, I'll bet I can get there in fifteen minutes," Rep said. "And if I don't get too mixed up on the freeways, I should be able to get you to General Mitchell Field with a few minutes to spare."

"I hate to ask, but I would deeply appreciate it."

"Don't be silly. It's the least I can do."

"If you sense on your way over here that anything funny is going on, by the way," Stewart said, "don't take any chances. Just give me a call on my cell phone and I'll make other arrangements.

Staying overnight in Milwaukee wouldn't be any tragedy, if it came to that."

"What are you talking about?"

"I hate to sound melodramatic, but the Gulfstream is too reliable to just throw a rod all of a sudden. We both know that Vance Hayes wasn't any boy scout. Coming on top of the adventures that have befallen you and your lovely wife, I can't help wondering whether he was mixed up with bad people who are afraid that we're somehow about to kick over the wrong rock."

"Well, I, for one, have stopped kicking," Rep said. "But between now and the time I drop you at Billy Mitchell Field, I expect cops with radar guns will be a greater threat to me than thugs from Vance Hayes' past."

Milwaukee's rush hour lasts about twenty minutes. At least on the west side, it's easy even for a newcomer to find his way around. Rep didn't have any trouble getting back to Timmerman Field and thence to the strip mall Stewart had described. He saw Stewart standing on the parking lot next to a FedEx drop box. He was speaking into what Rep assumed was a Dictaphone in his right hand while he waved his left arm at Rep. At his feet was a trial bag—not a subtly elegant briefcase like IP lawyers carry, but one of those massive, boxy, trial lawyer things that look like anvil salesmen's sample cases.

The parking lot would have been about the right size if everyone in America drove Mini Coopers. As it was, Rep pulled his Sable as close to the storefronts as he could to make sure he cleared PVC pipes that jutted from the bed of a Dakota pickup truck angle-parked on the street side of the lot.

"You made good time," Stewart said as he approached.

"No bad guys on the way," Rep said. He turned the engine off and got out so that he could open the trunk for Stewart's trial bag.

Out of the corner of his eye, as he turned toward the back of the car, Rep glimpsed Stewart's smile twist suddenly into a shocked grimace.

"Reppert, look out!" Stewart shouted, dropping his trial bag and pointing emphatically with his right arm.

Before Rep could jerk his head very far in that direction, his surroundings pinwheeled kaleidoscopically around him as Stewart's body thudded into his and slammed him into unforgiving concrete.

"What the hell?" he demanded, in eloquent incoherence.

"Stay down!" Stewart ordered. "We just got shot at!"

Stewart, sprawled on top of Rep, rolled onto the parking lot, shifted his weight to his hips, and hoisted his torso for a cautious look around.

"I don't see him," he said. "He must have driven off." Stewart climbed laboriously to his feet and began brushing off his Marks and Spencer tweeds.

"What happened?"

"I saw a muzzle flash from a reddish sedan speeding by."

"That's incredible," Rep said, abrasions smarting under his clothes as he stood up. He remembered Kuchinski thinking that a maroon sedan had followed him and Melissa on their escape from Dreyfus' studio.

"Believe it," Stewart said. He pointed to the driver's side front window on the Sable, now starred with spidery cracks radiating from an ugly impact point near the middle. "I have a feeling I'm not going to make my flight."

"I guess the next thing to do is call the police." Rep reached for the Sable's door handle so that he could retrieve his cell phone.

"You might want to use the pay phone around the corner, so you don't disturb the car before the police look it over."

"Right, absolutely right," Rep muttered distractedly.

It took fifteen seconds to get through to someone on nine-one-one, and forty more for the dispatcher to satisfy herself that no one was bleeding or suffocating, which put this call low on her priority list. Rep needed another three minutes to find fifty cents in his pocket, dial Melissa's number, and tell her not to worry but he probably wouldn't be there by six after all and she might want to take a cab home. When he got back to the car Stewart was striding back from the direction of the FedEx drop-box.

"Hell of a note," Stewart said, smiling mordantly. "To quote Justice Holmes, 'What a loss to American jurisprudence if it had gotten us both.'"

A squad car got there nine minutes later, and a second three minutes after that. By the time the second arrived the first cop had verified that Rep and Stewart weren't hurt and was getting their account of what had happened.

"Forgive the cliché," Stewart said, "but it happened so fast. We were getting ready to stow my trial bag and get in the car, and all of sudden I saw a bright flash from the window of a car going by about two hundred feet away. We hit the deck, and by the time we got up the car was nowhere in sight."

"Car," the cop said. "Make, model, color, license?"

"Reddish," Stewart said. "I think it was Japanese, but I couldn't pin it down any farther than that. I don't have a clue about the license plate."

"How about you?" the cop asked, turning toward Rep.

"I didn't see a thing," Rep said, shaking his head. "It completely blindsided me."

The second cop had been examining Rep's Sable. Now he came over, cradling a lump of dark metal in the palm of his hand.

"What do you think of this?" he asked his colleague.

"Thirty-eight," the first cop said without hesitation.

"Three fifty-seven maybe?" the second cop asked.

"Nah, too big. Even from two hundred feet off, a three fifty-seven with any powder grain count at all would have blown the whole window out." He looked back at Stewart. "You sure that was a muzzle flash you saw?"

"I saw plenty of muzzle flashes in Vietnam," Stewart said. "I know what muzzle flashes look like, and that was a muzzle flash."

"Hey, this thing came out of a gun all right," the second cop said. "You can see the striations just with the naked eye."

"Oh, well, we'll just skip ballistics then," the first cop said. Smiling at Rep and Stewart, he cocked his head toward his colleague. "Polish cowboy." He turned back to the other cop. "I *know* it came out of a gun. How else would it have gotten here? What I was thinking was maybe it came from a gun a lot farther off. We have drive-bys now and then in Milwaukee, but usually on the near north side, not way out here—and these two don't look like guys in the middle of a turf war to me. I'm wondering if some Nimrod was out there plinking and really blew one."

"I'll leave that to you," Stewart said. "Anything else from us?"

"Guess not," the first cop said. "We'll do a standard area check. You two can be on your way and wait for a call from the guys with gold shields."

"Great," Rep said numbly. "Oh, you might want to let Detective Latrobe Washington know about this right away. He'll be interested."

As understatements go, this one turned out to be world-class.

Chapter Eighteen

"Where are you right now, honey?" Melissa asked Rep over his cell phone just before nine that night.

"I'm headed north on I-94, just passing the Allen Bradley clock. I should be home in ten minutes."

"That's good, because Detective Washington is here and is quite keen about talking to you. They finally got a warrant for Dreyfus' studio."

"And how is Mr. Dreyfus?" Rep asked, his pulse quickening.

"Absent. He seems to have decamped hurriedly not too long before their visit. They did, however, find a handgun which I gather Detective Washington is anxious to show you."

"What kind of handgun?"

"I'm a bit hopeless in that area, I'm afraid," Melissa said. "It reminds me of the 'Faster Than a Speeding Bullet!' gun they used to fire at the beginning of the old *Superman* TV show in the fifties. A professor in a Post-War American Popular Culture course I took used it as an example of masculine modes of iconic discourse."

"You mean you got college credit for watching television?"

"Well, there *was* a paper."

Rep found his wife and Washington sitting over coffee cups in the apartment's dining area at a sturdy wooden table brought from Indianapolis that Rep and Melissa were now provisionally using as an all-purpose work space. A steel-blue revolver with a brown, cross-hatched grip lay in a Baggie between them.

"You're right," Rep said, "it does look a lot like the *Superman* gun. Although the barrel on this one seems a bit longer, and I don't remember a lanyard ring."

"This is a Smith and Wesson thirty-eight caliber revolver," Washington said. "When I was a kid, thirty-eights were the universal handgun in almost every cop show and gangster movie that came along."

"That rings a bell," Rep confirmed.

"Those shows were realistic, too," Washington said, in a let's-be-friends tone. Like they were shooting the bull in Rep's den before the Packer game. "Thirty-eights were the standard urban police handgun for a long time. Smith and Wesson even had a higher-powered cartridge that it called 'Thirty-eight Police Positive.' Two -hundred-thirty grains of powder instead of one-eighty, or something like that."

"You're using the past tense a lot," Melissa said.

"Thirty-eights have been out of style for quite a while. Most cops under forty these days are gonna pack a Glock automatic or a Browning nine millimeter parabellum."

"I remember reading something about that in the *New York Times* a couple of years ago," Melissa said. Just chatting, putting on the same act Washington was. No hurry. Not impatient about where this was going.

"Point is, even though thirty-eights aren't all that common anymore, we've had two shootings within a few days involving connected people, one of them fatal, and they were both with thirty-eights."

"Like the one there that you found in Dreyfus' studio," Rep said.

"Maybe. If this were a TV show we'd magically have a ballistics test done already and we'd know. Here in the real world, it's gonna take a few days. But while I wouldn't bet my pension on this weapon matching up with the Levitan ballistics and the bullet fired at you this afternoon, I might take a flyer with a week's pay. I'll tell you why."

"Okay," Melissa said.

"There were no recoverable fingerprints on this gun. Nor on the bullets loaded in it. Nor the shell casings for the two bullets fired from it. What does that tell you?"

"Pelham Dreyfus wiped the gun and the cartridges clean," Rep said. "Or someone did. Not something you'd do with a weapon you have for home protection or target shooting. That gun was almost certainly used to commit at least one crime."

"Bingo. Which is why I was so anxious to see you."

"Here I am," Rep said.

"After you got shot at this afternoon, you called nine-one-one at four-forty-four p.m. How long after the shot was fired did you make that call?"

"Couple of minutes, max," Rep said. "I found a pay phone maybe eighty feet away and made the call."

"It couldn't have been longer, could it?" Washington asked innocently. "Like maybe forty-five minutes or an hour? You know, like maybe it took a few minutes to make sure you weren't hurt, and see if there were bad guys still in the area, and then call your wife? You know how time can really run away from you without you realizing it."

"No way," Rep said. "Two minutes at the outside."

"Here's what's bothering me, then. When we found out Dreyfus had skipped, we sent out the usual bulletins. A TSA officer at O'Hare Airport in Chicago thinks he saw someone who fits our description of Dreyfus clear security in Terminal Five around six p.m."

"Terminal Five is where most international flights take off."

"Right. Now, the i.d. could be wrong. TSA officers see thousands of people a day. This guy was an ex-MP, though, and he sounds pretty sure. If Dreyfus was clearing O'Hare security at six o'clock, he would've had a helluva time taking a potshot at you and your buddy ninety miles away only eighty minutes before. It wouldn't violate the laws of physics, but it would violate the laws of dealing with rush hour traffic in two cities."

"No way that happened," Melissa said, shaking her head.

"Right," Rep agreed. "And if Dreyfus wasn't the one who shot at Ken and me, maybe whoever did planted the gun at Dreyfus' studio to try to pin Levitan's murder on Dreyfus."

"That's one theory, all right. And before I drop it, someone is going to have to explain to me how Dreyfus could have been careful enough to get his computer files and his negative files and the deposition transcript we know he got and almost every other incriminating thing out of his apartment, but leave a murder weapon behind."

"*Almost* every other incriminating thing?" Melissa asked.

"He left a long list of raunchy phone numbers, including some to places overseas. But he cleaned out almost everything else except the gun. We didn't even find those copies of *Soldier for Hire* magazine that Ms. Pennyworth had noticed."

"If Levitan's murderer trying to frame Dreyfus is just one theory," Melissa said, "I'd like to hear the other ones."

"What I meant by that was, let's do this in baby steps," Washington said. "For example: where's Ken Stewart right about now?"

"God willing and weather permitting," Rep said, "he's getting ready to sleep in his own bed in Indianapolis."

"You mean even with having to wait around to report the shooting this afternoon you still got him to Mitchell in time for his flight?"

"No, I got him to O'Hare in time for a commuter flight from there."

"You just dropped everything on the spur of the moment at the end of a long day and made a hundred-eighty-mile round trip to and from O'Hare for this guy?" Washington demanded. "He must be a friend in a million."

"He is," Rep said, after a reflective pause. "That's exactly what he is."

Chapter Nineteen

The following Monday afternoon, in the twelfth-floor conference room of his firm's Indianapolis headquarters, Rep briefed three young associates on the delights of the upcoming IP audit. Buried in the file cabinets of this new client and squirreled away in the hard drives of its computers, he explained, they would find little sacks of gold. With contagious fervor—at least he hoped it was contagious—he depicted the elation that awaited them when they stumbled over trademarks whose registrations would have to be renewed in twenty-three countries, royalty arrearages that could now be happily collected, and long-forgotten cross licensing agreements screaming for synergistic exploitation.

This would, he warned, seem a bit tedious at first. Rather tedious, in fact. Indeed, when you got right down to it, a dreary slog through a Serbonian bog. In the end though, he assured them, they would find their efforts amply rewarded—not, to be sure, in money, which would all go to Rep and his partners, but in the infinitely more precious coin of professional satisfaction. He promised to meet them at General Mitchell Field in Milwaukee Tuesday afternoon, whence they would drive to a very nice Ramada near the client's exurban headquarters, away from the distractions of Milwaukee night life.

He then went back to the well-appointed office that the firm still kept for him in Indianapolis. The official rationale for this redundant work-space was that Rep had to spend a day or two every two weeks here, touching base with longstanding clients.

Less officially, the office symbolized the expectation that he would abandon the madcap Milwaukee adventure in less than a year and come back to Indianapolis for good.

As he settled behind his desk this afternoon and listened to voice-mails, that unwelcome possibility seemed to recede. He had no trouble imagining the pleasant computations whirring through the heads of the partners who had made it a point to cross paths with him and greet him warmly. Three associates times eight hours per day times three days times an effective billing rate of maybe two hundred fifty dollars an hour—and that's just for Phase One. Maybe this Milwaukee boondoggle could actually work.

Thank you, Ken Stewart.

"Hey, counselor," Kuchinski's voice said on the last voice-mail. "Just got a flash from a compadre down at the Safety Building. Ballistics did a quick and dirty check. It's not the test they'll use in court, but they're pretty sure about the match. The bullet that killed Levitan and the one fired at you and Stewart both came from the gun they found in Dreyfus' studio."

Rep was still thinking about that when the phone rang and he answered it.

"I may need a copyright lawyer in the Midwest." The voice was friendly but no-nonsense. "Someone recommended you."

Rep caught his breath. His mother knew that he'd call her Tuesday night. If she felt the need to call him—the riskiest thing she could possibly do—something major had to be behind it.

"I see. What's the nature of the problem?"

"I got a report that someone is misappropriating my commercially valuable phone number," Rep's mother said.

"Five-five-six-six-eight-five-four-nine-six-eight?" Rep asked, glancing at the caller i.d. box on his phone.

"The numbers after the area code spell out 'OTK-4YOU,'" the woman patiently explained. "'OTK' stands for 'over-the-knee,' which has a special significance for a certain market—you might call it my target audience."

"Right, right." *If I'd noticed THAT mnemonic aid, I wouldn't have had to put the number in my Palm Pilot.*

"I just got a call from a Milwaukee police officer, who said he found the number in unsavory company."

"I can see why you'd be sensitive about that," Rep said. "But first I'll need to know who the adverse party is, so that I can check for conflicts."

"Roger Leopold."

"Definitely not a client. Is he in the same business you are?"

"He was in a business related to mine for quite a while. One of his catalogues was called *Cahiers du Sinema*. With an S instead of a C. He also owned a gentlemen's club in your neck of the woods called Hoosier Daddy."

"Got it. Would he have been interested in your number?"

"I can't imagine. He and I never did business with each other, and I heard that a couple of years ago he sold out and went into a different field. The people I talked to thought Leopold was offshore these days. Even so, the cops found that number with a search warrant after I started asking questions about Leopold, and I can't help wondering if that's just happenstance."

"Whom did he sell out to?" Rep asked.

"Who do you usually sell out to in this business?"

"And so he got out clean?"

"He got out by the skin of his teeth. Had some legal problems right at the end. Local choir boys wanted to shut his Internet channel down, and you can't survive these days doing just catalogue and retail. That made his buyers think maybe they should forget the whole thing. Problem was, Leopold had already spent a good chunk of the earnest money. And buyers like he had—let's just say lawsuits aren't their idea of conflict resolution. He managed to scrape through somehow, though."

"Sounds like a pretty bad dude," Rep said.

"That's fair. Maybe a little too rough for a practice like yours, huh?"

"Oh, I don't know. I just handled a problem a little like this for a client up in Milwaukee, involving someone named Pelham Dreyfus. He wasn't any altar boy himself."

"Counselor," Rep's mother said, "mentioning Roger Leopold and Pelham Dreyfus in the same breath is like comparing Vlad the Impaler with a proctologist. I'm going to think about this and get back to you."

"Right. I'll look forward to your call."

He frowned at the phone for several seconds after he hung up. Mom wasn't mixed up with Leopold. Never had been. So far, so good. She had looked into Leopold as he'd asked her to do and dug up some useful data. Great. But what she'd found out had worried her, and she'd called to warn Rep. Okay, fair enough. That's what moms are for, even if they work in a field where riding crops and leather paddles are a business expense.

What bothered him, though, was that her number had been on the raunchy list found in Dreyfus' studio and she had no explanation for that. Blaming Leopold was pure speculation, and calling it happenstance was way too convenient. So what did that leave? Whatever the answer, he could hardly go to Detective Washington with questions like these.

Doubts unresolved and worries lingering, he returned the calls that needed a response yet this afternoon, launched himself from his chair, snatched his briefcase, and almost sprinted out of his office.

"A taxi is waiting downstairs," his secretary said as she handed a modest bundle to him. "Here are some faxes that came in this afternoon."

"Thanks."

Rep reached his gate twenty-five minutes before the originally scheduled boarding time, and discovered—naturally—that the flight was now running forty-five minutes late. Squirming uncomfortably into a chair in the departure lounge, he started reviewing the faxes his secretary had handed him on his way out the door. The first one was from Hayes' former secretary.

Hayes again. Just when Rep thought he had lifted himself and Melissa above the battle, Hayes' clammy hand reached back from beyond the grave and pulled him right back into the middle of the fray. He desperately wanted to keep himself and Mclissa off the casualty list without getting Mom a one-way ticket back to the Oklahoma Women's Correctional Facility in the process. The most sensible way to do that was to do nothing—stand aside and let the cops carry the ball. Hayes, though, was the orphan link, the one that didn't logically connect to anything. If Hayes' death were connected to Levitan's death and Dreyfus' disappearance, helping Washington understand that connection was one thing no one but Rep was likely to do.

Unbidden images from Hayes' burial jostled their way rudely back into his memory, along with the nagging thought that something about it was somehow off. Again he saw the modest crowd, the cars spattered from fender to wheel well with muddy slush and road salt, the sparse mourners treading uncertainly over sodden cedar chips covering the pathway through the cemetery's spongy sod. Again he smelled the damp wool odor of the overcoats, the acrid smoke from a couple of furtive cigarettes. Again he heard the sharp report as the wind whipped the flag draping the casket—

Scattered applause pulled him from his reverie. He glanced up in surprise. A handful of soldiers in desert camouflage uniforms were walking through the concourse. Six or seven of them, Indiana National Guardsmen probably, coming home from Iraq. Waiting passengers clapped for them as they passed, and Rep joined in. The soldiers seemed embarrassed by the attention. They didn't acknowledge the tribute, didn't smile or nod. Just walked on, staring self-consciously straight ahead.

Rep was only thirty-four, but three of the soldiers seemed impossibly young to him. Barely out of high school. A couple of years before they could have been Junior ROTC cadets like the—

Like the honor guard at Vance Hayes' burial. Except that Vance Hayes had never worn a uniform. He'd never served in the military. He didn't have a right to an honor guard or a flag-draped coffin. THAT'S what was wrong—the thing that had been bothering him, the anomaly that he couldn't quite put his finger on because he just hadn't cared enough to think it through carefully.

Rep fumbled feverishly with the fax pile.

"This is the Leopold order I mentioned," a handwritten scrawl on the cover page said, just above Polly Allbright's signature. "Your secretary called a while back to be sure she had the complete file because she said you'd asked for it. This wasn't in it, so I thought I'd send it along."

He flipped over to the second page. At first he couldn't believe what he saw. Literally could not believe it.

The document was dated December 2, 2003. The heading read, "In the Supreme Court of the United States." A legal caption identified the City of Cincinnati, Ohio as the plaintiff-respondent and Roger Leopold as the defendant-petitioner. In other words, Cincinnati had sued Leopold and so far Leopold had lost. Then came twenty words worth of polite, understated prose: "The Court issued the following order in your case today: The petition for a writ of certiorari is granted."

Granted!

Rep didn't bother reading the stuff about briefing schedules that followed. He double-checked the document's date. No mistake. The very month he died, Vance Hayes had learned that he would be arguing a case before the United States Supreme Court. For ninety-nine percent of the lawyers in the United States—certainly including Hayes—that would be the highlight of their careers by several orders of magnitude. The legal equivalent of playing in the World Series, the Super Bowl, the Masters, and the NCAA Final Four rolled into one. A once in a lifetime opportunity.

Rep dropped the magic piece of paper to his lap and stared in front of him. On one topic he no longer entertained the slightest doubt. He knew. *Knew.* Adult onset diabetes or not, there was no way Vance Hayes had consciously or subconsciously thrown his life away in some manic, death-defying stunt a few months before he'd be pleading Roger Leopold's case to the nine justices of the United States Supreme Court.

Rep vaulted from his seat and began hustling back toward the security checkpoint. He pulled out his cell phone on the run, found Ken Stewart's office number on his phone's menu and hit SEND.

"Ken, Rep," he said after the voice-mail prompt. "Two things. First, I think Vance Hayes was murdered, which means one or both of us may be in more danger than we realize. Second, if you have the name and number of the guy in charge of arrangements for Hayes' burial, that'll save me having to track it down. There's something I need to ask him."

He hit END and took a deep breath. Now he could call his secretary for later flight times. And call Melissa to tell her he'd be very late. And call the telephone number on the cover sheet of the fax he'd just read, hoping against hope that he'd reach Polly Allbright.

Still a bit down about Rep's call saying he'd be late, Melissa finished emailing a colleague at the Bowling Green University Center for the Study of American Popular Culture. Her email asked whether, stashed among the demo disks of one-hit wonder garage bands and the copy-edited manuscripts of first novels by authors who never had second novels, the Center might have some early back issues of a very niche-market magazine called *Soldier for Hire*. If so, would the colleague mind Xeroxing a representative issue from each year and sending the copies to Melissa with a modest (she hoped) bill?

She was about to log off the Internet and go back to her paper when, impulsively, she decided to check one more thing. With a trio of clicks she Googled August 14, 2003, the date of the garbled email identified in Leopold's deposition. Twenty-eight seconds and four mouse-clicks later she was looking at a picture of thousands of New Yorkers straggling on foot across the Brooklyn Bridge, deprived of subways and buses by a massive power failure that had blacked out the eastern third of the United States. Amid elections, hurricanes, wars, and rumors of wars in the two busy years since then, she had largely forgotten about that little headline.

Eighty-seven minutes after Melissa began Googling, Rep started putting Redwell folders neatly back into banker's boxes in Polly Allbright's garage.

"You finding what you need?" Allbright asked, for the third time, through a screen door that led from the garage into the house.

"Yeah, I'm just about to get out of your hair. Do you mind if I take a couple of these?"

"Go ahead. I was gonna get rid of 'em anyway at the next Boy Scout paper drive. No use to anyone anymore."

Rep tucked a thirty-two-page pleading into the thin Roger Leopold file jacket under his left arm. It didn't seem to have anything to do with Leopold, but it puzzled him and he wanted to examine it more systematically than he could here. The cover page said "Order of Proof" and referred to proof beyond a reasonable doubt and several statutes from Title 18 of the United States Code. That meant it dealt with a criminal case rather than a civil matter. Rep, though, had never heard of Hayes handling a criminal case. And even if he'd taken one on now and then, you tried criminal cases in court, not on paper. Correlating the evidence you had with each element of each offense was fine—that's what an order of proof was. But that might take eight or ten pages. Why had Hayes cobbled together this daunting pamphlet with tabbed affidavits and annotated documents appended to it?

His left arm encumbered, Rep tried to lift the last folder he wanted into the banker's box one-handed. Mistake. It slipped from his grasp and scattered miscellaneous paper over the oil-stained floor. Cussing mildly at his misjudgment, Rep cleaned the mess up. The final handful of paper included a three-and-one-half by five-inch color photograph. It caught his eye and he took a closer look at it.

Taken a long time ago, apparently. Two soldiers in khakis, three young women with Asian features, sitting at a lattice-work table in a sidewalk café.

"Do you know who this is?" he asked Allbright, turning the picture around and holding it between his thumb and index finger.

"Sure. That's Lieutenant Timothy Hayes. His brother."

In his fatigue, Rep hadn't asked the question as precisely as he should have. He had assumed that one of the soldiers in the picture was Tim Hayes—why else would it be in these files? He had intended to ask about the pretty young woman in between the two soldiers, leaning back in her chair, mouth open in an apparently carefree laugh, cigarette gripped insouciantly in her right hand a few inches from her cheek.

The precise image, in other words, of Sue Key's picture in *Pretty Girls Smoking Cigarettes*. Except that this picture had to have been taken years before Sue Key was born.

Chapter Twenty

"Hello, beloved," Rep said over the phone shortly after four-thirty on Tuesday afternoon. "How are things going?"

"I just spent twenty minutes with a graduate student, vetting the prospectus for his thesis before he shows it to his adviser. The title was *Corporal Punishment in Charlotte Brontë*. I'm afraid his interests might be misconstrued."

"Or even worse, construed correctly."

"I tried to be subtle," Melissa sighed. "I told him that he'd have to hide a topic like that behind opaque and pretentious jargon. Something like *Charlotte's Kink: Sublimated Sexual 'Deviance' as Mimesis of Patriarchal Repression in Mid-Victorian Proto-Gothic Fiction.*"

"Did he get the message?"

"On the contrary, he wrote my suggestion down word for word."

"Well, at least you're one step closer to determining the precise moment when academic satire in America became impossible."

"So, what can I do for you? Or did you call just because you couldn't wait to hear my delicately sculpted voice?"

"I was wondering if you still had Washington's card with his phone number. I'm in a ten-minute lull in the IP audit here, and I have some information for him."

"I do." Melissa rummaged in her purse. "I'll get it for you."

"Could you patch me through to him? You should hear this too."

"I'll try," Melissa said, "but be patient with me if I lose you. My degrees are in literature, not engineering."

This becoming modesty understated Melissa's technological dexterity. Twenty seconds later the two of them were on the line with Washington. While Rep told him something about Roger Leopold and the Supreme Court, Melissa flicked through five-by-eight index cards.

"Are you getting this, honey?" Rep asked. "Somehow I'm not sure I have your undivided attention."

"I'm multi-tasking, dear. Hayes was doing something *pro bono*. City trying to shut a naughty bookstore with a large Internet operation by using a civil nuisance action instead of a criminal obscenity charge. City's position looked dicey because Internet regulation statutes kept getting struck down on First Amendment grounds, but in this case the City was winning anyway. Leopold needed a lawyer several cuts above the breed he usually engaged."

"Right," Washington said, his voice crackling through static. "And Hayes saved Leopold's bacon by taking his case and getting it all the way to the Supreme Court, where Leopold eventually came out on top. Which I agree is an interesting coincidence, but isn't that what lawyers do?"

"*Pro bono* means for free," Rep said. "Hayes wouldn't have represented his own mother *pro bono*. If he took a case for free, he was getting more than professional satisfaction out of it."

"Information, maybe," Washington said.

"Right. I'll give you five to one that Hayes walked into that deposition in Milwaukee already knowing that Roger Leopold would say something that would make the case settle fast."

"Namely?" Washington pressed.

"I don't know. It has to be somewhere in the deposition transcript, but none of us can spot it."

"I'd like to ask Roger Leopold himself about it," Washington said. "But the last anyone heard he was in Hong Kong and I've somehow misplaced my passport. I'll come up with something, though. Thanks for the information."

"Sure," Rep said.

"And if you happen on any bright ideas about that letter from the Senate Judiciary Committee, feel free to give me a ring about them, too. Half our senators are busy running for president, and the staff apparently has more important things to do than return my phone calls."

"Will do," Rep said, although he still couldn't imagine what Levitan's contact with that committee could have to do with him or Sue Key. "Melissa, I'll call tonight."

"Counting the minutes," Melissa said.

She got up to make sure her office door was securely closed. Turned off half her overhead lights and flipped on a small, goose-neck desk lamp. Popped a Richard Eliot CD in the boombox perched precariously on the corner of her desk. Filled a plastic cup with water from a carafe she had replenished five minutes before the graduate student walked in. And got to work. Junior faculty don't get tenure by making fun of academic jargon. They get it by publishing, and in the next three hours she wanted to move five serviceable pages closer to that goal. She zipped the cursor past her title—*Peel-and-Eat Shrimp and Material Breach: Exploring the Sub-Textual Vitality of Commercial Rhetoric*—and the two pages she had managed already.

Twenty minutes later she had typed perhaps four hundred additional words, but her DELETE key had sent most of them to cyberheaven. Another hour's work produced three more paragraphs.

Knuckles rapped at her door. She ignored the knock. A card taped to the door said clearly that she would next have office hours at 11:00 the following morning. She didn't agree with colleagues who dismissed students as occupational hazards. But an assistant professor in the second month of her first tenure track position can't afford too many unscheduled demands on her time if she's going to commit high-concept literary criticism.

A second knock sounded. She ignored that one too. Then a male voice, sounding considerably older than your average undergraduate, said, "Doctor Pennyworth? Please give me sixty seconds. It's very important."

"'Very important' won't do," she muttered as she whipped from her chair and stalked to the door. "It had better be life-and-death."

She cracked the door wide enough to see a heavy-set man a head taller than she was, in his late forties or early fifties and with thinning reddish-brown hair. He wore a scruffy, brown corduroy sport coat over the kind of madras plaid shirt you might see at the hardware store on Saturday afternoon on a guy who planned to stop for a Miller Genuine Draft on the way home.

"You have ten seconds," she said. "Make it good."

"Pelham Dreyfus is dead," the man said.

"Good enough," Melissa gasped after a moment's shock. She opened the door fully, retreated to her desk, and gestured toward the visitor's chair.

"My name is Charlie Dressing." He handed her a card that listed an email address for something called spotlight.com. The card didn't list Charles Dressing or any other name.

"I thought Dreyfus was on the run. How do you know he's dead?"

"Security guards at O'Hare found his body in the trunk of his own car in one of the parking ramps."

"How did he die?" Melissa asked.

"I don't know. Who killed him? Don't know. How was he killed? Don't know. Who was the last person to see him alive? Don't know. What—"

"I get it," Melissa said. "You've told me everything you know."

"Beyond the fact that he's dead, I'm mayonnaise in a closed refrigerator, stuffing inside a turkey, a bandage applied to a wound on a moonless night—"

"*Capice*," Melissa sighed. "You're Dressing in the dark. Very droll."

"I do my best." Dressing sketched a what-can you do? smile. "It's all I have so far, but I thought you'd want to know it right away."

"You were absolutely right about that," Melissa said. She noticed that Dressing's eyes casually but systematically surveyed her office, checked out the detritus on her desk, scanned the pile of index cards and photocopies next to her computer. "So the next question is, why are you doing me this favor?"

"Because I want some information that you can help me with."

"Namely?"

"Namely, what you found in Dreyfus' place that led to all this fuss."

"Assuming that I found anything, why would I tell you?"

"It would be a very classy way of saying 'thank you,' for starters."

Melissa examined Dressing's card for a long moment. Then she rested her forearms on her desk and looked levelly at him.

"Whom are you with, Mr. Dressing?"

"I'm by myself. Spotlight is me."

"I take it you're a private investigator."

"Oh, no ma'am," Dressing said with mock earnestness worthy of Eddie Haskel. "Under the second sub-paragraph of sub-section one-a of section four-forty-point-twenty-six of the Wisconsin Statutes, a private investigator must hold a permit issued by the Wisconsin Department of Regulation and Licensing. I don't have such a permit, so it follows that I'm not a private investigator. I'm what you might call a freelance paralegal."

Dressing stood up and took a leisurely stroll around the exiguous space between Melissa's desk and the back wall of her office. Placing his hands on the back of his hips, he stretched luxuriantly. As if he owned the place, and could do whatever he wanted to there. Melissa wouldn't have called anything he did threatening, but a latent sense of menace radiated from him.

"How did you find out about Dreyfus being dead?" she asked him.

"Using freelance paralegal skills." Turning back to face her, he flashed a quit-wasting-my-time smile. "Telephone, police-band radio, friend on the force who likes to watch the Bucks from a luxury suite at the Bradley Center. That kind of thing."

"Who's paying you to deploy those skills in this matter?" she pressed.

"The same guy who's paying me to keep my mouth shut about things like that. Look, we're on the same side, okay? We both want to find out the same thing. It makes sense for us to work together. I've shown you mine, now you show me yours. How about it?"

His tone had become a bit more insistent. His words just barely qualified as a request. He leaned forward, resting one fist on the edge of her desk and smiled cajolingly. Melissa instinctively pushed her chair back as a cold, wet tickle of fear stirred in her belly.

"Does Detective Washington know you're here?"

"It's not his day to watch me," Dressing said. "And I think you can forget him anyway. If the stiff at O'Hare is in fact Pelham Dreyfus, then as far as he's concerned this case is over. Dreyfus gets tagged with the Levitan murder as well as the pot-shot at your husband, then dies of lead poisoning or whatever himself. Mob hit will probably be Washington's theory, and who cares if it holds water 'cause it clears two cases and there'll never be a trial."

"I give him more credit than that."

"Well, I've been in Milwaukee a lot longer than you have. You don't get to be a lieutenant here without knowing when to stop thinking."

"How do you know how long I've been in Milwaukee?"

Dressing swatted the question dismissively away as he straightened up.

"Listen," he said. "Three days ago a twelve year old girl was shot in her front yard about thirty blocks from downtown. She wasn't a blackmailer, she wasn't trying to hustle anyone—she was just in the wrong zip code when some drug dealer who couldn't shoot straight tried to take out a competitor. The shooter hasn't been arrested yet. That's the kind of case the City of Milwaukee needs Detective Washington on. If he can close the Levitan file with a murderer who's already conveniently dead, that's what he's going to do. Now, how about a little *quid pro quo*?"

Resisting the impulse to push her chair back again, Melissa found the plastic cup and took a generous sip from it. She put it down. She forced herself to look up and meet Dressing's gaze.

"Watch out for the high hopper on your way out," she said.

"Sorry," Dressing said, "you lost me on that one."

"Charlie Dressen," Melissa explained in the icy tone she generally saved for students who'd bought their term papers over the Internet, "managed the Milwaukee Braves during the 1960s. 'Watch out for the high hopper' was his way of calling a squeeze play."

"Uh-huh," Dressing said. "There aren't many thirty-year-old women who know that."

"Thirty-three," Melissa said. "There aren't many who like instrumental jazz, either, and there's only one who's spent hours talking old-school baseball with Rep Pennyworth. Your name isn't Charlie Dressing, you won't tell me whom you're working with or for or why, I don't have any reason to believe a word you've said, and I have a paper to write. Get lost."

"I've heard that your husband says you're brilliant," he said. "Well, let me tell you something: you're not as smart as he thinks you are."

"No one in the world is as smart as Rep thinks I am. Now beat it before I call security."

"I'm on my way," the guy said. "But keep the card. You've got a dog in this fight whether you like it or not."

He left before Melissa could have come back with a clever riposte even if she'd thought of one, which she hadn't. She drained the cup, refilled it, drank half of it down, and dabbed sweat from her forehead and the corners of her mouth. With a conscious effort of will, she turned back to the computer and the arcana of deconstructive language theory.

Fake-name's intrusion had shaken her up. She had typed three more doomed sentences before she focused on the probability that she wasn't the only person this dime-store cowboy planned on hustling for information about what Pelham Dreyfus had known. She dug up Sue Key's business number, dialed it, and did her best to leave a voice-mail that would sound urgent but not hysterical. If Key had a home phone it wasn't listed, so the first message was the best Melissa could do.

Then she got back to her paper. For the next forty-five minutes she dissected academic commentary that snidely dismissed "peel-and-eat shrimp" as mindless ad-babble and "material breach" as pompous jargon. People in the real world, she explained, found it quite useful to know that they didn't have to cook packaged shrimp before eating them—that *all* they had to do to the seafood was peel it. And when one found oneself construing, say, a contract (or, perhaps, a UN resolution), one might be well advised to distinguish between material breaches and technical or insubstantial ones before starting a lawsuit—or a war.

Her phone rang. Thinking it might be Key calling back, she answered it.

"Hi, this is Holly, one of the library assistants at Alverno College?" the caller said, adopting the contemporary habit of turning her statement into a question by inflecting her voice at the end. "You called about the Bourroughs monograph?"

"Yes," Melissa said. "I couldn't get it on-line."

"We have a copy, but it isn't scanned. I can mail you a photocopy, or if you're in a hurry for it I could just leave a copy at the desk for you here."

"I'd really like to pick it up tonight," Melissa said, knowing that she had to make as much progress as she could while Rep was out of town. "I'm new to the area. Can you give me directions to Alverno?"

"If you haven't driven on the south side yet," the librarian said, "frankly, I'd take a cab? It's kind of a different world down here."

"Good idea," Melissa said, beginning the SAVE-LOG OFF process with her right hand even as she hung up with her left.

Taxis don't just cruise Milwaukee's streets as they do Chicago's or New York's. As Melissa hustled out of Curtin Hall she figured her best bet was to drive down to the cab stand at the Pfister Hotel on the east side of downtown and take a taxi from there. When she crossed Hartford, though, still a good block from her parking lot, she saw a blue Veterans Taxi just dropping off a fare on Downer Avenue. Her shrill whistle and arm-snap got the attention of the driver, who reached her by driving up Downer.

Up Downer, Melissa thought. *God not only exists, He or She has a sense of humor.* The driver winced when he heard her ask for Alverno College.

"Any problem with taking the Lake route to the south side? It's a little longer, but it'll be faster. The work they're doing on the Marquette Interchange makes the north-south freeway a long, skinny parking lot this time of day."

"Go ahead," Melissa said distractedly.

During the ride she left voice-mails for Washington and Rep. By the time she'd completed those chores she could see the Italian Community Center on her right, which meant they were on the south side. A straight mile or so later and a few twists and turns after the cab turned away from Lake Michigan, she noticed a long, odd name on a street sign: Kinnikinnick. She remembered the name from Rep's account of driving Key back home after the Cold Coast settlement.

Like a ham actor in a provincial theater, Fake-name had been edging his way back to center stage in her mind throughout the cab ride. She'd thought the voice-mail was all she could do to warn Key, but maybe now she could go one better than that. Fumbling a bit with nervousness, she managed to find Key's address on her Palm Pilot.

"Tell you what," she said to the cabbie. "On your way to Alverno, stop at this address." She recited it.

"That's not exactly on the way, but it's your nickel."

Ten minutes later the cab stopped in the middle of a street chock-a-block with curb-parked cars on both sides. Promising to take only a minute, Melissa strode down the alley-way toward Key's flat, climbed the stairs to the second-story apartment and rang the bell. Nothing happened. She could hear the bell sounding inside, but heard no movement and saw no lights. She tried again, accompanying the bell-push this time with an authoritative rap on the door. Same result.

Figuring that as long as she was here she might as well leave a note, Melissa began to write one. She had just begun the process when the door cracked just wide enough for her to see half of Key's face.

"Oh, hi," Melissa said. "There's something I wanted—"

"This isn't really a good time," Key said. "I've got, uh, like this monster transcript that has to be done by tomorrow. As long as you're here, though, could I bum a couple of cigarettes? I'm all out, and I don't want to take time away from the transcript to go out for some."

Huh? Melissa thought. Missing only a beat or two from surprise, she managed to ad lib a response.

"Sorry, I don't have any myself right now. Would you like me to run out and get some for you?"

"No, no, that's okay," Key said. "My bro will be over before too much longer, and he'll have a pack for me. Thanks anyway."

The door closed decisively.

On her way back to the cab, Melissa tried Washington's number again. Not there. She sensed impatience radiating from the cabbie, and she didn't blame him. She pulled two twenties from her purse and tendered them.

"Listen," she said, "for forty dollars can you go over to Alverno, pick up an envelope being held for me at the library desk, and bring it back here?"

"Are you kidding?" the cabbie asked. "For forty bucks I can bring it to you gift-wrapped with an Italian sausage on the side."

He sped off, leaving Melissa at the curb, wondering what she should do. The only logical explanation for Key's performance just now was unwanted company and quick thinking. Maybe Melissa could call nine-one-one and spin that into an emergency. Maybe—

Or maybe, you precious goose, you could call Nguyen AS SUE ALL BUT EXPRESSLY TOLD YOU TO. Sheesh.

Four-one-one had Don Nguyen's home number, and Melissa dialed it. She got an answering machine and left a message.

Chapter Twenty-One

Melissa gave Nguyen three hundred impatient seconds to call her back and tell her he was on his way. Then, figuring that she was out of options, she squared her shoulders and, affecting the determinedly resolute tread of a bailiff bringing bad news to Grantley Manor, headed back for Key's flat. As much for form's sake as anything else she banged again on the door.

"Sue, it's me," she called, sacrificing grammar to efficiency. "I don't know what's going on, but I've got something for you that your brother sent over. C'mon, open up."

Then she knocked again. No response. She rattled the door and rapped on its glass portion.

"Hey, Sue?" Melissa called then. "I really do have to get this to you. It's not something I can just leave on the doorstep—you know what I mean? I need to get it inside your flat, and I need to get it there in the next ten minutes." She paused and took a deep breath. "I mean it, Sue. I'll set the burglar alarm off if I have to."

That did the trick. Within three seconds she saw light spill into the hallway and heard footsteps scurrying toward the door. She could make out two shadowy figures. Bolts snapped and the door flew open. In the muted light Melissa saw Fake-name and Key.

"I didn't mean for—" the young woman began.

"Well, well, well," Fake-name interrupted. "Professor Penny-worth. Come on in—and bring your pot or ecstasy or meth or whatever it is with you."

Melissa stayed where she was. Fake-name had interpreted her necessarily vague comments about what she'd brought for Key as amateurish allusions to a drug delivery. He must have thought that such guilty knowledge would give him leverage to pry information out of both her and Key, and that's why he'd finally had Key open up.

"Where I grew up," Melissa said, "you don't barge into other people's homes without their permission. Sue, may I come in?"

"I really don't—I mean, ah—that is, okay, I guess so, sure."

Melissa stepped into the hall and followed Key to the flat's kitchen, all under Fake-name's close supervision. As at her office, he stopped short of anything you could call an overt physical threat. He didn't lay his hands on them or show a weapon or raise his fist. He just made it clear what he wanted them to do, and let the danger implicit in his size and attitude take care of the rest.

"You know this guy?" Key asked Melissa in a tone combining accusation with astonishment as she parked her hips irritably against the small counter near the refrigerator.

"Not really," Melissa said. "I never saw him before he accosted me in my office a couple of hours ago and told me his name was Charlie Dressing."

"Charlie Dressing?" Key said disgustedly to the man. "You told *me* your name was Bobby Bragan."

"You'd better get this case wrapped up fast," Melissa said to him, "before you run out of Milwaukee Braves ex-managers to steal names from."

"Let's quit wasting time," the guy said. "I really do have friends on the Milwaukee police force, and every cop likes an easy collar. I could arrange a drug bust here by snapping my fingers. I know pot isn't any big deal anymore, but even if that's all you're delivering it's not going to do your academic career any good to have your mug shot in the Metro section of the *Journal-Sentinel* under a headline saying something about 'Drug-Dealing Professor.' I've already told you the information I need. Give it to me and I'll get out of your hair so you two can complete your business and blow a little weed."

"You do have an active imagination," Melissa said. She felt hollow-bellied and jelly-legged, and the only way she knew to deal with that was to act a lot braver than she felt. "You're blowing smoke up your own orifice."

"You wanna show me what's in your purse?" the guy asked casually, offering her an I've-been-bluffed-by-pros smile.

Melissa ignored him and turned to Key.

"Has he threatened you?" she asked.

"Yes," Key hissed.

"No, I have not," the guy interjected. "'Threat' is a defined term under case law interpreting subsection one of section nine-forty-three-point-thirty of the Wisconsin Statutes, and nothing I have said or done qualifies."

Then the Wisconsin Statutes could stand another look, Melissa thought, *because right now I'm scared stiff.*

"He told me he had information about Don," Key told Melissa, her voice breaking for the first time. "He said Don could be in a lot of trouble. He said he could help, but he needed information from me. I couldn't tell him anything and I told him that and asked him to leave, but he wouldn't go."

"Did he force you to let him stay here?"

"I don't know if I can say that," Key said, after a moment's confused pause. "When I asked him to leave, he just wouldn't go. Instead he'd smile and talk about how Don has a record already and bad things could happen to him and didn't I want to help him because he could do something to help but only if he had my cooperation."

"How about when I knocked the first time? Did he say he'd do something to you if you just asked me to get some help?"

"Not really," Key said. "He said something like he'd strongly suggest I get rid of you fast because we, like, really had to have this talk. I was afraid he *would* do something, but he never actually said he would."

"You see?" Fake-name asked, smiling smugly. "Now, let's talk about protecting both Sue's brother and your career at the same time, shall we?"

Melissa's cell phone rang. Skipping the apologies customary in her understanding of cell-phone protocol, she answered.

"Hi, honey," Rep said. "What's up?"

"Oh, hi, Detective Washington. Thanks for calling back."

"Uh, right," Rep said.

"This is actually well timed. There's a gentlemen here who's interested in arranging a drug bust by the Milwaukee Police Department. Let me put him on so that he can tell you where to have the officers come."

She held the phone out to Fake-name. It would be imprecise to say that assurance drained from his face, because "drained" implies a process that takes some time, whereas the change here was instantaneous. He backed away toward the kitchen door and pushed the palms of his hands toward Melissa, as if the phone were a rodent particularly redolent of vermin.

"Don't you want to talk to Detective Washington?" Melissa coaxed.

A key sounded in the outside lock. The guy's eyes widened, as if Washington might somehow have magically appeared at the flat in response to Melissa's comment a few seconds before.

"That would either be my seldom seen flat-mate or Don," Key said.

"All right, I'm going now," Fake-name said—superfluously, for he was already into the hallway. "But think about what I said."

"And don't come back," Key shouted.

"Who's this guy, Sis?" a voice that Melissa took to be Nguyen's called loudly from the hallway. "Is he giving you any trouble?"

"Not anymore," Key yelled. "Just let him go."

And that's probably just what would have happened had the interloper not chosen this moment for an ill-advised effort to recover his manhood.

"Watch it, slope," they heard him sneer from the hallway. "You're a little guy. Little guys don't do too well in jail."

Melissa and Key didn't hear the contact between Nguyen's right fist and Fake-name's solar plexus that apparently followed this comment. They did hear an audible expulsion of breath and the sound of someone about to be sick, which drew them to the hallway. They found Fake-name on his knees, hugging himself around the midsection. He was muttering something about a felony in violation of section nine-forty-point-twenty of the Wisconsin Statutes.

"Ordinary battery is only a misdemeanor," Nguyen said. "Felony requires substantial bodily harm. Wanna try for that one?"

"Bro," Key said fiercely, "get in here before I bust you one. I don't want this creep vomiting all over my hallway."

Fake-name took advantage of the brief diversion caused by Key's admonition to half-crawl and half-walk out the door. At that point, Melissa remembered Rep and raised the cell phone back to her ear.

"How much of that did I hear?" Rep asked.

"Not a word. Call me back at home in about two hours."

"Check."

Lowering the phone, Melissa looked at Key and Nguyen.

"I'll leave right now if you'd like me to," she said, figuring that Key had probably had her fill of verbal strong-arming for one night. "But I really would like to talk to you if you don't mind."

"You kidding?" Key trilled. "You just saved my cute little first-generation American butt. Come back into the kitchen so I can whip up some traditional Vietnamese-American cuisine."

This turned out to be Oolong tea and frozen personal pan pizzas nuked in the microwave. The food proved to be better than the conversation that went with it.

After Melissa and Key rehashed their encounters, Nguyen swore that he wasn't in any more trouble than the average mechanic trying to procure beer, food, rent, tunes, basic cable, a decent ride, and an occasional slap-and-tickle on book-rate small engine work in Milwaukee. Watching his face as he relayed this to Key, Melissa believed him. She'd known plenty of boisterous micks in Kansas City who could feed cops blarney until they sweated corned beef and cabbage but couldn't lie to a nun to save their lives. Melissa suspected that Nguyen was the same way with Key.

Then, taking a calculated risk, Melissa gave them the highlights of what she and Rep had learned, with the bracing implication that the seemingly petty theft from Key's apartment might be related to two murders. She had hoped by doing this to win their trust. She could tell from the younger woman's eyes, though, that instead of extending trust Key had ducked under a shell too hard for Melissa to penetrate.

"You sound like you know a lot more about this than I do," she said guardedly when Melissa had finished. "I don't see what I could tell you that would be any help."

"Well," Melissa said carefully, "you could tell me what the deal was between your mom and Vance Hayes."

"I just don't have any idea," Key said with a high school drama class smile-and-shrug. "That letter she gave me came like a bolt from the blue."

I hope she never plays poker with that face. She'll go broke fast.

"Perhaps, then," Melissa said, "you could call your mom and ask her if she'd be willing to talk to me."

"I don't think so," Key said, lowering her eyes and sagging miserably in her chair. "I've gotten too many people involved in my own troubles already. I can't drag Mother into this as well."

Melissa rejected any idea of debating the point. Increased mental and emotional pressure wouldn't do Key any good right now.

"I understand," Melissa said, touching Key's hand in what she hoped was a comforting gesture. "After I leave, though, please call your mother and tell her that she might be the next person the jerk who stopped here tonight has on his list."

As she walked outside to wait for the cabbie to return from Alverno, she hoped he'd been kidding about the Italian sausage.

Chapter Twenty-Two

"So this poor man's Travis McGee thinks I'm going to pin it all on Dreyfus and call it a day, huh?" Detective Washington asked as he approached Melissa after she had darted across Hartford Avenue the next day.

"And good afternoon to you, Lieutenant," Melissa said, slowing her brisk pace slightly as Washington began walking beside her. "I take it you've heard my voice-mail about yesterday's little adventure."

"That's the main reason I'm here. That plus the photograph and other material your husband had messengered over to me."

"What about Pelham Dreyfus?"

"Still don't have a line on him. Around the time he supposedly got to O'Hare he could have caught flights for the Far East or Latin America, but we haven't even confirmed that he was the one who went through security then."

Melissa stopped and turned, open-mouthed, to face Washington.

"But Fake-name—the guy calling himself Dressing and then Bragan—said Dreyfus was dead."

"He was making that up."

For some reason, amid the deceit that had run through her encounter with Fake-name, the sheer effrontery of that particular lie flustered Melissa for a moment. The phony name, the tacit threats, the *noir* movie swagger—those aggravated her, but they didn't make her feel like an idiot. She had just assumed that

Dreyfus' death actually had triggered the guy's visit. It hadn't even occurred to her that he might have invented that as well.

"He just told me a bare-faced lie about that," Melissa sputtered, furious at her own gullibility.

"Yeah. He probably missed church last Sunday too."

"Well, I hope you find him quickly."

"So do I," Washington said, as he fell back into step beside her. "I'd like to hear what he has to say when he's been provided with the proper motivation. Unfortunately, we don't have a lot to go on. The dot com on that card he gave you is offshore, and we can't get any details about who's behind it."

"I wouldn't think Milwaukee would have that many characters who are interesting in quite the way this guy is."

"I'm not sure he's local. At least not recently. If any low-rent, unlicensed P.I. had been flaming around Milwaukee for long the way this guy was yesterday, he would've come to my attention. And I would've come to his."

"He was citing chapter and verse from Wisconsin statutes and spouting inside information like a precinct captain."

"Ex-jailbirds can quote statutes like a preacher quotes the Bible. I think that whole routine was a scam, including the local insider stuff."

"That makes a lot of sense, now that you've spelled it out for me," Melissa said.

"Dreyfus was just about dumb enough to try to shoot someone with a handgun from two hundred feet away," Washington said, "which would be a good trick for Wyatt Earp, but I don't see him having the guts to kill Levitan."

"Too much of a bottom-feeder?"

"He makes catfish look like gourmets. He was a penny-ante grifter."

"In other words," Melissa said, "somebody tougher and smarter and more dangerous than Dreyfus has been deeply involved in this from the start. Someone like Fake-name—or perhaps like Roger Leopold."

"Who went to Hong Kong for his health shortly after a deposition apparently made Milwaukee too warm for him. If this mess really is tied to Vance Hayes in some way, it's interesting that bad guys who get involved in it find ways to make sudden trips overseas."

"I'm not sure what you' re saying."

"Hayes makes a lot of trips to Southeast Asia with no good reason to go there, and no evidence that the bad reason is drugs. Low-life hoods and rough customers keep showing up in the background with money suddenly coming out of their ears just when they need to change climates. How do you put it together?"

How do I put it together? What, I smoke a couple of cigarettes and all of a sudden I'm Harriet Vane? "Excuse me, Lord Peter, but as you were such a great help with that unpleasantness at the Bellona Club, Scotland Yard wonders if you'd do your bit on this little matter of the lawyer in the lake."

Still, Washington's question intrigued her, so as they walked into Curtin Hall and headed for the stairs to the second floor she took a stab at an answer.

"I suppose it could add up to sexual tourism," she said.

"I suppose the same thing. So the next question is, how does sexual tourism in Southeast Asia get people killed in southeast Wisconsin?"

They strolled into a tiered, one-hundred-twenty-seat lecture room where Melissa would soon be teaching ninety-eight freshmen who'd tested their way out of Survey of English Literature I.

"You want me to say honor killings," Melissa said as she set a book and lecture notes on the desk, "so I will. Although I associate them more with Islamic regions."

"Don't kid yourself. Catholic, Protestant, Buddhist, or stone cold atheist, there's plenty of places right here in the USA where messing with the wrong guy's sister can get your cranium ventilated for you."

"Wrong guy's *sister*? Where did that come from?"

"Nguyen has a record, and he knows how to handle a gun."

"Maybe so," Melissa said, "but he's a long way from the scariest guy in this little drama."

"I'd like to show you something," Washington said, snapping open an ancient black fiberglass Samsonite attaché case.

"I'll be happy to look, but in about seventeen minutes you'll be competing with *Much Ado About Nothing*," Melissa said, glancing at her watch.

"I mentioned that when we searched Dreyfus' studio we couldn't find the copies of *Soldier for Hire* magazine that you'd noticed. But after Hayes' death, the Lake Delton police found these in the hotel safe, where Hayes had left them as soon as he checked in."

He laid a snapshot and a copy of *Soldier for Hire* on the desk. Melissa examined the photograph. It looked like the one from 1960s Saigon that Rep had found in Polly Albright's garage.

"Now look at the magazine."

"I have, actually. I'd noticed a copy in Dreyfus' studio, and after everything that happened I asked a colleague to send me some back issues and I glanced through half-a-dozen of them. It seems aimed at gun nuts, anti-government fanatics, and survivalists. It has more phallic substitutes per column inch than anything I've ever read before, including *Mandate* and *Tropic of Cancer*."

"I'm blushing," Washington said, "but I'll bet you can't tell. Look at the classified ads."

Melissa obediently flipped to the small-type pages in the back of the magazine. The three- to six-line ads here offered survival manuals, freeze-dried food that would last for decades, correspondence courses for people who wanted to become private investigators, services to find loved ones reported as missing in action in Vietnam, and vast arrays of exotic weaponry. After thirty seconds of skimming, Melissa's eyes fell on a circled ad in the lower third of the middle column:

```
        PEST CONTROL
Extermination services. Quick, efficient, no
questions asked. Results guaranteed.
```

"I can't believe this," she said. "It sounds like a hit-man looking for work. Can that possibly be legal?"

"I'd need more than this before I went to a DA. Point is, let's say Dreyfus sent Vance Hayes the altered calendar picture, along with a copy of *Soldier for Hire* magazine with that ad circled. What would you conclude?"

"That Dreyfus was trying to blackmail Hayes without leaving an explicit paper trail."

"Right. Connect the dots for me."

"Okay," Melissa said, as fascinated by the intellectual challenge as she was appalled by its implications. "Somewhere, somehow, Dreyfus stumbles over the old picture of Vance Hayes' brother with Xu Ky in South Vietnam. He learns that Hayes has been helping Xu Ky for years. Maybe he has an inkling from his softcore on-line business that Hayes has unhealthy predilections. Maybe he finds out about Hayes' unusual trips to Southeast Asia and figures that's what they were about."

"Uh huh," Washington said. "Maybe he even gets his mitts on one of Hayes' credit card numbers when Hayes was buying something reflecting that unhealthy taste you talked about."

"So the theory becomes even more vile. Dreyfus concludes that Hayes was extracting sexual favors from Xu Ky—like access to Sue Key when she was barely a teenager—in exchange for the services that he provided. I'm not a lawyer, but I hope that would amount to extortion and rape."

"I'm not a lawyer either, but it sounds to me like it would."

"Okay. Dreyfus wants money from Hayes, but he doesn't tell him to pay up or Dreyfus will go to the cops. Hayes would know that Dreyfus couldn't do that without putting himself in the soup as well. Instead, Dreyfus threatens to expose Hayes to Nguyen, leading to a once-in-a-lifetime experience for Hayes. If Hayes accuses Dreyfus of blackmailing him, Dreyfus will say that Hayes was just reading too much into a couple of innocent curiosities."

"Not a bad theory, right?"

"Right," Melissa said, as she noticed early-arriving students begin to drift into the room. "But you clearly had all this figured out yourself. Why are you running it by me?"

"Because whether it's Nguyen or someone else, that stronger and tougher guy you mentioned is still out there, and I don't want the body count going any higher. If I don't get a line on Leopold in a few days, I'm going to ask for some unorthodox help from you and your husband."

"Neither of us is known for orthodoxy."

"Meanwhile, don't let your guard down—with Nguyen or anyone else. Like the newsies say, if your mother says she loves you, check it out."

"Always good advice," Melissa said.

As Washington left, she sat on the top of the desk, closed her eyes, and tried to compose herself for the lecture to come. Shakespearean comedy seemed breathtakingly trivial at the moment. After a few deep breaths, she thought she had herself calmed down. Chilling or not, she told herself, Washington's idea was still just a theory.

"Good afternoon," she said to the now fully assembled class. "After two weeks of howling on the moor with King Lear, we've earned a little dessert. We'll be focusing on *Much Ado About Nguyen*."

"I thought Ben Jonson wrote that," a smart alec in the front row said.

◇◇◇

Rep's phone rang just as he was about to leave his hotel room for dinner with his client and the associates. He answered the phone anyway. If it was the client with a change of plans, this was the time to find out.

"Hello, Mr. Pennyworth," a deep, smooth, comforting voice said. "Roger Ormsby here, returning your call."

Rep blanked on the name for a second, then remembered the message he'd left at the funeral parlor that had handled Vance Hayes' burial.

"Thanks for calling back," Rep said, glancing at his watch. "I know it's almost eight o'clock in Indianapolis now. I was expecting to hear from you tomorrow morning."

"Yes, of course. At difficult times like these, however, we try to be as available to the family as we can."

Oops.

"Ah, actually, this is about an, ah, interment you have already taken care of. Over a year ago."

"Yes, of course. There are no…difficulties, I trust?"

"Just a question that occurred to me recently. The decedent was Vance Hayes. I remember an honor guard and a flag-draped coffin at the burial, but I'm sure Hayes never served in the armed forces. I was just wondering who authorized the military honors."

"Yes, of course," Ormsby said. "This is a matter of great sensitivity to veterans' groups, so we're pretty careful about it. Ordinarily the family provides us with a DD-Two-fourteen. That's a Defense Department form documenting discharge from the armed forces."

"What if there is no such form?"

"Then we check with the Defense Department or the VA ourselves. Or a local VFW or American Legion post will check for us."

"Well, then," Rep said cautiously, "perhaps I was mistaken about Mr. Hayes' service. Was the appropriate documentation presented in his case?"

"One moment, please."

Ormsby couldn't completely disguise his disappointment at the news that this call wouldn't lead to another stiff making its way into the velvety discretion of his funeral home, but he kept his tone professional.

"Yes, of course," Ormsby said after nearly a minute. "The Hayes situation was out of the ordinary. The deceased had no family members involved in the planning. The overall arrangements were made by the trustee of the deceased's estate." *Namely Ken Stewart*, Rep thought. "The issue of military honors was brought up by a third party, rather late in the day. He couldn't produce a DD-Two-fourteen, but we received an official letter from a Colonel Englehardt, retired and writing in his capacity as VFW liaison, confirming that Mr. Hayes was entitled to military honors."

"Did Colonel Englehardt provide any details?"

"Well, that was the unusual aspect of it. His letter didn't actually say that the deceased had served. He said, 'I can confirm without qualification that Vance Hayes has merited the honors contemplated by Title Ten of the United States Code, and accordingly a burial detail is authorized and will be provided through this post.' No specification of branch or date of discharge. But he enclosed an official flag, which we used to drape the coffin. So that was that."

"I see," Rep said, trying to hide his impatience. "And who would the third party who got Colonel Englehardt's attention be?"

"Yes, of course. I can't really see why this would be confidential. It was a Mr. Walter Kuchinski. He seems to have covered the additional expense out of his own pocket."

"Thank you," Rep murmured. "Thank you very much."

He hung up before Ormsby could say, "Yes, of course" again.

Chapter Twenty-Three

Neither the Milwaukee white pages nor information had a listing for Xu Ky when Melissa checked them that evening. Melissa didn't think Rep had the number. He'd apparently picked up only odd scraps of trivia about her, like the "weapon of Mass destruction" joke.

Whoa. *Hello.*

Melissa called Internet Explorer up on her computer and punched Archdiocese of Milwaukee into Google. No home page headings for liturgical directors (much less for their assistants), so she clicked on "Parishes." The Milwaukee Archdiocese had *a lot* of parishes.

She tried to think of Catholic saints associated with Asia. The only one she came up with was Francis Xavier, who lost his life bringing Christianity to Japan. She knew this much only from a pious video she and Grammy Seton had watched together on a VCR (a Sony, in fact, which added a certain poignancy to the saint's heroic sacrifice). No help here, for St. Francis Xavier hadn't made it onto the canon of Milwaukee parish patrons. A quick scroll disclosed no other obvious possibilities. She'd just have to go through the parishes one by one.

Luckily for her, St. Anselm's on South 6th Street appeared early in the alphabetical listing. It offered a hefty total of six Sunday masses. The schedule included a "Bilingual Mass English/ Spanish," a mass in English without music, *i.e.*, a short one, and, at eight o'clock on Sunday mornings, a "Vietnamese mass."

The site noted that lectors and Eucharistic ministers met every Wednesday evening at seven-thirty.

Melissa reached St. Anselm's at seven-fifty, which was almost too late. Even in the church's muted light, she could tell from the fidgety body language of the first people she saw that tonight's meetings were about to break up. She spotted two collections of about a dozen people each gathered just in front of the sanctuary, on opposite sides of the church. The leader of the nearer group was recapping who would cover the nursing homes, the hospitals, shut-ins, and so forth. Eucharistic ministers. She turned toward the other group.

They were focusing at the moment on how to pronounce "Achimelech" in English, Spanish, and Vietnamese. Nearly hidden within a double semi-circle of listeners, a speaker with a reedy, oddly melodic voice finished her review of that topic. Then she reminded lectors doing the second reading at each service not to leave their pews to go up to the sanctuary until the choir had finished singing the responsorial psalm.

"Our choir master doesn't like you walking on the choir's lines," she said in a gently mocking tone. "People can wait an extra twenty seconds to hear from St. Paul, so save your humble assistant liturgist a little heartburn, okay? That's about it. God be with you and have a blessed week."

Amid mild laughter the semi-circles disintegrated to reveal a petite, chubby woman with a laughing-Buddha face and graying hair. She wore a denim shirt, a dark brown corduroy skirt, and black Converse All Star high-top basketball shoes with white socks. Melissa figured the odds at about fifty-fifty, and she played longer shots than that during the NCAA basketball tournament.

"Excuse me," she said to the woman, "are you Xu Ky?"

"Yes," the woman said as she looked over at Melissa. "New lector? I'm sorry, but I don't recognize you." Melissa noted with interest that Ky spoke English with a slight southern accent, something like Georgia filtered through west Texas: "Ahm sorruh, but Ah don' recognize yew."

"No. My name is Melissa Pennyworth. My husband represented your daughter in that legal case she had recently."

"Oh, yes, my little calendar girl," Ky said, rolling her eyes. "She should know better than to sign that silly paper. I oughtta be stricter with her growing up. She always have that trace of mischief. We can talk. Come."

Ky led Melissa to the center aisle, where Ky genuflected and Melissa didn't, then down the aisle to the vestibule. A door on the left side of the vestibule opened to a stairway, which led down to a large multi-purpose room. The sight of that room instantly brought parochial school recollections surging from the depths of Melissa's memory: the din of indoor recess on torrential days, the whiff of macaroni and cheese on Lenten Fridays, the distinctive smell of mimeographed copies in a school that couldn't afford a Xerox machine.

Several people from the groups upstairs gathered around coffee urns on the far side. Ky unstacked two orange, molded fiberglass chairs and set them at one of the lunch tables that were now pushed against the nearer wall. With a gesture she invited Melissa to sit, then ambled across the room and returned with two Styrofoam cups of coffee. Melissa gratefully took one of them.

"You were raised in the Church, I'm guessing?" Ky asked.

"In a way," Melissa said. "My parents were lapsed Catholics. They had me receive the sacraments and go to parochial schools to placate my grandmother, but I didn't end up buying into it. How could you tell?"

"When you passed the altar, you didn't genuflect but you thought about it a little. For a non-Catholic there is nothing to think about."

"That's very perceptive." Melissa wondered if skipping the genuflection had gotten her off to a needlessly bad start, and thought she'd better explain herself. "I did think about genuflecting, just to be polite. I didn't do it because I decided it would have been a kind of lie—passing myself off as something I wasn't. As I said, I didn't really buy into it."

"I don't wonder," Ky said, nodding. "Having to go through the motions, form without faith, I'm surprised you didn't turn into a snarling atheist."

"That's pretty much what I was in my late teens. By twenty-three or so I had mellowed into a complacent agnostic. Since then I've experienced a reduction in complacency."

"Losing faith in your lack of faith?" Ky asked with a mischievous smile.

"Perhaps. But I'm nowhere near believing the way you do."

"Better a searching agnostic than a complacent formalist. Better doubt about the truth than certainty in error. You are here, though, to talk about Sue. Her little legal scrap is all over, I think? She bought me a lovely porcelain miniature with part of the money she got."

"That case is wrapped up," Melissa said. "But then there was the burglary of her apartment and Max Levitan's murder."

"Yes," Ky said as deep sadness clouded her face. "Truly terrible."

"I don't know whether Sue told you, but someone using a phony name has recently tried to pry information out of both me and her."

Ky said nothing.

"I can't make any sense out of it yet," Melissa said. "The pattern seems troublesome, though, so it's hard not to worry a little."

"That is true," Ky said, nodding. "I warn Sue when I give her Mr. Kuchinski's name that once you start with a lawyer it goes on and on. The famous ancient Chinese curse was supposedly, 'May your children live in interesting times.' The American equivalent would be, 'May your lawyer prosper and grow rich.'"

"That was the main thing I wanted to talk to you about. I know that you got Walt Kuchinski's name from a letter that Vance Hayes wrote. But Vance Hayes practiced law in Indianapolis. I was wondering how you ever happened to cross paths with him."

Ky paused, her face impassive.

"It is a very long story," she said at last.

"I have all the time you're willing to spare," Melissa said. "Whatever is going on, it affects Sue, as well as my husband and me, and maybe even you."

After a reflective look at Melissa, Ky swallowed the last of her coffee. She took a green Bic lighter from a pocket in her skirt and picked up her purse.

"Do you smoke?"

"No, but it won't bother me if you do."

"It will bother plenty of other people if I do it here," Ky said, standing up. "I live two blocks away. Come along."

As soon as they were outside, and without breaking stride, Ky extracted a Virginia Slim from a pack in her purse, parked the cigarette in one corner of her lips, lit it in a brusque, no-nonsense way, and blew smoke out around it before removing it from her mouth.

"I start smoking when I am fourteen," she said in a mildly apologetic tone. "The GIs pay us with packs of Marlboros and Winstons. Southern boys mostly, at first. Later on from all over, but southern to start. Not what you think. I mean they pay us for drinks and even rooms and just to talk, you know? The other too, yes, but I never do that. At PX they can get cigarettes fifteen cents a pack—much cheaper than we buy them anywhere in Saigon."

"Americans are so sheltered," Melissa mused aloud. "I can scarcely imagine what it was like growing up in the middle of a war."

"A terrible time in many, many ways, of course," Ky said. "But you know what? If an angel came down from heaven this very minute and told me I could live the rest of my life in one time and place, God forgive me, I would pick Saigon in the summer of 1967. I wouldn't have to be sixteen and thin as an arrow again. Fifty-five and fat would be okay by me. Just to be back there, in that city, when it was my city, with all the excitement and all the color and all the smells and everything that was special about it, even the danger, at a time when we could still hope—that's all I would ask. Well, here we are."

Melissa followed Ky up three concrete steps to the tiny porch of a two-story clapboard house. Ky led Melissa down a short hallway to the kitchen. Finishing her cigarette and grinding it out in a much-used ashtray on the counter nearest the door, she struck a kitchen match and lit one of the burners on an ancient white enamel stove. As soon as she had a steady flame going, she put a kettle over the burner. Then she took a china teapot from the dish-drainer near the sink and fit a small mesh tea strainer over its top.

"When did you leave South Vietnam?" Melissa asked as Ky spooned Oolong tea onto the strainer.

"About six months before it stopped being South Vietnam," Ky said with a trace of bitterness. She took two small cups out of the cupboard, each without handles and featuring a gold dragon enameled on a midnight blue background.

"Saigon to Milwaukee must have been a very difficult change for you."

"Sure," Ky said matter of factly. "My son is, what, less than three. We get to Milwaukee. Many people here are warm and open, but factory jobs are leaving the city. Workers feel threatened. Resentment very deep. Vietnamese men at that time, when we first get here, the young workers call them 'slopes.' Like GIs call the VC. Later, when my Don is maybe sixteen, seventeen, some whites call him 'timber nigger.'"

"What?" Melissa asked in astonishment.

"They thought he was Indian." Ky offered a mordant smile. "Native American. 'Timber nigger' was even worse than 'slope.'"

A shrill peep escaped from the kettle. Ky turned the burner off, grabbed the kettle's handle with a potholder, and poured scalding water through the strainer into the teapot. Removing the strainer, she left the tea to steep while she dumped the sodden grains in the trash.

"I am going the long way around to answer your question about Mr. Hayes," Ky said then. "Don is one tough kid."

"Yeah, I picked that up."

"Oh, he is much mellower now. Back then he fights a lot. One time there is very bad trouble. One of the whites hurt pretty bad, maybe going to die. I am not sure where to turn. Vance Hayes helps us. He gets everything pretty much worked out. And he helps us out now and then after that."

Ky poured tea from the pot into each of the cups. She brought the cups over to the kitchen table and set one in front of Melissa.

"But Hayes didn't just show up out of the blue, did he?"

Melissa could have kicked herself for her impatience. Ky looked at her shrewdly. For a moment Melissa thought she was going to shut her off. Ky, though, just took a long sip of tea as the indulgent tilt of her smile subtly changed.

"I know, I leave too many blanks," she said. "For instance, getting out of South Vietnam is pretty good trick six months before Saigon falls. Poor young girl with a three-year old brat and no husband—how do you suppose I manage that exit?"

"I don't know. How?"

Without leaving her chair, Ky reached for the ashtray, moved it from the counter to the table, and lit another cigarette. Melissa found Ky's steady gaze through the curling smoke bracing. She thought she read a challenge there—not a warning, exactly, but an admonition: *Before you stick your nose into someone else's business, you'd better think about whom you'll leave behind when the last helicopter pulls you off the embassy roof.*

"You know why I am going to tell you this story? Because you did not genuflect, because that would be a lie for you."

"Thank you."

"Don's father was Timmy Hayes. Lieutenant Timothy Hayes, Vance Hayes' brother. I made up the family name Duong for him to keep Lieutenant Tim out of trouble."

"I see."

"Not yet, you don't see anything," Ky said with an I've-got-twenty-years-on-you smile. "I am not Lieutenant Tim's 'geisha,' his 'mama-san.' He want to bring me to U.S. and marry. I know, I know. How many Vietnamese girls hear that from GIs? I believe my Lieutenant Tim, though. He told me the truth."

"So he got you out?"

"No. He is killed three weeks before his tour ends. I am, what, three months pregnant. Vance Hayes eventually gets us out. Takes a long time. Vance Hayes gets us here. And when Don has scrapes here and there, Vance Hayes helps out. This is what you want to know, I think?"

"Yes," Melissa said. "It's exactly what I wanted to know. I can't tell you how grateful I am to you for sharing it with me."

"That's okay, missy," Ky said with a joshing little nudge.

Relaxed, now, Ky settled back in the chair, propped her right elbow on the table, and held the cigarette in a relaxed grip about two inches from her cheekbone. Melissa caught her breath, just as Rep had looking at the aging photograph from Hayes' files. In her mind's eye the years and pounds and inches melted away, and she saw a happy-go-lucky Xu Ky in her teens, flirting in a Saigon sidewalk café with American soldiers. And she knew there was no way on earth this woman had let Vance Hayes or anyone else use her daughter as a sexual toy.

The only problem with Detective Washington's neat theory was that it was wrong.

Chapter Twenty-Four

When Rep pulled his ringing cell phone from the Sable's nearer cup-holder at one-thirteen on Friday afternoon, he sighed a quick prayer that the call relate to the on-site part of the IP audit he'd just finished, or to tonight's dinner plans, or to anything except the Vance Hayes/Max Levitan mess.

It did. Terry Hutchinson, a law school classmate, wanted Rep to recommend an Indianapolis litigator for a contract dispute that Hutchinson's large Washington firm couldn't be bothered with handling. Rep promised to email a couple of names and phone numbers when he got back to the office.

"So," Rep said then, "things can't be too bad if you're handing off ninety-thousand-dollar cases."

"Guilty as charged. I paid my dues in the public sector right out of Michigan, and now I'm shamelessly making money. Twenty-nine months on the Senate Judiciary Committee staff, and I remember it like it was last week. That's because last week I had root canal work."

"I'd forgotten about that line on your resumé. Too bad you're not still there. I could make a cop up here happy if I could get some inside attention on that staff."

"Lotsa luck on that one, pal. With two Supreme Court vacancies to worry about, it'll be awhile before anyone on Judiciary finds time for civics class stuff like citizen contact or intergovernmental cooperation."

They signed off and Rep drove for another ten seconds before Hutchinson's last comment triggered the right synapse. He picked up his phone and tried to remember Detective Washington's number. Then he put the phone back into the cup-holder. He wanted to think some implications through before he called anyone.

He accomplished that in eight highway miles, which was a good thing because by then he was just about out of freeway. Approaching Lake Michigan, he swung right instead of exiting left and headed for Milwaukee's south side. On the way down, he had Sprint's computer tell him Cold Coast's number and patch him through to it. He asked the gruff male who answered if he could talk to the plant manager.

"Speaking," the voice said.

"This is Rep Pennyworth, the lawyer who was there a while back. I'd like to speak with you face to face for about ten minutes. I need some advice."

"The best advice I can give you is not to bother coming down here. I'm still writing a check every month from the last time I talked to a lawyer. Far as I'm concerned, if it weren't for people who sell heroin to school children lawyers would be the lowest form of human life."

"I get that a lot. But I'm trying to decide whether I should tell the detective investigating Max Levitan's murder about something I just thought of, or whether it's too trivial to bother him about. I'd like your input."

Rep didn't hear a click. On the other hand, for about seven seconds he didn't hear anything else either.

"This a shakedown?"

"The Board of Attorneys Professional Responsibility frowns on extortion. I don't want money. I want Max Levitan's murderer behind bars. I need ten minutes of your time."

Another pause, this one lasting three or four seconds.

"Okay," the guy said finally. "Don't come in the building. Meet me at the flagpoles out front."

The guy Rep saw standing between the two flagpoles five minutes later looked exactly the same as he had the morning he had shown Rep and Sue Key into Cold Coast's conference room. Same short-sleeved white dress shirt with the collar open, same bullet-shaped head and crewcut, same fireplug posture. The American flag, on his right as Rep approached him, was at half-staff. So was the black and white POW/MIA flag hanging limply from the pole on his left. He surprised Rep by holding out his right hand as Rep reached him.

"Dave Pavick." He flourished an unfiltered Camel in his left hand. "This is my excuse for being out here. So we've got about ten minutes."

"Okay," Rep said. "When Detective Washington was questioning me about Mr. Levitan's murder, he showed me a letter in Levitan's file on Sue Key's claim. The letter was from the staff of the Senate Judiciary Committee."

"Right, a blow-off. I remember him telling me about it. 'We'll get back to you.' Right, and the check is in the mail."

"What I was wondering was what happened to the stuff you took out of the file before Washington found it."

"Whatinhell izzat 'sposed ta mean?" Pavick's words came in an angry rush, but his tone was defensive instead of indignant.

"The letter was a reply. But a reply to what? Mr. Levitan's letter to the committee wasn't in the file."

"No idea." Pavick shrugged. "Maybe he phoned it in."

"I don't think so," Rep said. "I might be able to get a written answer to a phoned-in request if I spent half a morning trying to track down a staff contact through colleagues and law school classmates. But Max Levitan had complete contempt for contemporary politicians. Even if he started with a phone call he couldn't have reached anyone beyond clerks or interns. All they would have told him is to put it in writing."

"Maybe so, I don't know. What I do know is, I can't help you."

"That's too bad, because it wouldn't be hard to get the wrong idea about this. That letter was in the Sue Key file, so Detective Washington and I assumed that Levitan had gotten in touch with the Judiciary Committee because it has jurisdiction over copyright matters. Maybe hoping for free legal advice, maybe trying to put political pressure on me."

"Neither one makes any sense to me."

"Me either," Rep said. "But the Senate Judiciary Committee also has responsibility for reviewing federal judicial appointments. What if Levitan had written to ask for information from one of those files?"

"Why would he do that?"

"Exactly. And if he did, why would he put the letters in Sue Key's file? Unless there was some connection. You see, that's why it's such a pity that the letter he wrote has disappeared. If that letter should turn up, then we'd know. Of course, the police will find out eventually, because sooner or later Detective Washington's questions will get to the top of some staffer's in-box. But it would be nice to know now."

"Like I said, can't help you."

"There might have been other things taken out of that file as well before it was turned over," Rep said. "Things that, together with Levitan's letter, might have given the police the idea that Levitan was thinking of doing a shakedown. Maybe they disappeared to protect Levitan's reputation."

"No way Max did anything like that," Pavick said hotly. "He absolutely refused to get into anything like that. You should have heard him chew out that little weasel, Dreyfus, after he got your letter. I mean he reamed him a new one. He was screaming at him."

"Screaming what?"

"'I told that sonofabitch never to ask me for anything again. You have no idea what you're getting into. You could get yourself killed and me with you.' That kind of thing."

"Pretty provocative—especially after he was killed."

"I told all that part to the cops. About yelling at Dreyfus, I mean. But I guess they didn't let you in on it, huh?"

"No, and I don't blame them," Rep said. "It's none of my business. My point is that someone who thought the file would give the police the wrong impression might have scrubbed it a bit on the way from the file room to Detective Washington. Maybe Washington would think I was a pest if I took up his valuable time with these speculations. But maybe not."

Pavick's mouth twisted into a frown as he stewed in angry concentration for ten long seconds. The cliché about plant managers is that they only have to be smart six times a year, but they only get to be dumb once. Rep thought that he could almost hear the man thinking.

"Did you lock your car after you parked it over there?" Pavick asked.

"I don't think so." Rep took a startled glance over his shoulder at the Sable. "Why?"

"'Cause I saw someone messing around near it. He's gone now, though."

"I'll be more careful next time." Rep sketched a baffled shrug.

"Tell you what. There's a diner right around the corner from where you parked. Go have yourself a cup of coffee. Take about fifteen minutes at it. Skip the potato pancakes, though. Those are for professionals."

"Right," Rep said, nodding as understanding gradually seeped through.

After shaking hands with Pavick, he strode away, found Paula's Cracow Diner, and lingered over a cup of coffee that tasted like a cross between battery acid and high-viscosity grease from the Gdansk shipyards. When he'd made his leisurely way back to the Sable, he found about half an inch of paper scattered on the front passenger seat.

The top page was Levitan's letter to the Judiciary Committee. It asked for copies of letters or anything else sent to the committee by Vance Hayes in the last five years.

Hayes? For a moment Rep gazed unseeing through the windshield. Then he rifled through the rest of the pile. All Hayes. Copies of the same police report on Hayes' death that Rep had seen. Copies of news stories about his drowning. A time-line tracking Hayes' whereabouts during the week leading up to his plunge through the ice, with annotations to various sources, showing that Levitan had worked hard to come up with this information. Someone who didn't know him might have accused Levitan of stalking.

It doesn't make sense as extortion. But it doesn't make sense as anything else, either.

He started the car and headed downtown. The sooner Detective Washington started worrying about this new puzzle-piece, the happier Rep would be.

"Back before the end of the week, technically, huh?" Kuchinski asked Rep about forty-five minutes later.

"Yeah, we wrapped things up with the client before noon." Rep swiveled around in his chair to face Kuchinski. "My fresh-faced young associates are headed back to Indianapolis. I'm on the sixth page of a letter explaining how the client can stop leaving eighty thousand a year on the table."

"In that case, I have an important question for you. Do you know the first three rules of firearm safety?"

"Sure." Every red-blooded Midwestern male knows the first three rules of firearm safety. "One: don't take the safety off until you have the target clearly in sight. Two: don't put your finger on the trigger until you're ready to fire. Three: always maintain muzzle control."

"By providential coincidence, those are exactly the same as the first three rules of prudent cross-examination. So we now know that you are fully qualified either to try a lawsuit or go deer hunting."

"I can't do either one until I finish this letter."

"Plenty of time for that," Kuchinski scoffed breezily. "Deer season doesn't start 'til Thanksgiving week."

"Uh, yeah," Rep said. "I'm not real big on hunting."

"Well, you might wanna get big on it, my friend. The Brady Street Ski Club will not be alone at deer camp this year. We will be joined by Simeon David, the owner of La Crosse Metrics. LCM is hip-deep in trademark litigation, and Simeon might be in the mood for a second opinion."

"Hmm." *Ka-ching! ka-ching!* rang in Rep's head.

"I was expecting something a little stronger than 'hmm,'" Kuchinski said. "Something more along the lines of, 'When do we start and can I borrow a rifle from someone?'"

"That's my first reaction, all right. But there's another element in play here, from Levitan's murder. A new joker has jumped out of the deck—and the first one he jumped at was Melissa."

"What're you talkin' about, boy?"

Rep provided a quick rundown of Melissa's encounters with the cowboy who stole phony names from the yellowing roster of the old Milwaukee Braves. Rep passed on what he could remember of the description Melissa had given him. Kuchinski shook his head.

"You just described half the Marquette High School class of 1958. Why don't you get your missus on the phone and have *her* describe Mr. No-name for me?"

"Good idea." Rep picked up the receiver of his desk phone but then put it back down. "Before I call Melissa, though, there's something I wanted to ask you about. I learned while I was out of town that you were the one who arranged military honors for Hayes' burial. I was wondering why."

The warmth in Kuchinski's expression dropped about five degrees and an unmistakable wariness clouded his eyes. He waited five seconds before answering.

"You gave the guy's eulogy, right?" he said at last.

"Yes."

"Because he'd picked you to do it, right?"

"Yes."

"Well, I guess if he'd wanted you to know, he'd have made sure you did."

"Okay," Rep said. "If it's private, it's private."

"It's private."

"Fair enough. I'll see if I can reach Melissa."

Us/Them. Rep hadn't been through Vietnam. The black wall memorial in Washington wasn't his the way it was Kuchinski's. The POW/MIA banner flying at Cold Coast didn't belong to

Rep in the way it did to Kuchinski and Skupnievich and the rest of the Brady Street Ski Club. There were some places he couldn't go. Some places marked Members Only.

He got Melissa on the fourth ring and explained why he had called.

"You're on the speaker phone now, honey," he said after pushing the right button. "Go."

Melissa repeated the description she'd given to Washington. As she spoke, the hale-fellow joviality habitual with Kuchinski faded even further from his face, replaced by a look of sharp interest and acute concentration that Rep suspected Milwaukee's insurance defense bar had come to dread.

"Moved kind of fluidly, like he'd had concentrated physical training at some point in his life?" Kuchinski asked after Melissa had finished.

"That's fair."

"Not hulking, but seemed to fill a lot of space?"

"You could say that."

"Just a little flabby, like an athlete right on the verge of going to seed?"

"Definitely."

"You don't work as a trial lawyer for twenty-five years without learning to get a good look at people when they come to your office for a deposition," Kuchinski said. "If that guy isn't Roger Leopold, it's his twin brother."

"Hmm," Rep said, remembering his mother's chilling assessment of Leopold. "Walt, I think this rules out any jaunt to deer camp for me this year. I can't spend a week out of touch with Melissa with this guy running around."

"Actually, honey," Melissa interjected, "I haven't had a chance to talk with you about it yet, but Detective Washington wants to come over to meet with us tonight. I think it might put deer camp back in the picture."

"You go, girl!" Kuchinski said with delight. Then, pointing his finger at Rep, "Sighting in is a week from Monday at the Dan'l Morgan Shooting Range in Ozaukee County, soldier. Be there."

"I was reluctant to call you," MacKenzie Stewart told the policeman who'd just spent an hour tramping over the four acres of Stewart's estate nearest the *faux* Georgian mansion where he and Gael lived when they weren't in Washington. "But it looks like we've had uninvited company."

"I'd say you're right about that, sir," the cop said. He said "sir" automatically, the way recruits fresh out of basic training do. "Bits of fabric snagged on bushes, fresh stems snapped at ankle level, plantings trampled—and all of it inside your wall here."

"Do you think it might be teenagers looking for a little privacy?"

The cop shook his head.

"If they can get out to this neighborhood they have a car, and in Indianapolis in November a car is a lot warmer place for nookie. You've had someone giving your house a real careful look recently. I'll make a report."

◇◇◇

"I'm not one of the Jones Boys," Washington said to Rep and Melissa across their kitchen table a little after seven-thirty that evening.

"I don't know what that means," Melissa said.

"Arthur Jones was the first African-American police chief Milwaukee ever had," Washington explained. "A while back a federal jury found that he had discriminated against white officers in promoting detectives from lieutenant to captain. Well, that jury was wrong. Arthur Jones didn't discriminate on the basis of skin color. He discriminated on the basis of how good a job you did of kissing his butt."

"And you're still a lieutenant," Rep said. "So you apparently didn't see anal osculation on your job description."

"Right. I mention that because I'm about to step way outside the box, and I need you to trust me."

"Okay," Melissa said.

"Here's the way I see things. Dreyfus obviously thought there was valuable information in that transcript of Roger Leopold's deposition. Someone else apparently thinks Dreyfus was on to something, and it looks like that someone else is probably Leopold himself."

"Which would explain his coming after me and Sue Key," Melissa said. "Especially if he was the one who tried to follow me after I left Dreyfus' studio. But Leopold obviously knows what he said in the deposition."

"Exactly," Washington said. "So he must think Dreyfus had some other data that becomes valuable when you put it together with the transcript."

"And he thinks there's a chance Melissa has that data now, because she was in Dreyfus' studio shortly before he decamped."

"Right again," Washington said. "And sooner or later, we have to expect him to come for it. So let's invite him in. Leave your apartment and go somewhere Thanksgiving week. Over the river and through the woods to grandmother's house, or deer hunting, or somewhere else—just go. We'll have your apartment under close surveillance. If Leopold takes the bait, we'll grab him—and whether the murderer is Nguyen or Leopold or someone else, I'll bet we'll have him after Leopold spends four hours in the squeal room."

"I love this plan," Rep said. "But can you get away, honey?"

"I can double up on one class and have people cover for me on the others," Melissa said. "The trick will be figuring out where I go, because I don't plan on spending a week reeking of cosmolene and cheap cigars in the middle of people trying to kill Bambi's mom."

"We'll work that part out," Rep said. "Lieutenant, we have a deal. As of eight a.m. on the Saturday before Thanksgiving, Melissa and I are out of here."

"Okay," Washington said as he rose. "You're doing your part. Now we have to do ours."

Exactly what Melissa would do with herself during the Thanksgiving week sabbatical remained a puzzle until the following Monday afternoon—the first Monday in November, with the air just a bit "fresher," as Milwaukeeans say (or "colder," as the rest of the human race would put it). The answer came when Rep answered his phone, assuming that Melissa was calling him.

"Hello, beloved," he said.

"Well, well," Ken Stewart said. "This is a side of you we haven't seen before, Rep."

"Sorry, I'm a bit distracted. Things have gotten a little hairy here in the last couple of weeks."

"Down here as well," Stewart said. "We've had an intruder."

"Did you tell the police?"

"Sure, but there's a limit to what they can do. At the risk of seeming melodramatic, I called Wackenhut this morning. That's one of the top private investigation firms in the country. I asked them to see what they could find out about Roger Leopold. It took them only two hours and six phone calls to ascertain that he's no longer in Hong Kong."

"We think he's in Milwaukee, at least when he's not trespassing on your estate in Indianapolis," Rep said. "The police here have a plan. The problem is that it involves an unplanned vacation for Melissa and me during Thanksgiving week. I'll be hunting a client while pretending to hunt deer. We haven't figured out what Melissa will be doing."

"You've just given me a fantastic idea," Stewart said. "I talked this morning with a client who has a cabin in central Wisconsin, an hour or so from Stevens Point. Right in the heart of deer country, and he's not a hunter. I've been thinking that until we get our arms wrapped around this intruder business, it wouldn't be a terrible idea for Gael to hang out up there, out of harm's way. I can't go, and she's naturally reluctant to go up there by herself. But if Melissa would stay there with her, they'd both be safer and you could go out blithely hustling clients."

"You're right, that is a fantastic idea."

"Splendid. I'll wait to hear from you."

And so it was with a clear conscience that Rep one week later rolled with Kuchinski and Splinters in Kuchinski's Riviera onto the rutted gravel parking lot of the Dan'l Morgan Shooting Range. As they were unloading the trunk, Kuchinski hefted a large, black pistol that looked like a mutated Luger.

"Tell me what you think of this," he said.

He pointed the pistol at a newsmagazine cover shot of Saddam Hussein, which was taped to a bundle of newsprint at least two feet thick. He squeezed the trigger, producing the kind of small, soft *pop!* that well-raised guests at a dinner party would ignore. A bright red splotch appeared on Hussein's cheek.

"Paintball gun," Splinters said with disgust. "What I think is that real men use live ammunition."

"Not on squirrels on the east side of Milwaukee they don't. But that's just an excuse. I saw that thing at the sporting goods store when I was having my Weatherby tapped for its scope, and I told myself, 'Walt, you must own this. You must own it tonight. It is God's will.'"

Kuchinski put the paintball gun back in the trunk and the three of them lifted gun cases, a spotting scope, and the bundle of newsprint out. They walked with measured steps toward the range, for Sighting In is a solemn exercise. They waited with serene patience while the round of firing already under way proceeded. Let their ears get used once again to the sharp cracks of rifle fire in crisp autumn air. Watched the puffs of blue smoke float toward the sky. Greedily inhaled the rich aroma of vaporized cordite.

The firing let up. Five seconds of silence intervened before someone yelled, "Target check!" Everyone waited another five seconds, for live fire encourages discretion. Then the line of shooters trod warily toward piles of sandbags exactly one hundred yards away. Some went empty-handed, to pick up targets. Others carried paper bull's-eye and deer-face targets of various sizes. A couple of jokers had six-foot-tall plastic sheets with human figures outlined in black. Kuchinski was the only one who set a bundle of newsprint on the ground as his target.

The shooters retreated to their original positions. They waited until, as etiquette required, voices called, "Ready on the left!"

"Ready on the right!" "Ready on the firing line!" Very shortly after that the fusillade began anew.

Rep played along while Kuchinski and Splinters proceeded as deliberately as they could. They clearly didn't want it to end anytime soon. Even so, lining up shots as if they were million-dollar putts on the eighteenth green at Augusta and adjusting their sights by micrometers, it took less than fifteen minutes for them to shred Saddam Hussein's face with three-shot groups that a silver dollar could have covered.

"Is that a Leupold scope on the brand-new Wetherby, Mr. Kuchinski?" Splinters asked. "My poor little Remington with its paltry Weaver scope feels humbled to be in their presence. You must be having a prosperous year."

"Life is good." Kuchinski's tone didn't encourage follow-up.

They packed up while the firing around them again slowly tapered off. When the next target check came, Kuchinski trudged to the sandbags to retrieve his bundled newsprint. Rep expected him to chuck the awkward burden in a fifty-five gallon oil drum at the right of the firing line, but Kuchinski carried it all the way back to his car.

"What're you gonna do with that thing?" Rep asked.

"Dig the lead out of it," Kuchinski said. "I always take the sighting-in bullets along for good luck when I go deer hunting."

Chapter Twenty-Five

On the Thursday before Thanksgiving it snowed. Relatively well-mannered as upper Midwestern weather systems go, the snowstorm didn't start until after the evening rush hour. Snow fell steadily for hours, tapering off around two a.m.—just in time for the snowplows to get it cleared before morning drive-time. Milwaukeeans hadn't seen serious snow in mid-November for years, and few adults rejoiced at seeing it now. School administrators worried about burning a snow-day this early in the year, homeowners who hadn't prepped their snowblowers cursed their procrastination, and working parents wondered what they were going to do if the snow closed schools but not the factories or offices where they labored.

One group of grown-ups, however, watched the white stuff accumulate with unalloyed delight. Eight inches of snow blanketing Wisconsin answered longings that had long gone unrequited. This contingent consisted of deer hunters. The normal deer-hunting protocol is stationary: you set up your tree-stand, try to climb into it without blowing off your foot or some even more important part of your body, and wait there, bored and shivering, in the hope that a legal whitetail will wander into range.

The snow changed all that. A deep snow would drive deer to more aggressive foraging. And even more important, it didn't take a Native American guide or a charter subscriber to *Field and Stream* to follow deer tracks through snow. The opportune

snowfall made this Good Tracking Weather—a phrase uttered
by deer hunters with even more reverence than Sighting In.

The Friday before Thanksgiving Rep received a copy of the
Probate Court report on disposition of Vance Hayes' estate. Rep
had asked for this nearly six weeks before, but it hadn't seemed
urgent and he hadn't pressed the associate involved. It didn't seem
urgent now, either. Rep stuffed the document into the backpack
he was preparing for his trip to deer camp.

Late Friday afternoon, Don Nguyen zippered his M-14 and
thirty boxed cartridges into a leather scabbard. He strapped the
scabbard to the back of his Harley, checked to make sure he had
his deer tag and Buck skinning knife, and peeled away from
his flat. Twenty minutes later he was headed north over freshly
plowed highways, four car-lengths behind a maroon Mazda.

"At this rate," Melissa said to Rep Saturday morning as he pointed
the Sable north on Highway 45, "you're going to be at Teal Peaks
Camping and Sporting Goods an hour before you're supposed to
meet Walt there. I thought you didn't have to buy a rifle."

"I don't. Walt's lending me his old one. But if I'm going to
be in deer camp for a whole week I might need a second pair of
socks or something."

"Yeeccch," Melissa said then under her breath.

Rep didn't have to ask where her sudden disgust came from,
for he saw the southbound Chevy Blazer at the same time she
did. A glassy-eyed, stiff-legged, broken-necked, gutted buck's
carcass was lashed to the cargo rack on top. They both knew the
hunters' defenses, which have the virtue of being true: steers in
the slaughterhouse look a lot worse, so no one who eats steak
has any business being squeamish; and if a thirty-ought-six
hadn't snapped that Buck's spine and shattered his heart, he'd
probably have starved to death or been hit by a semi or died a
slow and agonizing death in the claws of a predator. But none
of that made the carcass any less repulsive to Melissa.

"You're not actually going to shoot a deer, are you?"

"Ever hear the one about the doctor, the lawyer, and the economist who went deer hunting? They spot a deer. The lawyer fires first and misses five feet to the right. The doctor fires second and misses five feet to the left. The economist claps his hands and shouts, 'We got 'im, we got 'im!'"

"That means no?" Melissa asked with a don't-feed-me-any-crap smile.

"That means not a chance."

Thirty minutes later Melissa noticed Rep intently studying a handgun in a glass case near the cash register at Teal Peaks. She didn't imagine he was thinking about buying it but she decided to intervene, just in case.

"Don't you have enough *impedimenta* for one trip, honey? I don't think anyone has outfitted himself quite this thoroughly since William Boot in *Black Mischief*."

Standing as he was in the midst of La Crosse Footwear insulated leather hunting boots (one pair), Wigwam bulk-knit, knee-length socks (two pairs), Weaver hunting gloves lined with Thinsulate (one pair), mustard brown heavy twill hunting pants (one pair), Pendleton flannel shirts in Black Watch tartan (two), UnderArmor insulated underwear (two sets), blaze orange Trooper-brand cap with pull-down ear-flaps (one), waterproof, screw-top metal cylinder for keeping matches dry (one), Maglite four-cell, heavy duty flashlight (one), Thomas quart-sized thermos with stainless steel liner (one), and a Timberline down-filled sleeping bag with ground cloth and tuck sack (one), Rep couldn't challenge her assessment. He imagined that he did look a lot like Evelyn Waugh's rural *naïf* blundering off to Ethiopia loaded down with enough gear for an infantry platoon. But that didn't mean he had to take it lying down.

"Up to a point, Lady Zinc," he murmured, alluding to the same satiric novel. "Look at this revolver. Does it remind you of any pop culture allusion you've committed recently?"

"Opening of *Superman* on TV," Melissa said as she examined it.

"That's right," the weathered proprietor said as he strolled behind the counter toward the cash register. "Smith and Wesson thirty-eight caliber Police Positive. I remember watching *The Adventures of Superman* as an original series in black-and-white, on a Zenith console TV in our living room."

"That's interesting," Melissa murmured. "This doesn't look quite the same as the gun I was looking at when I made that savvy comment."

"Smith and Wesson does make a number of different models," the proprietor said, in the dry tone you might use to comment that Imelda Marcos had a number of different pairs of shoes.

"Do they make one that looks like this one's big brother, with a longer barrel and a lanyard ring?" Rep asked.

The guy walked down to the far end of the counter, unlocked the back of the case, squatted, and took a dusty blue cardboard box from the bottom shelf. Bringing it back to Rep and Melissa, he removed the lid to reveal exactly what Rep had just described. The barrel was two inches longer, and a lanyard ring dangled from the bottom of the checkered grip.

"Smith and Wesson thirty-eight caliber Model Ten," he said. "Six-inch barrel, six-shot cylinder, double-action, center-fire."

"That's it," Rep said.

The merchant lifted the gun, released the cylinder and spun it, peered down the barrel, snapped the cylinder back into place, and dry-fired the weapon once. This routine generally got juices flowing in American males.

"Like to take a closer look at it?"

"No, thanks. Just trying to satisfy my curiosity. I'll be using something bigger than that to hunt deer."

"Deer?" the guy asked. "You leave your blaze orange in the car?"

"Well, I have the cap," Rep said defensively.

"I would most strongly recommend more than that. Parka at least, if not overalls. There will be seven hundred thousand armed men and women in the north Wisconsin woods this weekend, and they won't all be sober."

"A blaze orange parka isn't required, is it?" Rep asked, as he sensed his sales resistance crumbling and Melissa's bemused exasperation rising.

"No, it's not. But it's like that *Reader's Digest* story from the Vietnam days. Seems there was this real gung-ho second lieutenant going through advanced infantry training and doing okay, except he couldn't hit a house with a thirty-eight. So he asks the sergeant who's training him, 'Will failure to qualify with the thirty-eight keep me from going to Vietnam?' And the sergeant says, 'No sir. But it might keep you from coming back.'"

"Hmm," Rep said eloquently.

"One parka, coming up. What are you, about a thirty-six regular?"

"Wait a minute," Rep said, looking up. "I thought the standard sidearm in the U.S. Army during the Vietnam War was the Colt forty-five automatic."

"That's been the most common U.S. military sidearm for a long time, back to World War I if not before. But it wasn't the only one we used in Vietnam. Smith and Wesson designed that Model Ten specifically for the military. Both army and marines in Vietnam used it. Guards handling prisoner transport on helicopters would wear it in a shoulder holster, where it would be secure in close quarters and readily accessible if needed."

"Vietnam, huh?" Rep glanced at Melissa, thinking about Nguyen, while she glanced back at him and thought about Kuchinski.

"Yep. I'd say if you see a Model Ten more than thirty-five years old, it probably saw action in South Vietnam. I'll go see about that parka."

Ten minutes later, Rep stood in Teal Peaks' parking lot, gazing longingly at the Sable as it carried away Melissa and the jacket and shoes he had put on that morning. In their stead he wore his new hunting boots and a blaze orange parka and hat that could be seen from outer space. A glance at his watch confirmed that he had some time to kill before Kuchinski showed up.

"Idle time" is a blasphemous phrase in the legal lexicon. Lawyers read or dictate or talk on the phone or type while they're gulping down lunch, driving to and from work, waiting at airports, and on their way to the bathroom. Rep wasn't that compulsive himself, but he wasn't going to spend twenty minutes counting the cars on Main Street in New Berlin, Wisconsin. He dug the probate report out of his knapsack. He had reached the second page when he heard Kuchinski's voice—or, more accurately, his bellow.

"Hey, counselor! Get in before you draw fire!"

This surprised Rep, for he'd kept half an eye on the road, looking for Kuchinski's Riviera and not seeing it. Now he realized why. Kuchinski perched behind the wheel of a silver gray Cadillac Escalade SUV.

Which is very interesting. Because this report says that Walter Kuchinski, Esq. received a payment of $100,000 from the Estate of Vance Hayes.

Now that's what I call a kiss.

Melissa watched Gael Cunningham-Stewart's right foot rise off the tarmac during her goodbye clinch with Ken Stewart. The two were standing in the shadow of Stewart's Gulfstream jet on a landing strip at the Experimental Aircraft Association airfield in Oshkosh, Wisconsin. Even from a discreet thirty yards away, Melissa could sense the passion in their embrace. After Gael had walked over to the Sable and greeted Melissa, she turned around and watched the Gulfstream taxi back down the strip and take off. She waved until it had disappeared in the piercingly sunlit sky.

"All right," she said then to Melissa as they climbed into the car, "I'm in your hands. I have directions from the client-owner, but I don't know how much confidence I have in them."

"We'll do the best we can with that and the driving instructions I printed out from Mapquest," Melissa said. "If we start seeing mounties and roadside stands selling French fries with gravy, we'll know we blew it."

"I'm traveling pretty light," Gael said as Melissa pulled the car back onto Highway 41. "Should we stop somewhere before we get too far from civilization so that I can chip in for some Lean Cuisine or something?"

"I have a cooler in the trunk full of yogurt, fresh fruit, vegetables, juice, a few salmon filets and a cooked roast."

"That should hold us for a while, all right," Gael said. "I should mention one complication. I learned just before Ken and I left that an emergency motion is being heard by a panel of my court at noon on Monday. I'll take part by phone from the federal courthouse in Madison, which means I'll have to leave by nine-thirty in the morning or so. I feel terrible about imposing, but would it be a huge problem if I borrowed your car for the trip?"

"Not at all."

Wisconsin has a large tourist industry and correspondingly good, toll-free highways. Even feeling their way through unfamiliar territory, it took Gael and Melissa only a little over two hours to reach the general vicinity of the alleged cabin. As they cruised along state highways and then for a few miles along Interstate Thirty-nine, they passed more than a dozen pickup trucks and SUVs with dead deer tied to their luggage racks or lying in their beds. Deer season was only eleven hours or so old, and lots of hunters apparently already had their kill. Melissa noticed that the repugnance she'd felt this morning when she saw the first carcass progressively diminished. She was getting used to it.

"Well," Melissa said as they turned onto the last numbered road mentioned by Mapquest, "we're now pretty close to 'Here Be Dragons' territory. We're going to have to rely on the owner's directions from here on in."

"They say we should look for a left turn on County Road B," Gael said, consulting a much-folded page in her lap. "Then it mentions an old logging road, and that's where I begin to worry."

Melissa drove for just over a mile before she spotted a sign promising junction with B. She noticed two bulletholes in the sign, which for some hunters represented a less elusive target than deer. She turned left and started to wonder what an old logging road might look like.

Eight-tenths of a mile later, she found out. A wooden sign at the top of a slight grade said OLD LOGGING ROAD LANE. The road was gravel rather than asphalt, but someone had cleared enough snow from it to permit the Sable to negotiate the path. They parked on the side of the road, at the bottom of the grade, about forty feet from the front door of the promised cabin.

"Well done," Gael said.

"Lewis and Clark, that's us."

It took them less than an hour to carry their things in and get set up. They had all the cold running water they wanted once they gassed up a generator in the back yard and turned on the pump. No telephone, but lights, refrigerator, and stove would work as long as the generator did. For heat they'd depend on a cord of firewood and kindling stacked beside the cabin.

"Not exactly roughing it, are we?" Gael said.

"I'm already connecting with Laura Ingalls Wilder," Melissa said. "I may have the urge to fetch something at any moment."

"We're going to get along just fine."

"I'll call Rep just to let him know we arrived."

She punched his number into her cell phone and pushed SEND. Nothing happened. She looked at the screen: NO SERVICE.

Oops. I hadn't thought of that.

Chapter Twenty-Six

Rep knew from teenage experience that Hunting—with a capital H—means a lot more than tracking and shooting game. It involves, for example, drinking beer, including for breakfast; playing cards; telling jokes that would never find voice in the presence of women, people wearing ties, or other spoilsports; making pictures in the snow while performing biological functions; and driving on frontage roads to waysides to purchase more beer.

Even so, Rep had assumed that at *some* point in this excursion they would do some actual hunter stuff—get up before dawn, load rifles, fan out in search of deer, stuff like that. As the light paled toward evening on Sunday, though, he began to entertain doubts. Logs had gone from the woodpile to the fire, fliptops had popped, hamburgers had sizzled on messkit frypans, and tales about electoral campaigns in Milwaukee and women with talented lips in Vegas and Saigon had made the rounds. But no one so far had done anything that would threaten the life or serenity of any quadrupeds.

Rep had spent the drive up with Kuchinski trying to think of some polite way to raise awkward questions. Questions like: *What's with the sixty-thousand-dollar car all of a sudden? You know, the one that fits in with that brand-new, top-line rifle Splinters was drooling over. Do they have anything to do with Vance Hayes' six-figure bequest that you hadn't mentioned?*

The right words, though, hadn't come. Rep had mentioned that the Cadillac Escalade looked like quite a step up from the

Riviera, and Kuchinski had shrugged that off with a casual, "Yeah, sometimes things just work out." Rep couldn't figure out how to push things beyond that without making their conversation sound like a cross-examination.

His encounter with Simeon David, the prospective client, had likewise gone pretty much nowhere. Rep liked baseball and David liked hockey. Rep read *Forbes* and David skimmed *Business Week*. David was livid about his lawyers' recommending an eighty-thousand-dollar customer confusion survey, but Rep said he'd have recommended the same thing. The best approach to trademark litigation was never to have to do any. Once you were in a case, though, you had to do whatever it took to win. That was where things stood when the poker game started Sunday night. By eleven Rep had netted out forty dollars down and said he was calling it a night.

"Good idea," Kuchinski said as Rep unrolled his sleeping bag and arranged his backpack to serve as a pillow. "The weekend woodsmen will be back in Milwaukee tomorrow morning instead of cluttering up the forest, so we real hunters can go out and promote survival of the fittest."

Kuchinski woke him up before first light Monday morning. Rep had a what's-wrong-with-this-picture? feeling as he rolled up his sleeping bag, but he couldn't figure out why. When he got back from relieving himself, Kuchinski offered him a deer camp breakfast: instant coffee and pastry from the wayside.

"The others are all out already?"

"Except for Splinters," Kuchinski said, nodding at a sleeping bag almost invisible in the dim light, even though it was only twelve feet away.

They pulled themselves into blaze orange parkas and caps. Checked to make sure their deer tags showed through plastic pockets on the parkas' backs. Checked the safeties on their rifles. And headed out.

Well, almost out.

"You got any jerky?" Kuchinski asked three strides past the door.

"Nope. Didn't even think about it."

"Better take some along in case we end up chasing an eight-pointer through lunch."

He walked over to his Escalade and opened the back. As Kuchinski stuffed Baggies full of ambiguous brown food sticks into his parka pocket, Rep noticed a large, bulky apparatus that had apparently been buried under other gear when Rep stowed his backpack there Saturday morning.

"*Semper paratus* and all that," he said, "but is that a garage door opener? Why did you bring it up here?"

"Never can tell what you're gonna need in deer camp," Kuchinski said, pointing a milky flashlight beam toward the path in front of them. "Let's go."

"Wait a minute," Rep said. "I forgot my flashlight."

He hustled back inside to fetch it from his backpack. As he opened the flap and saw the disordered jumble inside, he froze for a second. He suddenly understood the off-kilter feeling he'd had when Kuchinski woke him up. Someone had rummaged through the backpack while he was sleeping on it. The contents weren't they way he'd left them, and one of the things that seemed out of place was the Vance Hayes bequest list.

The last time I was up at dawn, it was because I was working on a dissertation and hadn't gotten to bed the night before. Melissa cradled a steaming mug of pan-boiled coffee clumsily through thick mittens as she walked along the back of the cabin, gazing at the frozen lake that lay a hundred gently sloping feet to the west. She had found two blaze orange field jackets in a closet and slipped into one of them. Just in case.

Even if I only get half an hour of this view while I'm up here, it's worth the price of admission.

The dawn light showed orange-pink on the horizon but reflected with a gentle, blue-tinged whiteness from the ice that covered the lake. A pier jutted out over the crystal surface. A sailboat perhaps twelve feet long, mastless and tarpaulin covered, hung from a pulley a few feet above the dock's end, buttoned up tightly against winter but by its very presence promising spring.

Melissa crunched gingerly through snow that, this far north, came well over her ankle and was already crusted over. It took her almost a minute to cover the modest distance. *Is this what Lake Delton had looked like when Vance Hayes had ventured madly onto it?* She recalled Kuchinski talking about the first hard freeze up here only in October—a little over a month ago. From the shoreline, though, once she reached it, the ice looked hard and thick enough to support a tank.

Setting her coffee down on the land end of the pier she walked to the other end, lay on her belly, and looked straight down over the edge at ice fifteen or twenty feet from shore. Everything she saw suggested a rock-solid surface several inches thick. No visual clues to the eddies or currents that might well be swirling just a couple of inches below the surface. Perhaps as solid as it looked, and perhaps pure silver treachery.

A cheerfully piercing yell from the back door broke Melissa's reverie.

"Come and get it! Breakfast is served!"

Melissa pulled herself to her feet and waved to show that she'd heard the summons. Retrieving her coffee cup, she leaped a bit too confidently from the dock. Her right foot slipped out from under her, her right knee hit the frosty ground hard, and she plunged past mid-thigh into snow.

"Nuts," she said, for she didn't believe in wasting more robust cuss words with impeccable Anglo-Saxon credentials on trivia like this.

Praying that the mug hadn't broken, she looked down the slope and toward the dock, where it had to have fallen. She found it jauntily intact, half buried in a mound of conveniently cushioning snow. As she recovered it, though, she saw something else. She duck-walked toward the dock to get a closer look at a bulky shape buried deep in the shadows beneath it. She came close enough to make out skids and the lettering SKI-DOO on one side.

"What were you investigating down there?" Gael asked when Melissa had mushed her way back to the cabin.

"A snowmobile stashed under the dock. It seems odd."

"It sure does. The owners don't use the cabin in winter, or they wouldn't disconnect the phone. Why would they have a snowmobile here?"

"And if they did, why would they just stash it under the dock like that, without any protection? Look at how careful they are with the boat."

"Maybe they let a neighbor who's into winter sports keep it there," Gael suggested. "Anyway, are you all right?"

"Fine. These jeans will dry out in ten minutes. What's for breakfast?"

"Nothing special. Yogurt and fruit and orange juice."

"Sounds wonderful," Melissa said.

The mysterious snowmobile seemed much more than a hundred feet away.

Chapter Twenty-Seven

"When are you gonna get around to bracing me about the hundred thousand bucks?" Kuchinski asked.

The question, with its let's-pick-a-fight timbre, startled Rep. It came after forty-five minutes of tramping that had taken them two miles-plus northwest of their camp, and roughly doubled the syllables exchanged between the two of them since sunrise.

"As soon as I figure out how to ask without implying that you've been pawing through my insulated undies," Rep said. He kept his voice jovial, leaving it up to Kuchinski whether to treat his answer as a josh or a challenge.

"Your undies weren't what interested me, that's for sure," Kuchinski said quietly but with unmistakable irritation. "When I pulled into that parking lot Saturday morning I saw you studying a piece of paper like it was a cross between a draft notice and a bar exam. It seemed to leave you with a bad case of curiosity and a hard time getting to the point while we were driving up. I was kind of wondering what was going on."

"You weren't exactly chatty yourself."

They crunched another hundred yards or so, following no trail that Rep could see. Tracks abundantly pocked the snow, criss-crossing and overlapping. Kuchinski sent a half-accusing, half-disappointed look in Rep's direction as he resumed the conversation, his voice even chillier than the twenty-two-degree temperature.

"I'd feel better if you'd just come to me with any questions you had, instead of having some gumshoe go digging through records two states away."

"He was a young lawyer, not a gumshoe. I didn't ask him to peep through any keyholes of yours. I sure wasn't expecting your name to turn up on that bequest list."

"Fine. Just seems to me like you were playing 'em a little close to the vest—and this ain't poker."

Rep surmised that he had violated some unwritten masculine code, failed some test of intuitive faith. In Kuchinski's mind, apparently, the bequest list should have made Rep talkative instead of tongue-tied. Rep should have volunteered the information with a hey-isn't-this-interesting attitude. He should have shrugged off any sinister interpretation, should have known without having to be told that it meant nothing, should have understood and accepted its irrelevance without thinking about it.

But he hadn't. So Kuchinski had convinced himself that Rep suspected him of complicity in crimes trailing in the vaporous wake of Vance Hayes' ghost. The silence between them as they covered another fifty yards wasn't familiar but sullen, like a summer day heavy with approaching rain. Rep knew that he wasn't going to get another useful word out of Kuchinski about Vance Hayes or anything else unless he reversed Kuchinski's impression.

Rep stopped. Looking at him with sharp surprise, Kuchinski stopped as well. He opened his mouth but before he could speak Rep raised his right arm in an urgent *QUIET!* signal. Trying not to ham it up too much, he gazed straight in front of him, head slightly forward, eyes focusing with fierce intensity, the tip of his nose quivering slightly. Glancing at Kuchinski, he pointed at a birch with a divided trunk about eighty yards off. He raised his eyebrows questioningly. Kuchinski nodded with a puzzled expression that Rep interpreted as meaning *Yeah, that's a tree. So what?*

Rep set the rifle Kuchinski had lent him butt-first in the snow and leaned the barrel against a tree to his left. He started forward with a careful but steady pace, intended to hide the hollowness in his gut and the tremor in his calves. He didn't look back. Just moved ahead, offering Kuchinski an unarmed, can't-miss target. Six or seven Wisconsin hunters would be accidentally killed this deer season. It would be absolutely no trick for Kuchinski to make Rep one of them, except without the accident. Wait for Rep to get about fifty yards off, put a thirty-ought-six sized hole in his skull, remove his blaze orange coat and ditch it somewhere, and chalk it up to just another seasonal mishap. *Why the HELL did he shuck that coat? Tenderfoot and all but even so. What was he thinking? Can't figure it out.*

Rep was ten feet from the split-trunk birch when Kuchinski's rifle-shot split the air behind him.

Thirty miles away, Melissa didn't hear that shot. She'd heard plenty of other rifle fire since breakfast, but the vague uneasiness she felt as she looked out the back window of the cabin came from another source altogether. She'd heard an engine roar—not a car or truck engine, but a full-throated growl that sounded like a motorcycle with muscle. The howl had come from the woods.

She sipped coffee and shrugged. The article she should be working on right this minute nagged at her conscience. She didn't see how she could accomplish much by standing here gazing at woods where someone might or might not be lurking. She turned away from the window with every intention of getting back to work. As she crossed the room to get to her laptop, however, she noticed the photocopies of *Soldier for Hire* peeking out of the canvas carry bag where she'd stashed them. She'd gone to the trouble of hauling the things up here so that she'd have them available over the Thanksgiving break, on the off-chance that reviewing them might generate some insight beyond Detective Washington's coded-blackmail-message theory.

Dropping onto the couch, she pulled out the first issue and began paging through it. Forty minutes later she'd made it through a dozen of the things, for she came across nothing in them that required close reading. The articles, columns, and letters focused with grinding monotony on the short list of recurring subjects she had identified in her discussion with Washington.

The only topic that struck Melissa as something that would interest sensible people was MIAs. The insistent theme was that the United States government was systematically and deliberately suppressing evidence of Americans being held by communists in Vietnam. And not just the articles and columns. In every single issue, the first ad at the beginning of the classified section and the last ad at the end offered the services of WE'RE GOING HOME, INC., which apparently had one specialty: Finding loved ones who had been reported missing in action in South Vietnam.

Melissa put the twelve issues she'd reviewed back in her carry-all and reached for the most recent couple included in the package her colleague had sent her. Maybe a comparison of recent issues with those produced at the beginning of the magazine's history would tell her something. And if it didn't, maybe she'd just give up and get to work on her article after all.

The contrast with the earlier issues seemed more cosmetic than substantive. The type struck her as a little cleaner, the pictures a little sharper. References to MIAs had disappeared, but the copy otherwise covered the same gamut she had seen in the first issues she looked at. The only other change she noticed was that the magazine had acquired a professional-looking masthead, running one column wide down the second page inside the cover. She saw with mild interest that it identified a company called WE'RE GOING HOME, INC. as the publisher. In the beginning, in other words, *Soldier for Hire*'s parent company had also apparently been one of its key advertisers.

Wait a minute. Was that the point? Did the real money at the beginning come from getting people to pay WE'RE GOING HOME to try to find sons or husbands or buddies who'd never made it back from Vietnam? Had the magazine started out as just an elaborate tool for getting a line on people who'd fall for that kind of pitch? Had WE'RE GOING HOME always been the publisher?

A re-check of the first few issues confirmed her recollection that they included no masthead. The early issues went right from the table of contents to the first article, on page five.

She blinked. *Huh? Page FIVE?* She thumbed again through the first year's issues. One two-sided page—three on the recto and four on the verso, or the other way around, she couldn't remember—was missing from each copy. She couldn't imagine how that had happened.

Well, it would be easy enough to check once she got back to Milwaukee. Telling herself that Washington would probably have Leopold under lock and key and the case wrapped up by then, she tucked the carry-all away and strode with grim determination toward her laptop.

Just about the time Melissa managed to boot the computer up, Roger Leopold looked at Nguyen's prone body, the blood from a gash on the top of his head congealing rapidly in the cold air. Leopold hesitated. His ribs ached, his lip was split, and his teeth throbbed. Even taking Nguyen by surprise and having forty pounds and four inches on him, Leopold had absorbed a beating while he overwhelmed the smaller man. He desperately wanted to kill the little slope, but he couldn't take that chance. Cops around here had to know more about hunting accidents than he did. He couldn't count on faking one convincingly.

Then he smiled as inspiration came flooding in. Straddling Nguyen's body, he removed the deer tag encased in plastic on the back. If Nguyen started wandering around the woods again with his rifle after he woke up, he'd be begging to get arrested. Just to be safe, Leopold removed the clip from Nguyen's M-14 as well. Then, with his own handgun, he put a bullet through the front tire on Nguyen's Harley.

Chapter Twenty-Eight

Sound travels around seven hundred fifty miles per hour. The muzzle velocity of a thirty-ought-six has to be more than fifteen hundred feet per second. I heard the shot. Therefore I'm probably still alive.

Rep complimented himself on this elegant syllogism. Then he figured that someone lying face down in the snow with an armed man approaching him should move on to something more useful than self-congratulation very soon. Unfortunately, he couldn't think of anything in that category.

"Geez, Rep," he heard Kuchinski say then, "did I startle you?"

"Not at all. I've just always wondered what snow looked like really close up."

"Sorry." Kuchinski helped him up. "I didn't have time to warn you."

"Something come up all of a sudden, did it?"

"Something with a white tail and an impressive rack—and I don't mean my favorite bunny at the Lake Geneva Playboy Club."

"Are you saying there was actually a deer out there?"

"Rep," Kuchinski said reverently, "that was the best shot I've ever made in my life. Moving target, two hundred yards off with more timber than Paul Bunyan ever cut in between me and him—and I dropped him with one bullet."

"So I get credit for flushing a prize buck?"

"You weren't out there flushing any deer," Kuchinski said as he handed Rep the rifle Rep had left behind and began leading Rep forward. "That little piece of business about showing me your back and waltzing out there unarmed was you doing the Captain Titleman number, am I right?"

"I was just trying to show you I trusted you."

"Well, it was a hot dog stunt, but you made your point."

"Glad to hear it. I'm not sure my firm's group plan covers hypothermia, and I'd hate to die uninsured without accomplishing anything."

They hiked in silence for a couple of minutes before Kuchinski came to a respectful halt and pointed straight ahead of them. Twenty yards farther on Rep saw a vivid splotch of blood staining the snow. Smaller spots at irregular intervals led his eyes to a light brown bulge lying at the next tree line.

They closed eagerly on the slain deer. Neither spoke—Kuchinski because he was absorbing the moment, and Rep because he knew when to keep his mouth shut. Over the next fifteen minutes the only words exchanged between them were, "Thirteen points," and "Yep."

What happened during those fifteen minutes involved the judicious use of hunting knives, the removal and disposition of entrails, the manifestation of certain biological consequences of sudden death in mammals, and the attachment of Kuchinski's deer tag to one of the thirteen prongs on the dead buck's antlers. Then they trussed the buck's legs with a coil of manilla hemp and began retracing their steps, dragging the animal laboriously behind them.

"How long do you think it'll take us to get him back to camp?" Rep panted after ten minutes of slogging had taken them about a quarter of a mile.

"I don't figure on pulling him all the way back to camp," Kuchinski said. "We're a little over half a mile from a trail wide enough for the Escalade. I'm thinking we drag him that far, then hike to camp and four-wheel back."

"Sounds good," Rep managed. He now felt bathed in sweat, despite the frigid weather. "It's a good thing you didn't drive up here in the Riviera."

"That was subtle."

"I'm locally famous for subtle segues."

"Okay," Kuchinski sighed. "Even Splinters was ragging on me about the Escalade, so I guess I can't blame you for wondering about it. It is an oh-five, but it's more than slightly used. Contraband of the flourishing trade in crack cocaine, forfeited to Uncle Sam as an instrumentality of crime. I have some buddies at Alcohol, Tobacco and Firearms, so I knew about the auction in time to sell my Durango and make a decent bid."

"You mean you had an SUV even before this one?"

"For at least ten years," Kuchinski said.

"You just hang onto the Riviera as kind of a nostalgia thing?"

"Oh my word, son, you have *a lot* to learn about life as a trial lawyer in Milwaukee. You do *not* let *any* potential juror see you driving to court in a car that looks like it cost more than his first house. The Escalade and this new rifle are the fruits of a long career promoting the cause of law and justice and judicious friendships with ATF personnel—not a windfall from helping Vance Hayes launch his bark on the dark seas of eternity. That hundred thousand bucks came as a complete surprise—and not a particularly pleasant one."

"Sounds like a problem I'd like to have," Rep said.

"Careful what you ask for. The hundred grand had enough strings attached to moor a Lake Superior ore boat. I'm basically an uncompensated trustee. I'm supposed to use that money to help a peppy young court reporter named Sue Key."

"*Hello.*"

"You got that right, buddy."

"Why didn't he just leave the money to her?"

"He figured Nguyen would get his hands on it and run through it," Kuchinski said. "And he didn't want to fuss with a formal trust, 'cause then she'd know about it. He left the money to me, without telling her, so that I can help her out when she's ready to set up her own shop."

"He did that in memory of his dead brother's relationship with Key's mother, right?"

"You're not wrong," Kuchinski said, "but it's a little more complicated than that."

"Would the complicated part have something to do with the military honors you arranged for his burial?"

"Yep."

"You gonna tell me about it?"

"I guess that snow-dive you just took in homage to one of my war stories has earned you that much." Kuchinski took a deep breath and swiveled his head as if to take in the austere surroundings. Then he went on. "There were a dozen ways to avoid the draft in the sixties. Vance chose one of the simplest. He just stayed in school and piled one student deferment on top of another. By the time Congress closed that loophole, Vance was past twenty-six and off the hook. He was probably the only guy in Indianapolis practicing law full time while studying for a master's degree in American history."

"Sounds like that could put a pretty big dent in the family college fund."

"There wasn't much left for Tim, that's for sure. He could have scraped his way through a state school, but he got admitted to Notre Dame. The only way he could swing that was ROTC. He got his sheepskin and his gold bars on the same day, shipped out for 'Nam, and came home in a body bag."

"And Vance spent the rest of his life guilt-tripping himself over Tim dying in his place," Rep mused as the backs of his thighs began to throb. "That explains some things. But get to the part about the flag-draped coffin."

"For decades after the war there was a cottage industry over American MIAs not accounted for. Sylvester Stallone and Chuck Norris built half their careers around it. The rumors were over-the-top. Underground slave-labor camps, Nazi-style human experiments, *et cetera*."

"Actually," Rep said, "some of that stuff sounds more interesting than the average Chuck Norris movie."

"MIA families naturally held onto some hope that their kids were really alive and might come home some day. Hustlers preyed on these families. They'd place ads in gun magazines and survivalist magazines promising help finding MIAs. Sweat a few hundred bucks out of grandparents in Appalachia and grieving widows in Texas. Do a public records search, make some stuff up. Put together a report that held out some hope and promised more progress for a few more bucks. Bleed it as long as they could."

"Where did Vance Hayes come in?"

"He went after these creeps like a pit bull with a toothache. He'd represent families for free, threaten to sue these outfits for fraud, breach of contract, unjust enrichment, bad breath, anything he could think of. If he couldn't get anywhere with a civil action, he'd put together an evidence package for local prosecutors, with the documents all indexed and the witness statements tabbed and highlighted. All for practically no money."

Rep nodded. The order of proof he'd found made sense if it were a prepackaged case for some prosecutor.

"Wouldn't he get a percentage of any recovery?"

"There'd almost never be a net recovery. These were fly-by-night, hole-in-the-wall operations. They'd string things out as long as they could, then close up shop and leave town owing rent."

"And you helped him?"

"Just a little local talent and professional courtesy from time to time, when he had something going in Wisconsin. Carried his briefcase once in a while. He was the hero, not me."

"Heroic enough to rate a flag-draped coffin."

"That was my opinion," Kuchinski said. "Colonel Englehardt saw it the same way after I explained it to him. I don't know if Hayes went to heaven or hell, but whether he was looking at his burial from above or below I wanted him to see that, as far as I was concerned, he'd made up for Tim taking the bullet he thought was meant for him."

Rep plodded in silence, tugging his half of the awkward burden for another hundred yards or so, as he thought things over. His thighs were no longer throbbing. Now they were burning.

"Was Hayes still crusading as late as two years ago?"

"I hadn't heard from him about one of those cases since the mid-nineties. I figured the MIA thing had just run its course. When he called me about setting up Roger Leopold's deposition, I didn't flash on MIA scams at all. Figured the deposition was just about the lawsuit."

"But maybe the lawsuit was about the deposition."

"I've been thinking the same thing," Kuchinski said. "The more I ponder it, the likelier it seems that Hayes recruited a plaintiff and filed a claim just so he'd have an excuse for a little Q and A with Leopold under oath."

"Well, he made the most of it," Rep said. "He stumbled over something in Leopold's testimony that someone was willing to pay a lot of money to hush up. But none of us can figure out what it was."

"True."

"This is starting to fit together," Rep said, panting now as much from excitement as exertion. "Gathering information about whatever MIA scam Leopold was involved with explains those trips Hayes took to the Far East a lot better than speculation about sexual tourism. He used the deposition to force the issue with someone who didn't want that information floating around."

"The deposition also provided cover for Leopold," Kuchinski said. "He could come across as a reluctant witness under thumbscrews instead of a venal informer. Although if he needed cover like that, why did he give Hayes the information in the first place?"

"Because Hayes was saving Leopold's bacon," Rep, said. "He was defusing a legal claim that threatened to turn an Internet porn business Leopold had sold the mob into a pig in a poke. That's what got Hayes to the Supreme Court. He was trading legal services for information."

"If all this is right," Kuchinski said, "then Leopold looks like the bad guy all the way around. The quick settlement that Hayes got showed Leopold the value of information that Leopold himself had. When he ran a little short of ready cash in Hong Kong, he came back here to take a bite out of the apple for himself. Maybe Hayes got in the way, or maybe Leopold just took him out to cut down on the competition. When it got down to the short strokes, Levitan figured out that he could finger Leopold for Hayes' murder, so Leopold killed him too. Then he took a shot at you with the same gun to try to frame Dreyfus for the Levitan murder and take him out of the picture at the same time."

"That was a pretty cheesy excuse for a frame."

"True," Kuchinski said, "but it did scare Dreyfus off."

"You're saying it was worth a shot, so to speak."

"You should save that one for Judges' Night next year."

"Let me think the whole thing over and see if it parses," Rep said. "In the meantime, are we anywhere near that trail you thought you remembered?"

"Right up over that rise," Kuchinski said, pointing slightly ahead.

As rises go, Rep thought with dismay, *that looks a lot like a hill.* Eighty feet is a long way to haul dead weight up a sixty-five degree grade.

"I know exactly what you're thinking, and I've got you covered," Kuchinski said. "We can tie my trophy up right here."

"You're not thinking of taking the Escalade down that hill through eight inches of snow, are you?"

"No one's that crazy, not even me. But I've got it figured out."

"If it means we can stop dragging, I'll cheerfully take your word for it."

The two of them looped the free end of the rope around a tree branch well off the ground and hoisted the deer high enough to thwart any timber wolves that couldn't fly. Then, with the pale, late autumn sun high enough to hint that nine a.m. couldn't be that far off, they began the trek back to deer camp.

"You parsed our theory yet?" Kuchinski asked about fifteen minutes into this leg of the journey. "Think we've got it figured out?"

"There are some loose ends we haven't tied up yet," Rep said, "but I can't come up with any alternative that makes as much sense."

"What clinches it for me is that Leopold is the only one with a motive that anyone could take seriously. Except me, and you've cleared me."

"Let's think that one through," Rep said. "How about Nguyen? Family honor and all that?"

"The only thing Vance Hayes did to Nguyen's family was help it. Based on the Vietnamese ideas about honor that I bumped up against in-country, I'd say it's whoever killed Hayes that better be worrying about Nguyen."

"Hard to argue with that," Rep said.

"I suppose we could confect a motive for Ken Stewart if we really wanted to," Kuchinski said. "You told me he was the executor for Hayes' estate. The trustee's fee would be a nice piece of change every year for quite a while. What if Hayes got irascible and decided to change trustees?"

"Now we're just making stuff up," Rep said dismissively. "In the first place, the trustee's fee for a million-dollar asset base would be pocket change for Ken Stewart. He wouldn't run a red light to hang onto it, much less commit a murder. And then there's the detail that Ken has been as much in the crosshairs as I have. Whoever fired at me, Ken was about three feet away when it happened. And he's had some kind of a stalker on his own grounds."

"So who else is there besides Leopold, then?"

"I can't think of anyone," Rep said. "I'm just glad Melissa and I are up here while Leopold is back in Milwaukee, ducking Detective Washington."

Chapter Twenty-Nine

Okay, Nancy Drew, Melissa's superego warned in its usual English-nanny tone, *put some pixels on that screen. Or the next time Rep drags you to a baseball game you're not going to take anything to read, even between innings.*

It was nine-thirty-five. Gael was on her way to Madison and Melissa had the cabin to herself. Melissa usually composed at the keyboard, but this morning she had written the next six paragraphs out in longhand. She'd found over the weekend that the computer gluttonously consumed electricity. She'd had to refill the generator Sunday afternoon. She wasn't sure how much more gasoline they had, and with Gael gone she couldn't count on getting any more until late this afternoon. She was doing everything she could to conserve juice.

Now, though, the time had come to incorporate her elegant script into digital text. Melissa focused on the first handwritten sentence: *The failure of academic professionals to perceive substantively meaningful significations in commercial discourse that, by definition, must convey effective meaning to casual readers—because it would quickly disappear if it didn't—casts far more doubt on the perception than on the discourse it disparages.* She winced at the jargon, but jargon was the disguise her subversive message needed to infiltrate the bastions of group-think that she'd targeted. Eyes still fastened on the script, her fingers flew over the keys to record this unpolished gem of commentary.

Then she looked at the screen to check what she had produced:

> .tge faukyre if acadenuc orifessuibaks ti oerceuve syb-
> stabtuvekgt neabubgfhyk sugbufucabtuibs ub ainnercaak
> dusciyrse tgat bt efubutuib nyst cibvert effecutve neabubg
> ti casyak readers 00 dusciyrse ut wiykd qyucjkt dusaooear
> uf ut dudb;t 00 casts far nire diybt ib tge oerceotuibn tgab
> ib tge dusciyrse ut dusoaragfes,

"I didn't even know I knew Swedish," she muttered.

She realized what had happened. With her eyes away from
the keyboard, she had mistakenly put the four fingers of her right
hand one key to the left of the home keys they were supposed to
cover: "academic" became "acaenuc," while "significations" became
"sugbufucatuibs" and so forth. *Well, easily fixed.* She moved the
cursor back to the beginning and hit DELETE. Then she abruptly
stopped. Her fingertips tingled and her gut fluttered.

She had seen gibberish like this before. Bolting from her chair,
Melissa scurried over to her carryall in search of the Leopold
deposition transcript.

◇◇◇

Standing next to Kuchinski in back of the Escalade, Rep gazed
at the dead buck awaiting them at the bottom of the hill.

"You've gotten us to within eighty feet of the deer," Rep said.
"But that last eighty feet still looks to me like a good morning's
work all by itself."

"We'll just see about *that*," Kuchinski said.

He opened the Escalade's hatch, where Rep saw the bulky
garage door opener and its long, narrow, U-shaped metal rail
with a chain tracked around it that he had commented on when
they set out this morning.

"Can you plug this DC power cord in for me?"

Rep obediently took the end of the cable, climbed into the
hatch, and found the PTO aperture on the dashboard. After
plugging it in he turned the key in the ignition to activate the

battery. Rep got out of the Escalade and stamped back to the rear. He found Kuchinski threading one end of a rope through a steel ring attached to a clip-hook. Kuchinski then played out twenty feet of rope and attached the clip to the chain on the garage door opener.

"Think I could get a patent on this?" he asked as he stepped back.

"Why don't you just license Rube Goldberg's?"

Kuchinski pointed a remote control at the garage door opener. He pressed the trigger bar. With a gear-grinding groan the opener sputtered to life. Its chain began to move around the U-shaped rail. It pulled the clip, which pulled the ring, which pulled the rope, dragging about nine feet of it into the Escalade's hatch before the cycle stopped. Cackling like a schoolboy with a contraband copy of *Hustler*, Kuchinski stretched into the hatch, unclipped the hook, and reattached it to the apex of the chain.

"It works!" he yelled. "It'll be tedious, but the Treasury Department was a little short on factory-option winches when I bought this baby. Okay, let's go down and get started on the hard part."

After extracting his paintball gun from a well in the hatch, Kuchinski turned and began leading Rep down the hill. Rep took the rope, playing it out behind him as he went. They still had twenty feet to go when Rep spotted two raccoons circling curiously beneath the deer's carcass. Kuchinski raised the paintball gun and splatted the haunches of the nearer one. The startled animal scampered away, followed quickly by his chum.

Kuchinski cut the buck down from the tree. Rep knotted the last six feet of the rope in a looping figure eight around the buck's ankles. Kuchinski checked the knot and nodded his satisfaction.

"Okay," he said. "One of us has to hike back up and do that number with the remote control. The other has to stay down here and nudge this noble corpse over or around any obstacles that pop up. Your option."

The obvious choice was back up the hill. Rep, though, had a premonition that the garage door opener, with its one-half horsepower motor, might need a lot of help in actually pulling the deer. A garage door weighs forty to fifty pounds, and this deer probably had four times that heft. He hated the idea of Kuchinski's delight with his contraption turning to disappointment when the engine started and the deer didn't budge.

"I'll stay down here," Rep said.

"Suit yourself."

As soon as Kuchinski was over the crest of the rise, Rep squatted and braced himself behind the buck's body. When he saw the rope pull taut, he lifted and pushed. With that bit of help and an extra little thrust here and there, Kuchinski's jury-rigged contraption actually managed to move the body eight or nine feet up the hill.

Rep had a ten-second break while Kuchinski presumably unclipped the hook and reattached it to the top of the chain. Then he repeated his earlier contribution and was rewarded with another eight feet of progress. Boring, but less effort than hauling the deer manually and, of course—and this was the real point—they were Using Tools.

The only mishap came on the fourth round of tugs. Just as Rep and the improvised winch got the deer in motion, an icicle two feet long, shaped like a crude club and just as hard, fell from a tree branch and smashed Rep's left shoulder. Wincing at the sharp and unexpected pain, Rep looked accusingly at the now partially splintered cudgel.

I'm lucky to get off with just a bruise. If that thing had hit my cap instead of this padded parka, it could have done some real damage.

Finally, after nine fits of heaving and pushing and watching, Rep was able to follow the buck's corpse triumphantly over the crest of the hill. He saw Kuchinski standing there, grinning broadly, holding the remote control as if he were dictating a seven-figure settlement agreement into it.

Rep stopped, right there, staring straight ahead.

"All right," Kuchinski said. "Next step is to heave this baby to the roof and tie him down. Then we're on our way."

Rep didn't move a muscle. He wasn't seeing Kuchinski and the Escalade. In a furious collage the sharp pain of the plummeting ice-club smashing his shoulder, the pictures in the Lake Delton bar and grill, the sounds of the flatlanders jokes there, that first breath-catching sight of Lake Delton's immense reach, and his glimpse just now of Kuchinski holding the remote control like a Dictaphone flashed at the speed of remembered light through his brain.

"What in hell's the matter with you, boy?" Kuchinski demanded.

"I've been bribed!" Rep yelled.

This is like grading freshman term papers. It isn't hard, it's just tedious.

Letter by tiresome letter, one tentative keystroke after another, the gibberish in the Leopold transcript resolved itself into recognizable words. As Melissa performed this mechanical chore, she tried to sort out what had to have happened that August day when the email was created. She imagined Levitan at a computer docking station in a cubicle in Ohio where he was visiting Cold Coast's parent company. She imagined him typing in the address and the subject of the email and about to start the text. Suddenly the power goes out. This is late on a summer afternoon, but maybe he's in an interior cubicle, cut off from natural light.

Startled, he looks around, takes his fingers off the keyboard. He's not sure what's just happened. Then, because for some reason he deems his message both critical and urgent, he puts his fingers back on the keyboard and resumes typing, in the dark, his four right fingers each one key off. The building has no electrical power but the computer's battery keeps the machine on and dutifully records each keystroke.

Wait a minute. If the battery was still providing power, why wouldn't the screen be lit? Why wouldn't he see that he was typing nonsense? Perhaps because the sudden cutoff of regular power had shocked the laptop into "sleeper" mode, drastically dimming the screen. Or maybe he'd just been too frantic or confused to notice. Anyway, he finishes the message. He hits SEND. If he'd had the cursor poised over that command at the start, which wouldn't be unusual, and if his email program didn't have automatic spell-check, he could have found the mouse in the dark and done that. Then he'd joined the probably half-panicked evacuation of his building.

With all electrical connections to the network cut off, though, how did the computer send the message? Were Wi-Fi connections available back then? Maybe. Even if they weren't, suppose the computer didn't send the message right away. Wouldn't it have done so when the power came back on? And here, she realized, was the key. Suppose the computer never sent the message at all. Suppose he'd never hit SEND at all. *The message would still have been stored on the hard drive; still have been recorded in the email tapes used by the network the docking station was plugged into; and with enough technical know-how, retrievable from either.*

She had finished decoding the message. She looked at the translation on her screen. She read it with such intense focus, such chilling absorption, that she didn't notice the man quietly enter the room and come to within about ten feet of her. She almost jumped out of her skin when she heard his voice.

"So," he said, "now you know."

Chapter Thirty

"Define 'know,'" Melissa told the intruder as she swiveled around in her chair to face him. "Because most of it I'd still have to guess. And, oh dear, where are my manners? Please take off your coat and find a seat."

"You do affected nonchalance very well," Ken Stewart said.

He shrugged off his parka. The coat and its hood were white, splashed with gray, black, and pale green camouflage shadings. Melissa tried for an expression as casual as her manner, but the pneumatic drill hammering in her chest made that a challenge. She felt color draining from her face. And this was with Stewart perching pleasantly on the arm of the couch, a good six feet from her. Not crowding, ostentatiously non-threatening. The anti-Leopold.

"You know what that bloody email said. And now that you do, I don't think you'll have much trouble with the rest."

"'Play the Gael card if you want, but leave me out of it. And never ask me for anything again,'" Melissa quoted. "'Gael' has to be your Gael. I'm guessing that early in her legal career she worked as counsel for WE'RE GOING HOME, INC., the company that produced *Soldier for Hire* magazine and ran MIA investigation scams. Leopold pressured Levitan into providing him with documentation of her involvement. He got free legal work from Hayes by dangling that information in front of him. If Gael's name shows up in the masthead of early issues of *Soldier for Hire*, that probably explains why pages disappeared from the copies that I brought here."

"Not her name, just the parent company that employed her. Before it took her sensible advice to put several layers of corporate insulation between itself and the MIA stuff."

"But the company name alone would be enough to trace back to Gael's connection through her resumé if the wrong person got the right hints. And that might have blocked Senate confirmation of her judicial appointment."

"Would have, not might have," Stewart said. "If she'd done something silly, like smoking pot in her late twenties, we might have been able to finesse it." *There's hope for me yet,* Melissa thought. "But the MIA stuff would have killed her. The opposition would have jumped all over it, played the patriotism card, wrapped itself in the flag, struck those self-righteous poses politicians are so good at. They wouldn't really have *cared* about those families and the cynical exploitation of their grief. They'd just have used the pretext for a cheap hit on the president, with Gael as collateral damage."

"Translation," Melissa said. "Her nomination would have been quietly withdrawn, and she would have continued in a prestigious job, earning six figures a year. More disappointment than tragedy, no?"

"But she wanted to be a judge," Stewart said with a kind of fervent wistfulness, as if this were an unanswerable rebuttal. "Wanted it with all her heart. God put her on this earth to be a federal judge. And so I wanted it for her, as fiercely as I've ever wanted anything."

Melissa remembered Rep's description of the dinner he had shared with Ken and Gael Stewart in Washington: their comfortable banter, the total adoration for Gael that Rep had seen in Ken's gaze. She recalled their passionate parting clinch in Oshkosh. And she remembered Gael's bitter observations to Rep about how she'd had to claw her way by her fingernails into positions that lawyers with more glittering credentials expected as a matter of natural entitlement.

You killed for love. A chivalric ideal from a medieval chanson of courtly romance. But instead of slaying dragons, you killed people—people who got in the way.

"Why did Hayes pick Rep to give his eulogy?"

"Oh, I did that," Stewart said dismissively. "Hayes hadn't even thought about dying, much less planned his funeral. I should've just done the eulogy myself, but I wouldn't have had any excuse for not mentioning the case he'd gotten to the Supreme Court. I couldn't possibly pretend not to have learned about it. I tabbed Rep precisely because of the grudge between them. I thought he'd go through the motions and then forget about it. I didn't know about this 'power of the past' hang-up he had."

"So it was just cosmic bad luck that landed us in the middle of this."

"That existential wail applies to the whole thing. Pelham Dreyfus was a world-class dunderhead. Leopold used him as cat's paw in a shakedown that Dreyfus thought was aimed at Hayes but in fact had targeted me. Two years later, Leopold decided to use him again, to try to leverage more cooperation out of Levitan. Dreyfus figured there was another payday in there somewhere—he just didn't know where."

"So he tried to find out by stealing the deposition notes."

"Right. He didn't have a prayer of figuring it out. All he managed to do was make Leopold think he had more information than he did."

"By that time, though, the Gael card was worthless. You had to pay off Leopold the first time around to keep him from cooperating with Hayes, because Hayes could have given the smear to opposition senators before the confirmation vote. You bought him off, got him out of the country—just as you recently did with Dreyfus—and hushed up the email by engineering a quick settlement of the lawsuit."

"No particular trick, that one. The precious idiot running Orlofsky Publications doesn't know much, but he knows enough to do what I tell him."

"After Gael was confirmed, though," Melissa said, "there was no way the MIA stuff was going to get her impeached. The smear would have kept her from getting on the bench, but it wasn't going to get her thrown off."

"Exactly right," Stewart said, as if this were just an amiable intellectual joust in a faculty lounge. "Because Levitan knew that, he asked himself why Leopold thought he could extort more money from me."

"That's why Levitan contacted the Senate Judiciary Committee," Melissa said. "He wasn't looking for some kind of political leverage on copyright legislation to use against Rep. He wanted to know if Vance Hayes had offered information about Gael to staff counsel."

"Right again. That could only mean that he thought Leopold's extortion plans related to awkward questions about Hayes' death."

"As they did," Melissa guessed.

"That was the Levitan/Leopold theory. The two of them decided that I had murdered Hayes." Stewart paused and offered Melissa an intrigued and quizzical look. "Do you think I murdered Hayes, by the way?"

"Of course not."

"Gentlemen are supposed to pretend to believe ladies who are lying through their teeth," Stewart said, smiling gallantly, "but in your case I just can't bring it off."

"*Did* you kill him?"

"No. He thought I was going to, but I didn't."

"Then who did?"

"No one. The police aren't morons and they got it right. He died in an absurd accident. I mean, think about it. How could anyone arrange for him to ride a snowmobile onto a frozen lake and fall through the ice?"

"And it was just a coincidence that it happened shortly before Gael's confirmation hearings?"

"Not at all. Hayes came to the resort to meet Leopold and have him sign an affidavit explaining the email and summarizing the *Soldier for Hire* smear. I found out about it, intercepted Leopold, and outbid Hayes. The Supreme Court had already agreed to hear the case, and Leopold knew that he wouldn't have any trouble finding a competent lawyer to take it from there, just for the chance to appear in the Supreme Court. When Hayes arrived, he found a message from Leopold saying there'd been a change of plans and Leopold was headed to the Far East."

"Which Hayes didn't take lying down," Melissa said.

"Hardly. The obvious way to get to East Asia from Wisconsin is to fly out of O'Hare in Chicago. Hayes bet that Leopold would take the non-obvious approach and fly out of Minneapolis. Hayes planned to drive through the night to Minneapolis, in the hope of intercepting Leopold at the airport there. If it turned out he'd bet wrong, he was prepared to fly to Hong Kong himself and try to meet Leopold when he eventually did come in."

"Zeal to make Captain Ahab blush," Melissa said. "But how do you know what Hayes was thinking?"

"He told me, while I was pleading with him not to ruin my wife."

"Pleading unsuccessfully, I take it."

"He was drunk, on power if not alcohol. He said that with or without a clinching affidavit from Leopold he was going to turn what he had over to a contact on the minority staff of the Senate Judiciary Committee. The only way I could save Gael's reputation was to have her withdraw her name within twenty-four hours. Then he told me to get out of his room."

"But you didn't kill him?" Melissa asked skeptically. "You just did an elegantly casual win-some-lose-some shrug and walked away?"

"Of course not. Plan B was pretty desperate, but it wasn't murder. I'd brought a bag of marbles along. I planned to drop them into his gas tank."

"What would that accomplish?"

"It would make his gas gauge read artificially high and almost certainly clog up the tank as well. Hayes would be cruising along through northwest Wisconsin thinking he still had almost half a tank of gas or so, when all of a sudden his engine would stop. While Hayes was standing beside the interstate waiting for Triple-A, Leopold would be going on his merry way and I'd be grabbing all the documentation I could from Hayes' room."

"Sounds brilliant," Melissa said.

"He moved much faster than I expected. I'd barely gotten his gas cap off when he came hustling across the parking lot at two a.m. in full mission-from-God mode. He spotted me, imputed homicidal intent, panicked, ran away, hopped the snowmobile, and took his last ride."

"That worked out very nicely for you, then, didn't it?"

"Sometimes it's better to be lucky than good."

"Right. So who killed Levitan and took a shot at Rep?"

"Leopold. Except he was taking a shot at me, not Rep. He thought I was cross about having to pay him off twice. He was right. He wanted to deter me from doing anything adventurous."

"Okay," Kuchinski said as the Escalade lurched onto State Highway 16. "You wanna tell me what we're in such a hurry about?"

Rep explained his theory. This required four full minutes, and Kuchinski spent three-point-two of them looking at Rep with undisguised skepticism and a trace of alarm. Rep wondered for a moment if Kuchinski were going to turn the Escalade around and head back to deer camp so that Rep could lie down with a cold compress on his brow.

"You don't look like you buy it," Rep said.

"I've heard more plausible stuff in Intake Court from guys wearing leg-irons. I think you're crazier than hell. But we're gonna play it safe. Sit tight, and this former crackmobile and I will get you there. We'll be butt-sprung and cranky as a circuit judge on motion day, but we'll get there."

"The reason you think I'm lying is that you love Rep enough to kill for him yourself if you had to," Stewart told Melissa. "You assume I've done the same thing for Gael. I've read it in your eyes during this chat. You've decided that I'm a mortal threat to Rep—and if you had a gun right now you'd empty a clip into me in a heartbeat. You wouldn't think twice about it."

"My eyes *are* my most flattering feature," Melissa said demurely, "but your assessment is what the deconstructionists call 'a strong misreading.'"

"You're kidding either me or yourself. As we used to say in 'Nam, I've had people mad at me with guns in their hands. I know what someone looks like when they're ready to kill."

The chilling ring of uncomfortable truth resonated in Melissa's soul. Would she kill him in cold blood to protect Rep? At first, her brain dismissed the idea. She couldn't imagine killing anyone. But Stewart was right: he had more experience with human depravity than she did. On this arcane issue, he might indeed know her better than she knew herself.

"Let's say you didn't kill anyone. Why are we having this conversation?"

"Because this gifted-amateur poking around you and Rep have been doing needs to stop. Your probing won't help the police get Leopold, but it will threaten the reputation of the only woman I've ever loved. I've come here and told you things I've never told anyone else, including Gael, for one reason and one reason only: to get a clear understanding that all of us are through muck-raking in this particular midden."

"Uncover relevant information and then suppress it? Sam Spade would be disappointed in me."

"You aren't married to Sam Spade."

"That sounds a bit like a threat."

"I couldn't be more shocked if you confused the *sorbet intermezzo* for dessert at a Skull and Bones reunion dinner," Stewart said, smiling with patrician charm at the self-parody. "I'm asking for something very important to me, but I'm asking solely on the basis of friendship and mutual esteem. You and Rep should know better than most people that if you search for the truth, every once in a while you're going to find it—and then you have to decide what to do about it. Sometimes the best course is to forget it. Oedipus ignored that sensible advice from Tiresias, and look where it got him."

The chilly insinuation in Stewart's last sentence sent a nauseating ripple surging through Melissa's gut. She needed to see his cards.

"As André Malraux used to say condescendingly to Louise de Vilmorin when she popped off," Melissa said, "'*Approfondissez. Developez.*'"

"Rep told me about his mother," Stewart said, his tone suggesting regret at having to mention such unpleasantness. "Accomplice to a cop-killing, escaped from prison and all that. But he left out the payoff. He didn't say that she'd died or that he'd tried to track her down and couldn't. Those would have been natural things to say if they were true, but he didn't say them, so they aren't. That means his mother is alive and a fugitive from justice; that Rep knows she's alive and knows where she is; and that he's almost certainly guilty of harboring or aiding and abetting. But there's no point in Rep's mom going to prison or Rep himself being disbarred, is there?"

"Got it," Melissa said. "You're not threatening us, you're blackmailing us. How ironic."

Did Stewart plant Mom's number along with the other raunchy contact data in Dreyfus' studio when he helped him clean it out and get out of town? Did he plant the gun that killed Levitan at the same time? Or did Leopold do that? Because whoever did that also killed Levitan. But how could Stewart have planted that gun in Dreyfus' studio BEFORE that same gun was used to take a shot at Rep? He couldn't have planted it afterward, because Rep was with him from the time the shot was fired until after the police had searched Dreyfus' studio. Am I going too fast here?

"I'm trying to make you understand," Stewart said. "Let me go at it in a different way, kind of off the wall. The second gulf war isn't very well thought of among academics, am I right?"

"The debate does tend to be rather one-sided," Melissa confirmed.

"We waged war on a country that, admittedly, had a cruelly tyrannical government based on a hateful ideology and that had committed many atrocities, but that hadn't attacked us."

"That's the consensus view on Iraq," Melissa said.

"Oh, I'm sorry, you're still talking about Iraq. My last comment was about what the United States did to Nazi Germany in World War II."

"Cute," Melissa said, shaking her head and smiling in admiration at the rhetorical *coup*. "But what's the point?"

"That you can spin high-sounding abstractions any way you want to. What really matters in the end, though, are concrete facts. The concrete facts that happen to interest you and me are Rep's and Gael's secrets. They should both stay secret. Tiresias was right and Sam Spade was wrong. Oedipus was a good king, Rep's a good lawyer, Gael's a good judge. Why ruin them just because it was Mom in the sack all those years, or a girl-woman panicked in a gunfight, or a shyster drowned?"

"Okay, I get it," Melissa said with a trace of asperity. "Standing trial for murder would make you cranky, and being convicted could ruin your whole weekend. And if you're unhappy, Rep and I are going to be unhappy."

"Take a cynical view if you like. Even if I had killed Hayes, what are the chances that the prosecuting attorney for Lickspittle County or wherever Lake Delton is would beat the lawyers I could afford to hire?"

"I don't know."

"Slim to none. Exposure wouldn't result in justice being done, even if I were guilty. But it would make you and Rep material witnesses. Discrediting material witnesses is part of every criminal lawyer's job."

"That does lend a certain perspective to Sam Spade and justice for its own sake," Melissa sighed, her shoulders slumping in resignation.

"There's a very straightforward way to put this together that avoids unpleasant consequences for everyone. Namely, Leopold did it."

"Leopold killed Hayes?"

"Works for me," Stewart said, "but the police will probably prefer, 'Leopold killed Levitan, and who says anyone killed Hayes?' Leopold will finger me, but as long as it's just his word against mine I win the swearing contest."

"Why would Leopold kill Levitan?"

"To reduce competition in the shakedown market and leave himself as the only one with salable information," Stewart said. "The Levitan homicide will be cleared if a jury sees it that way and finds that Leopold killed him."

"Which, however, might not be the truth."

"Aren't you academics always going on about how there is no 'truth,' that it's all just perceptions conditioned by race, class, and gender?"

"Many do take that view," Melissa said. "Some of us, though, see a certain irony in treating the relativity of truth as an absolute."

"Even so, you're not going to sacrifice your husband just to keep Roger Leopold out of prison."

"You're right," Melissa said with a defeated sigh. "Even if it means letting a scoundrel be convicted of the one crime he hasn't committed. But I need to talk to Rep."

"I think you should. Don't just talk to him, though. Guide him."

"Meaning what?"

"Do you know one of the big reasons I've sent Rep so much IP work over the years? Because I know he's not going to steal my clients' other business for his own firm. He's not cold blooded enough for the really predatory side of practicing law."

"And I am?"

"Most definitely, Doctor Pennyworth. You can do what you have to do and wake up the next morning with your conscience under control."

"I guess we'll find out for sure when I call Rep."

"Have him come here. We should talk to him together."

"Fine with me." Melissa kept her tone flat, the voice of someone who hates herself for giving in. "The cabin is a dead zone for cell phones, but I can sometimes get a signal about two hundred yards up the road."

Melissa glanced at Stewart's approving expression. It looked like she was better at lying through her teeth than he'd given her credit for being.

She stood up and shuffled dispiritedly over to the pegs by the front door where the blaze orange coats hung. She pulled one on, glancing over her shoulder at Stewart, who had re-donned his white winter camouflage jacket and was crossing the room toward her computer.

"I think I'll erase and save over before I turn it off, in case someone wanders in while we're out," he said.

"Whatever."

Melissa slumped against the door jamb, like a bored ingenue in a New Wave movie. She noticed that there was no car parked outside.

Did Stewart really just want the genteel understanding he'd described, or was he looking for something a lot more permanent? How confident did she have to be that Stewart was going to kill her and Rep before she could justify a preemptive strike of her own? Stewart's crack about the second gulf war echoed in her mind. How sure did you have to be about the risk of millions of Americans dying ghastly deaths before you went to war over it? Eighty percent? Sixty percent? She imagined President Bush grinning wickedly at her. *Not so damned clear when you're the one who has to make the decision, is it, professor?*

In an explosive surge of adrenaline, Melissa dashed through the door and began sprinting with long, loping strides away from the cabin, across Old Logging Road Lane, and through the calf-deep snow toward the austere woods.

Chapter Thirty-One

"Melissa! You're pulling a Hayes on me! Don't run off!"

Melissa heard Stewart's voice clearly but at a perceptible distance. Without looking back, she could tell he was running after her. She thought she had about two hundred yards on him. Striding through snow this deep felt like running in heavy sand, and her coat and winter boots didn't help. The crust of the snow cut into her shins. Her legs already felt heavy.

Come ON! When you were sixteen you could run three miles in twenty-two minutes thirty-eight point seven seconds. He may be super-fit, but you have twenty-five YEARS on him! Move it!

She darted into the woods, dodging white-barked trees and ducking leafless branches. In the virgin snow she was leaving a trail that anyone could follow, but the trees would provide some cover if he started shooting. She tacked to her left, seeking a route that would take her parallel to the lakeshore while keeping her in the woods. The sound of Stewart crashing through the timber twenty or thirty seconds behind her pumped her a bit.

But not enough. The frigid air she hungrily gulped seemed to sear her protesting lungs. She felt an ominous hollow in her diaphragm, the first warning that she was going to run out of wind before long. Those sub-eight-minute miles had come seventeen years ago, and thirty minutes on an elliptical now and then hadn't kept her in shape for something like this.

Stewart sounded like he'd fallen a bit farther behind. She sensed, though, that this reflected calculation rather than fatigue.

He was sacrificing distance to preserve endurance, figuring that he'd follow the clear trail she was leaving and then close the gap fast enough when she ran out of gas and collapsed. She'd had to start at a sprint instead of beginning slowly and building her pace gradually. The price in pain was steep, and she was already paying it.

Don't quit! She sought some distraction, some mental exercise to take her mind off the pain. *"You're not a loser just because you're defeated. You're a loser only if you quit."* Who said that? G. K. Chesterton? No, an American. Hemingway? No, a politician. Theodore Roosevelt? Not orotund enough for him. Nixon! That was it, Nixon said it. She was quoting Richard Nixon! Well, he'd gotten that one right. That and China. Give him those two.

Glancing to her left, she glimpsed the lake through an uneven screen of birch and pine. Running less than five minutes now, she felt sweat freezing on her face and soaking through her shirt. Sharp stitch in her rib cage, on the right side. *That's okay, that's okay.* You can run through pain. Pain just means you don't want to run, not that you can't. The way your body lets you know you *can't* run any more is that you start throwing up. Or you die, that's another way you can tell.

She tripped on something buried under the snow and sprawled spreadeagled, bruising one knee and lacerating the other on a pointed rock. She swore fluently under her breath but willed the sobs not to come. *You can cry later. What was Golda Meir's line? "Tell Kissinger he can sleep when the war is over."*

She scrambled franticly to her feet. For a terrible instant she thought her legs would refuse her command to run again. Then they moved, two strides, three, and she was off once more. She'd managed less than a mile so far, and her breath was coming now in shallow, scorching pants. If her plan was going to work it had better work pretty soon, because she didn't think she had much left.

She could still hear Stewart, a little farther behind than before but running steadily. No shouting and no shots. Just relentless mushing and an occasional branch snap.

Pumping her arms, she reached a little deeper. That bought her another hundred yards. That was it. She begged her body for more, pleaded for just ten more strides, and her body said no. With a piercing gasp she fell to both knees and began vomiting violently into the snow.

As soon as the retching stopped and she'd spat the last of the stomach acid from her mouth, she snapped her head around to look behind her. She saw trees and snow. She couldn't see Stewart, just a vague, indistinct movement in the middle distance through the timber. Whatever he'd paid for that white camouflage jacket, he'd gotten his money's worth.

She sagged back, resting her bottom on her heels. She lacked the strength even to stand. It wouldn't be long now. Thirty seconds? Forty? Well, she hadn't quit. Rep would know that, and he'd be proud of her.

She glanced back again. The obscure movement was much closer, no more than forty yards away. If she was right she had ten seconds to live.

Rifle shots barked crisp and clear through the frigid air. The indistinct movement abruptly stopped.

Melissa's eyes widened. She recoiled, and a quick, shrill shriek escaped from her. *If I was right, I just saved two lives. And whether I was right or wrong, I just killed a man.*

With standing up still out of the question, she lurched forward, catching herself on her hands as they sank into the snow in front of her. On all fours, head sagging, she sucked air in short, shallow drafts. She forced her mouth closed, made herself breathe through her nose, held the breath as long as she could, then pursed her lips and expelled it through her mouth. Nine more of those and then she chanced a deep breath, gulping cold air into her lungs. She winced as pain lanced through the right side of her body.

No fun, but she could handle it. She jerked her torso upright. Her bare hands were raw from their immersion in the snow, but she scarcely noticed. She was kneeling now, with no light-headedness and no black dots dancing in front of her eyes. That was the important thing. She brought her right leg up, planting her foot in the snow. Then, laboriously, she pushed herself erect. A queasy wave of nausea rippled from her belly to her throat, but she closed her eyes and held her breath and it passed.

Numbly, senses dulled, she began to stumble back the way she had come, toward where the indistinct mass had stopped after the rifle shots. She had her hands buried as deeply in the parka's pockets as she could get them. She couldn't feel her fingers. *So this is what it's like to be in shock.* She'd had that kind of reaction before. *So this is what it's like to smoke pot.* And not long after that: *So this is what it's like to make love.* Except that one had just been what it was like to have sex. Making love had come much later. Each time she'd had the same reaction, the reaction she was having now: *That's it? What's the big deal?*

She knew she was getting close when she heard chatter, first as a vague rumble and then sharpening into understandable words from three distinct voices. All male, she thought, one sounding a bit younger than the other two.

"It wasn't your fault."

"I was shooting at a deer. I didn't even see him."

"Wasn't your fault. Not a thing you coulda done."

"You saw the deer, didn't you? I had him in my sights, I swear. This guy just came outta nowhere."

"Look at him. No blaze orange, no red, no colors at all. Like he was trying to get shot."

Melissa came within sight of the trio. They stood around Stewart's body, splayed prone in blood-soaked snow. In a 1950s movie Stewart would still be alive, rolled over on his back, a gaping exit wound mysteriously reduced to a small puncture politely oozing manageable trickles of blood. He'd gasp out some helpful exit line. A confession, perhaps, but not necessarily. Maybe a wry, ironic commentary, a curtain speech with style and a touch of class.

But this wasn't a 1950s movie. Melissa didn't know if Stewart had been dead before he hit the ground. She didn't know if he'd heard the shot that killed him. But she knew he was dead now.

The three men looked up sharply at her, their expressions surprised and a bit shocked, as if she were naked. Then she realized that, in a sense, she was: she didn't have a rifle. One of the men hastily dug a flask from the side pocket of his hunting coat and offered it to her. Melissa hadn't had undiluted bourbon in more than ten years, but she accepted the proffer and helped herself to a modest swig. The occasion seemed to demand it, and she figured it would warm her up.

It did.

"Who are you?" one of the older men asked.

"My name is Melissa Seton Pennyworth. I'm staying in the cabin about a mile from here, on Old Logging Road Lane."

"Do you know who he is?"

"Listen," the younger guy blurted, before she could answer, "did you see a deer a few minutes ago, running through here?"

"Yes," Melissa said dully.

That was a lie, but she figured it was a lie he needed to hear. She glanced around the group. She hadn't told them the body was Ken Stewart's, and she didn't want to, at least not yet.

"Has someone sent for the police?" she asked.

"Sven went hiking off to look for a warden. If he doesn't come on one before he gets to a working phone, he'll call it in. Worst case is he has to go all the way to the highway and flag someone down. Shouldn't be too long. Is there a phone in that cottage?"

Melissa started to say, "Not working," but checked herself. She needed an exit line of her own. She didn't know the protocol for reacting to corpses lying in the forest, but she suspected it didn't involve just walking away without some kind of official sanction.

"I actually haven't tried the phone there yet." The second lie came more easily than the first, just as Grammy Seton had warned her when she was seven. "I'll go over and check."

As she began to move, the men parted to make room for her.

"Excuse me," one of the older ones said as she stepped past him, "but what were you doing out here? I mean, obviously you're not hunting."

Melissa supposed that, now that she'd started down the slippery slope of depravity, the third lie should have tripped effortlessly off her lips. But it didn't. She told the truth.

"I was running from him," she said, looking down at Stewart.

"Why was he chasing you?"

"I'm not sure."

The truth again. It might get to be a habit.

Chapter Thirty-Two

Melissa's cell phone double-chirped about halfway between Plover and Stevens Point, fifty-some freeway minutes south of the cabin. She was riding next to Rep, who was driving Kuchinski's Escalade.

"Please pull over as soon as you can, honey," she told Rep. "My cell phone just found a signal and I'm not sure how much farther we can go without losing coverage again."

"Okay. A sign back there said there's a rest area in a mile or so."

Melissa punched her voice-mail code into the phone and raised it to her ear. She played the latest message twice, and lowered the phone only eighty seconds later, just as Rep eased the Escalade into the rest area's parking lot. He pulled it over parallel to a bank of plowed snow on the far side of the lot instead of parking in one of the marked slots near the nondescript building housing pay phones and vending machines.

"That was a message from Gael," Melissa said. "She got the voice-mail I left from the pay phone before we got under way."

"So she knows you're headed to Madison to talk to her?"

"Yes, but she said she'll be heading back anyway and wants me to call her so we don't just drive past each other." Melissa was already punching a new number into her phone.

"Gael, this is Melissa Pennyworth," Melissa said a few seconds later in a tag-you're-it voice that told Rep she was responding to yet another voice-mail prompt. "I just picked up the message you left when you returned my call. I really want to talk to you face-to-face as soon as possible. Rep and I are at the rest area near Exit 153 on I-39. My phone is about out of power, but Rep and I will wait here for you."

"Melissa Pennyworth is planning on being back here mid-afternoon or so," Kuchinski told the deputy sheriff at the cottage door a few minutes later. "You're welcome to wait inside if you like."

The deputy looked reasonably trim for fifty-five or so. Unfortunately, Kuchinski figured, he was probably about twenty-eight. His khaki uniform shirt collar showed above a chocolate brown leather jacket. And no hat. The day had warmed slightly but it wasn't no-hat warm, not by a long shot.

"Are you *real* sure she's going to be back?" the deputy asked.

"Well, she's driving my SUV with the best buck I ever shot tied to its luggage rack, so if we don't see her by sundown I'll join the posse myself."

"Just what did she think was more important than a dead guy?"

"The dead guy's widow," Kuchinski said, lowering his voice. "Melissa wants Gael to hear about what's happened face-to-face, from her."

The deputy chewed that over for about three seconds and then gave Kuchinski the slightest head movement that could possibly qualify as a nod.

Leaning against the driver's side door of the Escalade, Rep glanced over at Melissa. She stood about five feet away, gazing glassy-eyed at the freeway. She had left her coat open during the long drive and didn't bother to re-zip it now. Without making a production out of it, Rep strolled behind her, slipped his right hand under the collar of her coat, and began kneading the tense muscles below her neck with practiced, circular movements of his fist.

"That's heaven," she murmured, arching her head back.

"The pitching coach for the Milwaukee Brewers always feels his pitchers' neck and shoulder muscles when he visits them on the mound, to see how worked up they are," he said. "If you were a pitcher, I'd be signaling the bullpen with both arms right now."

"You don't think of people from rich families fighting in Vietnam," she mused, out of nowhere, as much to herself as to him.

"That's true. Vietnam was a working class war. Hillbillies, farm boys, factory workers, ghetto kids. That was the stereotype."

"Ken made some crack about Vietnam. Some macho thing they used to say there. And I felt this little jolt inside my brain. Ken *had* served in that war. I guess I'd known that at some level, but it was buried."

"He certainly didn't have to go," Rep said. "He could have ducked the draft even more easily than Vance Hayes did. If he hadn't wanted to stay in school his family could have gotten him a National Guard slot, and that's just for starters. Instead he volunteered for Officer Candidate School."

"Vietnam would have been a logical place for Ken to pick up that special model revolver that killed Levitan."

"More logical than Roger Leopold buying it in the underworld equivalent of a flea market," Rep said, continuing the massage. "Detective Washington made that Smith and Wesson sound like it was two steps up from a flintlock. I suspect Leopold would have opted for something a bit more state of the art."

"You've been reading 'Crimestoppers Textbook' from the old Dick Tracy comic strips again, haven't you?" A trace of banter at last brought a glimmer to her voice.

"Was it the Vietnam crack that made you sure Ken was going to kill us instead of just bullying us into silence?"

"I never got to be sure. When I started running I was about sixty percent confident that I was right. I might not have led him into the woods if I hadn't noticed there was no car or a truck outside. How had he gotten there? I figured he must have come on the snowmobile I'd seen this morning, hidden under the dock."

"Implying that he'd snuck in and had been watching the cabin from hiding."

"That's the way I saw it. You don't have to cover your tracks like that if all you're interested in is a little heart-to-heart chat."

"It hangs together, all right."

"But it's not conclusive, is it?" Melissa asked—said, really, making it a question just to be polite.

"I don't have the slightest doubt that you did the right thing, if that's what you're asking."

"That's just because you love me unconditionally. You'd think I'd done the right thing if I'd shot him in the back while he was sleeping."

"That would depend on how many shots you took."

She shrugged her coat off her shoulders.

"A little farther down, on the right," she said. "Ahh, that's perfect."

"*In re* doing the right thing, your unconditional love comment hit it right across the seams. I figure in this discussion you need a husband more than a lawyer. If you'd like, though, I can do clinical and analytical too. But that will involve suspending the massage."

"Be my guest."

Rep freed his right hand and tramped toward the rear of the Escalade. He opened the hatch to reveal the garage door opener that Kuchinski had jury-rigged into a winch. The clip-ring still dangled from the chain. The paintball gun and the remote control lay on the floorboard beside it.

"This is a paintball gun," Rep said, picking up that item.

"So far I'm keeping up."

Rep dropped a round, red paint pellet into the chamber, then fired at the pavement ten feet away. A vivid, red splat stained the concrete.

"Very impressive," Melissa said with boys-will-be-boys archness.

"If you're twelve. It gets better."

He dropped a misshapen lump of gray lead into the chamber.

"Is that a bullet?"

"It used to be."

"Where in the world did you get it?"

"Walt always saves the spent slugs from when he sights in just before deer seasons starts. He brings them along on the hunt for good luck."

"Won't it be too big for the barrel?"

"Shouldn't be. The paintball gun is forty-two caliber, and the bullet is only a little over thirty."

"How confident are you this is going to work?"

"Nowhere near your sixty percent, that's for sure. A mental image of this snapped into my mind this morning when I saw Walt holding the remote control for this contraption as if it were a Dictaphone. But mental images don't count. We need a working model."

He took the paintball gun over to the garage door opener, pried the ring part of the clip-ring far enough apart to worry it through the trigger guard, and then closed the ring snugly against the front of the trigger. He raised the barrel of the paintball gun to about a thirty-degree angle. With his left hand he tossed the remote over to Melissa. Startled, she managed to catch it anyway.

"Press the remote while I'm holding the gun in place."

"That looks like something that could cost you a finger," she said.

"A small price to pay for advancing the frontiers of technology."

Warily, she raised the remote and pressed its bar. The garage door opener's motor hummed. The chain jolted into motion. It pulled the clip-ring with it. The ring pressed against the paintball gun's trigger. Rep held the gun against the chain's tug. The trigger moved. The gun spat the leaden lump from its barrel. The lump landed about twenty feet away.

"Whattaya know?" Rep said, unable to keep a hint of delight from his voice. "Looks like Newton was onto something."

"Your point being," she said, "that Ken could have faked the shooting in the parking lot."

"Exactly. I didn't hear a shot or see a muzzle flash. Ken said he did and I believed him. Why wouldn't I? I thought he'd just saved my life. When I drove up he looked like he was dictating, so I assumed he was holding a Dictaphone. I didn't look closely at it—why would I? But it didn't have to be a Dictaphone. It could have been the remote control for a garage door opener."

"Where was the garage door opener itself, in this theory?"

"Concealed in the bed of a nearby pickup truck, along with the paintball gun. Say he'd fired a bullet from the Smith and Wesson sometime before into a pillow or a tub or water or something and retrieved the slug. Then say the paintball gun was wired in place and pointed at a high enough angle to get the bullet that he'd put in its chamber over the tailgate. Push the remote, and bingo. The noise of the garage door opener wouldn't stand out over the sound of passing traffic."

"And because the ballistics on that bullet matched the ballistics on the bullet that killed Levitan," Melissa said, "his little stunt would make it look like you and he were the only people in the City of Milwaukee who couldn't possibly have committed that murder."

"Right."

"But how could Ken be sure the officers who came to investigate wouldn't look in the bed of the pickup truck and spot the gun?"

"Ken sent me around the corner to call the police from a pay phone. While I was doing that he had plenty of time to retrieve the paintball gun, stash it in a FedEx mailer he'd already addressed, and drop that mailer in a FedEx pickup box on the parking lot. When I came back from making the call, in fact, he was walking away from that pickup box, back toward my car."

"Didn't Indianapolis cops find evidence of an intruder on Ken's estate?"

"Yes—and I'm betting that Ken planted the evidence they found."

"Okay," Melissa said. "But what you've just proven is that he *could* have faked the shooting—not that he did."

"True. Other things *could* explain the established facts. Pelham Dreyfus could have written down my mother's business phone number even though he had no use for it. Roger Leopold could have decided to take a shot at me to try to frame Pelham Dreyfus for Levitan's murder, even though the frame would have fit a lot tighter without the shooting."

"Paging Doctor Occam," Melissa said. "We need your razor, stat."

"Right. The Ken theory is straightforward and any alternative explanation requires a lot of French pastry. We're never going to be absolutely sure, but my confidence level now is bumping up against ninety percent or so."

"You mean you're ninety percent sure that he faked the shooting at the strip mall," Melissa said. "How sure are you that he somehow found a way to drop Vance Hayes through an ice sheet into Lake Delton?"

"Eighty-six point five."

"Reppert, beloved, this isn't a particularly good time for flippancy."

"I'm not being flippant. Well, maybe a little. Faking the shooting doesn't make any sense unless Ken murdered Levitan. The only reason for him to kill Levitan would be to cover up his murder of Hayes."

"But Ken made it sound just as logical that Leopold killed Levitan because he thought he could blackmail Ken and didn't want Levitan competing with him," Melissa said.

"Ken was a good lawyer, so he stuck with the truth as far as he could. But his story fell apart when he tried to make Levitan into a blackmailer. Leopold thought he needed information from Levitan to blackmail Ken over Hayes' death. He was right. Levitan, though, refused to collaborate with him. I'm betting that Leopold had Dreyfus bring the calendar to Sue Key's attention just as a way of showing Levitan that Leopold would seriously mess with him if he didn't play along."

"But the plant manager at Cold Coast took stuff out of Levitan's files because he thought it made Levitan look like a blackmailer," Melissa pointed out. "He clearly was after some guilty information. If Levitan weren't planning on blackmailing

Ken, why did he have it? Why did he try to find out what Hayes had told the Judiciary Committee?"

"Because he wanted justice done for Vance Hayes, and he figured that what Hayes had told the committee was the motive for his murder. Hayes stood up for the working class stiffs who went to 'Nam and never came back. To Levitan, who made sure a POW/MIA flag flew outside Cold Coast every day, that made Hayes a hero. He was trying to build enough of a file to take to a cop. If Levitan had been after a payoff, Ken would have given him one. Levitan died because he couldn't be bought."

"But this all assumes that Hayes was murdered," Melissa said. "And I'm a little hazy on the nuts and bolts part of getting Hayes through the ice."

"That's because you've never been ice fishing."

"Neither have you."

"True. But I've sat in a bar in a place where ice-fishing is a big deal. I've heard locals make fun of flatlanders who can't quite grasp the concept of cutting fishing holes in the ice."

"I see your point," Melissa said tactfully. "But wouldn't cutting a hole big enough to squeeze Vance Hayes through be a daunting, time-consuming, and somewhat conspicuous task, even in the small hours of the morning, if you were doing it with his dead body nearby?"

"I think Ken cut the hole ahead of time. You can rent small, prefabricated shelters to use for ice-fishing. Ken could have sat in one of those things by himself for an entire day, cutting an ample hole in the ice and making it look jagged instead of symmetrical. No one would have seen the hole, and no one would have thought a thing about it. He could have clopped Hayes in the back of the head with a block of ice—I can tell you from recent and personal experience that one of those babies will work just as well as a billy club. Then he could have taken the body out under cover of darkness and dropped it through the hole. The cops would attribute Hayes' head wound to the edges of the ice-hole he supposedly fell through instead of the ice-club that Ken used."

"But the wound's indentation wouldn't match the edge of the ice-hole."

"Which the police would quite sensibly attribute to water working on the ice-hole edge during the lengthy time it took to retrieve Hayes' body."

"I suppose," Melissa said listlessly.

"That sounds more like a grudging concession than an exhilarated catharsis."

"I'd be devastated if I thought I'd gotten him killed because I was wrong," Melissa said. "Being right isn't devastating, but I can't be very elated, either."

"I understand, treasure." Rep's voice dropped almost to a whisper. He put his hands on her shoulders with a tender, first-date awkwardness. "You took on a terrible moral responsibility. A lot of people wouldn't have had the guts to do it, and a lot of others would have shrugged off the moral issue, if they thought about it at all. But if you hadn't done what you did you and I would be dead or in mortal danger."

"I think you're right about that part."

"That seems like a pretty important part to be right about."

"About which to be right," she said, smiling briefly and wagging her index finger at him in school-marmish mockery. "What's bothering me is that it turns out I am a cold-blooded predator, just as Ken said I was."

"Self-defense isn't predation."

"How much of it was self-defense and how much was convenience? I deliberately did something to get Ken killed even though I wasn't anywhere close to certain that I had to do it to keep myself and you alive."

"And we know now that if you'd waited until you were certain, we'd probably both be dead."

"I generally know I've done the right thing because it *feels* right, not because I've worked the problem out logically. Conscience should be instinctive. You're not supposed to have to think about it."

"Sometimes there are close questions. Today was one of them."

"Right. By getting Ken killed, I kept him from killing us. But I also kept him from telling what he knew about you and your mom, or from making us collaborate with him in framing Roger Leopold for Levitan's murder."

"Two birds with one stone," Rep said.

"Too convenient for me to feel comfortable about it. Ken read me right. He told me that if I thought he was a threat to you I'd kill him without a flicker of remorse. And that's exactly what I did. I killed him just as surely as if I'd gotten him in my sights and squeezed the trigger myself."

"What you're going through right now sounds a lot like remorse to me."

"I am feeling bad about it," Melissa said. "But if I had it to do over, I'd do it again. At least in the Catholic Church that doesn't count as remorse."

"Maybe not remorse, but at least regret. If it'll make you feel any better, we can practice perfect Acts of Contrition on the way back."

Grinning gamely at him, Melissa punched Rep lightly on the bicep.

"If you didn't exist, we'd have to invent you. Thanks for being a lover *and* a lawyer."

Her head snapped up. Out of the corner of her eye she saw their Sable pulling into the rest area, with Gael at the wheel. She waved at the car and began walking toward it. Gael pulled into the first parking space she could and jumped out.

"Has something happened to Rep or one of his friends?" Gael asked, her voice worried and puzzled at the same time.

Melissa sprinted over to the older woman so that she could talk to her without raising her voice.

"No," she said. "It's Ken."

"What? Ken? What's happened to Ken?"

"Gael, I would give anything on earth not to be the one who has to tell you this. Ken was killed in a hunting accident this morning. He was running through the woods near the cabin, and a deer hunter shot him."

Gael's face registered utter incomprehension.

"Near the cabin? That's impossible. He was supposed to be in Chicago. I was going to call him there this afternoon. What would he be doing up at the cabin?"

Melissa hesitated. Her lips moved soundlessly a couple of times.

"I can't be absolutely sure about that. But he was there. I saw him. I talked to him, and then I saw his body after he was killed. I am terribly, terribly sorry, but he's dead, Gael. Ken is dead."

Her mouth half open, Gael shook her head slightly in mute denial. She mouthed the word "no" without speaking it. Then she spoke it in a voice low in volume and shrill at the same time. Then she screamed it.

"NO! NO! Oh, God, no! Dear sweet Jesus no!"

She collapsed into Melissa's arms and Melissa hugged her as she would a child while Gael shook with panted sobs. As gently as she could, Melissa maneuvered her into the Sable, sat beside her on the front seat, and closed the door. Again she hugged the shaking and suddenly frail woman to her breast.

Rep watched from about thirty feet away, guilt gnawing at him. He felt guilty because he was glad that the comfort Gael in her grief needed from Melissa had for the moment displaced Melissa's own self-doubt and moral agony. And he felt guilty as well because he knew that he himself should be feeling sorrow a lot sharper than the hot tightness in his throat and the hollow pang in his diaphragm. He'd lost a friend in a million—and he'd lost him a long time before he knew he had.

Rep walked toward the rest area's service building to get three cups of lousy coffee. At the moment, that was the only remotely useful thing he could think of doing.

Chapter Thirty-Three

"Mr. Kuchinski, please step outside while Ms. Pennyworth and I talk."

"No can do, deputy. I'm her lawyer."

"You're also a possible witness," Deputy Sheriff Howard Oldenberg said, gazing steadily at Kuchinski. "I'd think that would make it ethically improper for you to represent anyone involved."

"Well, I left my copy of the *Code of Professional Responsibility* back at the office. If you'd like to postpone this interview until I can track that point down, I'm sure Ms. Pennyworth won't mind."

"It's OK, Walt," Melissa said, looking over her shoulder from the hearth. "I don't need a lawyer. Even if I had something to hide, all you could tell me is to shut up—and I'm not very good at that."

"If this weren't a new shirt I'd rend my garments at such blasphemy," Kuchinski said as he strode toward the door. "Deputy, you're interviewing a witness who's still in traumatic shock and you're doing it over the objection of her lawyer. Proceed at your peril." A loud door slam punctuated his exit.

Melissa poked at the listless fire. She had spent nearly an hour with Gael at the rest area while Gael wept herself dry. Then they had agreed that Melissa should come back alone in the Escalade while Rep drove Gael back about a half-hour behind in the Sable.

"My opinion of lawyers just went down," Oldenberg said. "And I didn't think that was possible."

"What can I help you with, deputy?" Melissa asked, husbanding a yellow tongue of flame that was trying bravely to wrap itself around a fresh log.

"Why were you running and why was the decedent chasing you?"

"I was running because I was afraid," Melissa said. "Your next question is what was I afraid of, and I don't have a very good answer. I heard strange noises on the property this morning. I had the feeling someone was watching the cabin from hiding. I had no idea Ken was anywhere in the area, and I was startled when he suddenly appeared. When we talked I got the idea he was obliquely trying to warn me about something. I overreacted, panicked, and ran." Every word literally true and, taken together, quite deceptive.

"What did you think he was trying to warn you about?"

"About a guy named Roger Leopold. There, I think that fire may finally be in good shape." She rose and found a perch on the couch. "Deputy, why don't you sit near the fire? You must be chilled after tramping around in the snow all day."

"Tell me about this Leopold character," Oldenberg said, as he accepted her invitation. Melissa gave him a thumbnail sketch of the theft from Sue Key's apartment and the events that had followed from it.

"Ken seemed to be saying there was something to the Leopold story that the police weren't getting at," she said then, "but he didn't really say what. He just implied that my husband and I needed to be very careful."

"What were his actual words?"

"The gist is what I just told you." Wood crackled and Melissa felt a burst of warmth from the hearth. "I can't remember his comments verbatim. Maybe they'll come back to me after I've calmed down a bit."

"Why was Stewart chasing you?"

"I'd say he was running after me, rather than chasing me. I suppose it was because he thought I was behaving oddly and he was worried about me."

"I see," Oldenberg said. "You say you were surprised when the decedent showed up here. We found a lightweight survival tent and a sleeping bag about twenty yards into the woods off the east edge of the property. Would you know anything about that?"

"No. If they're Ken's it doesn't make any sense. This is his client's cabin and he'd arranged for us to use it. He'd obviously be welcome here."

"It doesn't make any sense unless he didn't want you—or his wife—to know he was here," Oldenberg said.

"But that doesn't compute either."

For almost a minute Oldenberg said nothing. His eyes glinted with a simultaneously wary and expectant expression. As the seconds ticked by, Melissa felt an almost overwhelming urge to speak, to blurt *something* out just to fill the silent void. She suspected that the reason for Oldenberg's studied silence was to create that very pressure. She held her peace.

"Ms. Pennyworth, how much do you know about firearms?"

"I can talk a good game because I have to read a lot of crime novels in my work, but I've never actually fired a gun. I could tell you, for example, that a lot of professionals these days favor something called a Sig Sauer. If you showed me five handguns right now, though, I couldn't tell you which was a Sig Sauer and which were something else."

"Well, what I'm about to show you isn't a Sig Sauer. It's a Ruger."

Oldenberg extracted an unhandy bundle wrapped in an oily cloth from a backpack at his feet. Laying the thing on the floor, he unfolded the cloth to expose the largest handgun Melissa had ever seen—something that might be bought by a guy who had some *serious* compensation issues. It was a nickel-plated revolver. The barrel had to be eight inches long. A thin bar ran along the top of the gun. Mounted on the bar was a telescopic sight.

I'm finally sure. I almost wish I weren't. Almost.

"That looks very formidable," she said.

"It is. It's designed for hunters who want to go after big game with handguns. We found it on the decedent's body."

"But Ken wasn't a hunter. He hated the very idea of hunting."

"No, ma'am, I don't think he brought this gun up here for hunting. It's a forty-four magnum. Most rifle hunters use something considerably lighter—thirty-ought-six, three-oh-three, thirty-thirty. During deer season, though, you'll still find some hunters here and there with a forty-four/forty. That's an Old West rifle caliber, supposedly developed so that cowboys could use the same cartridge with their handguns and their rifles."

"I see."

"Ma'am, this Ruger is not a defensive weapon. It's heavy and inconvenient to carry, and it takes a good six seconds or more to haul it out and deploy it. The decedent brought this gun up here to kill a human being with it, and make it look like a deer hunter with a rifle had done it."

"You clearly know a lot more about it than I do," Melissa said. "But it's awfully hard for me to square that with the Ken Stewart I thought I knew."

"Who do you think he came up here to kill?"

"I can't think of a good reason for Ken to kill anybody."

"How about your husband?"

"Why in the world would Ken want to kill Rep?"

"Why would he sleep outside instead of with his wife?"

"Ah, comes the dawn," Melissa said. She supposed she ought to feel indignant, but instead she found herself intrigued by Oldenberg's idea. "You think Ken and I were having an affair. He came up here to kill Rep or Gael or both, with or without my connivance. Either I got cold feet or I found out what he was up to. Whichever, I panicked and ran terrified into the woods. He ran after me to keep from spoiling everything, but with fatal consequences for himself instead of me. Is that your theory?"

"I may have some details wrong here and there," Oldenberg said. "Why don't you tell me the way it actually was?"

"Okay, here's the way it actually was," Melissa said briskly. "The Milwaukee detective I told you about earlier wanted Rep and me to get out of town for a week to bait Leopold into burglarizing our apartment so the police could catch him. We agreed. Walt Kuchinski—the lawyer who stomped out at the beginning of our interview—invited Rep on a hunting trip, but that left the problem of finding a place to stash me. Ken solved that problem by coming up with this cabin. So your theory that this was all a plot to murder Rep requires either a lot of convenient coincidences or a conspiracy reaching into the heart of the Milwaukee Police Department."

"You're sticking with that, are you?"

"Deputy Oldenberg, I was not carrying on an affair with Ken Stewart or anyone else," Melissa said, her voice ringing effort-lessly with conviction now that she could tell the real truth. "I wasn't cheating on my husband. I'll agree to a vaginal swab if you'd like to have a nurse check me for Ken's DNA."

"I may, at that. But I think you've read too many of those crime stories you were talking about."

"Occupational hazard."

"Look, this is my job."

"I know it is, deputy. I'm not upset. Your questions were perfectly proper, and I'm not blaming you for asking them. But your premise is wrong. Ken Stewart's tragic death had nothing to do with a sexual affair between him and me, because nothing of the kind ever took place."

"The hunter who shot the decedent is a yooper, but the guys with him are from around here and they vouched for him. So I can't make the decedent's death into anything except a hunt-ing accident. But too many things don't fit. You're no hysterical schoolgirl, and you didn't go running into the woods in a blind panic just because you got bad vibes from this guy. There's something you're not telling me. You might want to re-think that approach, because if my theory is wrong, then right now I'd say the decedent was right about one thing: you were in danger, and you still are. The sheriff's office and the Highway Patrol can't do much for you if you won't tell me the whole truth."

Melissa lowered her eyes briefly to show respect for the intense law officer. After all, he was right.

"There's nothing more I can tell you," she said.

"Then you're on your own. Enjoy the rest of the day—what's left of it. And please get word to me when Ms. Stewart arrives."

It took Kuchinski forty seconds to come back in after Oldenberg went out. Melissa overheard a short, sharp conversation in the interim.

"How did it go?"

"Fine. What's a 'yooper'?"

"Someone from the UP—the Upper Peninsula of Michigan. It's a natural part of Wisconsin, but Michigan wanted it so we gave it to them. Raised the average IQ in both states."

"That's the second new thing I've learned today," Melissa said. "I also found out that Ruger makes hunting pistols that look like small cannons."

"Well, here's number three. Rep and Gael Stewart are about a hundred yards down Old Logging Road Lane, making themselves scarce until the deputy leaves. She'd like to speak with you alone before she talks to him."

Chapter Thirty-Four

"Do you think I was having an affair with Ken?"

Melissa and Gael were alone together at the cabin. They had been talking for about twenty minutes.

"I'm quite sure you weren't," Gael answered. "This will sound arrogant, but I don't think Ken was capable of cheating on me like that. He might have spent a night now and then with call girls on some of his out-of-town trips, although I'm not sure he even did that. But from the day we were engaged, there's no way he had a romantic relationship with anyone but me."

"He adored you."

"Yes, he did. He gave me everything he had emotionally."

"This must be a terrible loss for you," Melissa said. "I'm deeply sorry."

"Ken's death is an incredible jolt. I feel like several of my emotional circuit breakers have tripped. I'll have a lot more sobbing to do in the next few days, but for now it's comforting to focus on the needs of the moment."

Gael settled back a bit farther in the couch near the fire and sipped black coffee that Melissa had made. She glanced at the pint bottle of Jim Beam that she'd taken from a carry-all and put on the end table, then shook her head.

"Better save that until after I've talked to the constabulary," she said, glancing at her watch. "I'll be seeing them before long."

"They don't know you're here yet?"

"No. I plan to get to a ranger station by four o'clock to speak with the investigating officer. I'm not just a widow, though. I'm also a lawyer. As cold-blooded as it sounds, I'm hoping to learn what you told him before he questions me."

"I think I've covered it."

"I see." Long pause, deliberate coffee sip.

"You sound dubious," Melissa said.

"If what you've shared with me so far is everything you've told the deputy, then I think there must be a lot you didn't tell him. I'd like to know what it is. Feel free to tell me that it's none of my bloody business, if you like. I give you my word of honor that you won't hear anything you say to me repeated in front of a jury. You don't have to believe that, but I hope you will."

"I told him the truth but nothing close to the whole truth," Melissa said flatly. "My Grammy Seton would have said that what I did was worse than actually lying—that simply lying without making any bones about it would have been less dishonest than dancing around the real facts."

"That's uncomfortably close to what lawyers tell witnesses to do. Tell the truth about what you know, but don't volunteer information and don't talk about what you just think or suspect. If you don't mind sharing, what specifically didn't you tell Deputy Oldenberg?"

Melissa reminded herself that she was talking to a woman who had just lost a husband of almost thirty years. A man who had adored her. A man who had killed for her.

"I didn't tell him that I thought Ken had come here to kill me and Rep," Melissa said then, in the kind of flat, unenthusiastic, let's-get-this-over-with voice you might use to confess a petty theft. "I didn't tell him that I thought Ken had killed Vance Hayes to keep your confirmation from being blocked, and that he'd killed Max Levitan to cover up the Hayes killing. I didn't tell him that I thought Ken was trying to frame Leopold for the Levitan murder."

If any of this shocked or infuriated or even surprised Gael, no such reaction showed on her face. What Melissa read in her expression was something like *I asked for it and I got it, so no whining*.

"You'd be good at a pretrial deposition," Gael said. "I hope I'll be that good when I have my little chat with the deputy." She glanced at her watch and put her coffee down. "Speaking of which, I'd better get moving. With not much more than an hour of daylight left, I'd rather be early than late."

Melissa and Gael stepped out of the cottage to see Rep standing beside the Sable and Kuchinski next to his Escalade.

"Here's the theory, your Honor," Kuchinski said. "Rep will drive you. I'll lead the way, because I know where the place is. Rep will stay there during your interview and drive you back when it's done. That way, you three can head back tomorrow morning. I'll drive over to deer camp, show my trophy here off to my buddies, and pack Rep's gear up. He can collect it from me when we're both back in the office after Thanksgiving."

"That sounds fine," Gael said, "except that I don't need a chauffeur. I can follow you while Rep and Melissa spend some time together."

"No, no," Melissa said quickly, "Walt is absolutely right. The last thing you need to worry about right now is navigating rural Wisconsin."

"That's very kind of you. I can't say I was looking forward to the drive."

Melissa went back into the cottage. She would have loved spending the next two hours wrapped in her husband's arms in front of the fire, or cooking some improvised meal together, or just trading a little verbal by-play with him. But those thoughts only sharpened her sense of Gael's loss. Gael's needs took priority over Melissa's wants.

She started toward the work-table she'd been using, then turned back and bolted the front door behind her. No sense taking chances.

She intended to pack up tonight. Before she packed, though, she had an essential task to perform: making sure Ken had completely erased her transcription of the decoded email from her computer. She could do the work over again later, if necessary, but she wasn't going to leave the fatal words readily accessible to people who might have mischievous ideas about them.

As she booted up the computer, she felt a chilly intuition that someone else was in the cabin. She reproached herself for behaving like some frail and timid heroine in a gothic romance. Then she heard the voice.

"My God," Roger Leopold said as he strolled into the room, "I thought they'd never leave."

Chapter Thirty-Five

"Don't think about running," Leopold said. "There's nothing to run to. While I was looking for a place to hide on the property I stumbled over the snowmobile that Stewart stashed down there. I figure you know it's there as well. I know how to start one of those babies, but you don't. Anyway, there's nothing to run from. If you do what you're told you'll be okay, and if you don't—well, you can't outrun a bullet."

"Right," Melissa said. "Ken Stewart couldn't outrun one, could he?"

"Apparently not."

"Was it really that poor hunter who killed him, or did you do that?"

"I never made a shot that good the best day I ever had," Leopold said. "I wanted Stewart alive. He was going to pay me some more money."

"Well, in that case it was quite inconsiderate of him to pass away this morning," Melissa said. "Speaking of running, though, wouldn't this be an excellent time for you to start? If the police catch up to you, I think you'll find yourself short of character witnesses."

"Running is exactly what I have in mind. With the people I have after me, the Milwaukee cops are a vacation."

"Well, don't hesitate on my account."

"I need money. I spent what little I had left coming back here to get some more, and I haven't gotten any yet."

"There are some credit cards and about eighty dollars in my purse," Melissa said. "That's all I can contribute."

"Gael Stewart can contribute a lot more," Leopold said.

"You mean you plan on selling her the same Persian carpet you already sold her dead husband once and were trying to sell him again? Promise not to disclose compromising information if she'll write you a check?"

"More like if she'll go on-line and order an immediate wire transfer to an offshore bank account of mine. As soon as receipt is confirmed, I'll be on my way and out of your lives forever."

"You can't go on-line from here," Melissa pointed out. "You can't even make a cell-phone call from this cabin."

"I'll take care of that detail after I have Judge Stewart under control."

"You're going to kidnap a federal judge along with me, take us someplace private with Internet access, and extort money from her?"

"That's about the size of it," Leopold said. "And then get out of your hair. You probably don't believe that part, but what choice do you have?"

"Actually, I do believe it. You're smart enough to know that if you leave a dead federal judge behind they'll never stop looking for you. If you leave a quiet federal judge, they'll never start. What do you want me to do?"

"Keep your mouth shut. Don't scream when she comes back. Don't try anything. Let her walk into the cabin for a constructive dialogue. Then come along like a good girl while we take care of business."

"Makes sense. You want something to eat while we're waiting?"

"Food can wait. I need to take a thorough look around first."

There might be ranger stations somewhere in Wisconsin, but Rep and Gael didn't end up at one of them. Kuchinski led them instead to a squat, brown, wood frame building, roughly the size of a ranch house in a post-war subdivision. Gold letters and numerals on a brown signboard identified it as Wisconsin Department of Natural Resources District 16 Game Warden Post. It had taken them nearly forty minutes of driving down the lakeshore and then around the narrow lake's tip and finally back up the shore to cover the fifteen road miles that separated the post from the cabin.

Rep and Gael waved goodbye to Kuchinski as he drove off, and went inside. As soon as they did a young warden behind a waist-high counter noticed them and called, "Mrs. Stewart?"

"Yes," Gael said.

"We're very sorry about your husband," the warden said as she lifted a section of the counter to create an opening. "Deputy Oldenberg is waiting for you in the small office back here to your right."

Rep started to accompany Gael toward the indicated office, but the warden waved him back. Left alone, Rep wondered how much time he'd have to kill in the twenty-by-twenty-foot room. Full color posters decried the wickedness of shooting from moving vehicles or hunting on private land without permission. Small booklets offered details of Wisconsin fish and game regulations. That pretty much covered the available diversions. Ten minutes of pacing around it was all he could take. He went outside to see if the twenty-degree wind-chill could take the edge off his boredom.

He's taking his time—good. Melissa watched Leopold saunter around the cabin, checking doors, windows, and sight lines. For her benefit he flaunted the tan finish semi-automatic pistol he had stuck through his belt. He told her it was a Heckler and Koch Mark Twenty-three, in the reverential tone you might use to identify a Stradivarius.

She thought that about twenty minutes had passed. The only thing she'd accomplished so far was to turn on every light she could reach. Winter sunshine still poured into the cabin from the west and south, but she flipped on lamps all the same.

"Get that fire built back up," Leopold said, rubbing his arms as he looked through the window nearer the door.

Melissa moved to comply. As she walked past Leopold, he snap-kicked her from behind. The startling burst of pain filled her for an instant with white-hot fury, but she willed herself back under control. As coolly as she could, she analyzed the violent outburst. *Carefully calibrated. Hard enough to smart but not to bruise. Meant less to intimidate than to infantilize—to put me in my place.*

"What was that about?" she asked matter-of-factly as she knelt at the hearth to pile more wood in the fire.

"That was for what you were thinking."

"I wasn't thinking anything."

"That was in case you were."

Interesting. And important. He's afraid. He kicked me because he's scared. That means he's probably too much of a coward to leave Gael and me alive even though he knows that would be the smart thing to do.

With that conclusion, all doubt about her situation disappeared from Melissa's mind. She didn't know what she was going to do, but she now knew what she wasn't going to do. She wasn't going to sell Gael out. She already had the blood of one Stewart on her hands, and that was enough for one day.

She took her time with the fire. When the flames had caught and the wood was crackling, she stood up and turned toward Leopold.

"Do you want something to eat now?"

"Good idea."

Listening to the steady hum of the generator outside, Melissa strode ahead of Leopold into the tiny kitchen. As she passed the electric stove she turned its oven on. Then, in almost the same motion, she opened the refrigerator. In addition to a foil-wrapped salmon filet and what was left of the roast, she took out carrots and a bowl of mixed fruit. She left the vegetable compartment drawer pulled slightly out, so that the refrigerator door wouldn't close completely.

"That's all you have?" Leopold demanded indignantly.

"Yeah. Gael ate the last of the Beef Wellington and *pâté du foie gras.*"

"You've really got a lip on you, don't you?" Leopold asked, his tone more bemused than threatening.

"If you like. Take your pick of the food. I'll make some coffee."

"Just a minute. Stand right exactly where you are."

Gripping her left bicep roughly with his right hand, he jerked her around the confined space while he opened drawers and cabinet doors. He scooped handfuls of knives, forks, can-openers, and one corkscrew into the sink.

"All right," he said then. "Go ahead with the coffee."

After she had tap water heating in a saucepan on the stovetop, Melissa leaned her still tender fanny against the sink. She looked for a chance to grab the pot from the stove and hurl scalding water at him, but it didn't come. He watched her too closely, made sure she knew he was aware of the risk.

"Do you want me to make you a sandwich?"

"I'll take care of that part," he said, laying the words out in a now-hear-this tone. "And of anything else that involves a knife."

Rep stamped his boots, slapped his gloved hands against his arms, and strode around the parking area surrounding the DNR post. On the back end of his ninth circuit a cabin across the lake, perhaps fifteen degrees north of a straight line from the post, caught his eye. He thought for a second it must be the one Melissa and Gael were sharing, but then he realized it couldn't be. In the pale winter sun of late afternoon he could tell that all the cabin's lights were on. He remembered Melissa worrying about having enough gas to keep the generator going, and knew she wouldn't be squandering power like that.

As he circled back to the front, headlights blinking rapidly on a quickly approaching vehicle startled him. He wondered whether the DNR was bringing a poacher in. Then the SUV came within fifty feet or so and he saw that it was Kuchinski's Escalade. He hustled toward the road, and the behemoth crossed to the wrong side and screeched to a stop a few feet from him. Kuchinski already had his head out the window.

"I thought you were going back to deer camp," Rep said.

"I was, but I ran into someone on the way."

"Hey," a voice called from the passenger seat, "it's sis' mouthpiece. Sorry, shyster, you're too late. I've beaten the rap all by myself."

"Don?" Rep asked. "Don Nguyen? What are you talking about?"

"One of the grasshoppers found me this morning wandering in the woods with a rifle and no deer tag," Nguyen said. "Also an ugly head wound, but he jumped to conclusions anyway. He hauled me halfway to Minnesota and his buddies spent six hours verifying that I actually had bought a deer tag before they decided I was telling the truth about being mugged."

"Who mugged you?"

"Roger Leopold."

"Leopold?" Rep yelped. "He's supposed to be down in Milwaukee, falling into a trap the police have set."

"Well, when my lights went out this morning he was up here."

"I came across Mr. Nguyen while he was trying to hitchhike his way back to the last place he saw his Harley," Kuchinski said. "I heard Leopold's name and figured we'd better hook up with you stat."

"He could be at the cabin right now!" Rep shouted.

He clambered into the rear seat. As he pulled the door shut behind him, the lights on in the cabin across the lake winked again in his mind. So did his mother's reference to Vlad the Impaler.

"Wait a minute," he said urgently. "Before we head out, can you pull this thing around to the back parking lot?"

"You crazy? We have a forty-minute drive ahead of us."

"I'm not sure we have forty minutes to spare," Rep said.

"You haven't been wrong yet on this trip, but there's a first time for everything," Kuchinski grumbled.

Even as he spoke, though, the Escalade was rolling and turning. As soon as it stopped, at the back of the rear parking area and parallel to the lake front, Rep lunged across the back seat to gaze searchingly through the passenger side window at the cabin.

"What in hell you doin', boy?" Kuchinski asked.

"Trying to figure out if there are two people in the window of that lit-up cabin across the lake," Rep said, shading his eyes.

"Hell's bells, that's twelve hundred yards off if it's a foot. Natty Bumpo himself couldn't make out two people at that distance. Try this."

Kuchinski fetched the Weatherby from an improvised rack attached to the back of the front seat and handed it to Rep. Rolling down the window with one hand, Rep accepted the rifle, rested its stock on the side of the door, and squinted through the powerful scope that cut two-thirds of a mile to less than a football field. At first he saw a gray blur. He adjusted the focus ring, first with futile haste and then more deliberately. With agonizing slowness, the image resolved itself into a frozen lake, some cleared space, and the cabin.

But what was he seeing flickering past the cabin windows? One person? Two? Shadows?

Well, he thought, *shadows don't move unless someone moves them.* Rep sensed that Kuchinski was thinking the same thing he was. As he pulled the rifle back inside and spoke, his voice sounded absurdly deliberate to him, as if he'd popped a Quaalude.

"I don't know for sure. But I think that's their cabin. And I think there are two people in it. Why don't you and Nguyen go around the lake, in case I'm wrong? I'll take the Sable."

"Bull*shit*, counselor," Kuchinski said. "No way you're cuttin'me outta this kill. Besides, you don't even know where the best place is. Get your butt strapped in and I'll show you how it's done."

Rep obeyed. As he buckled up he noticed Nguyen putting loose cartridges from a box into his coat pocket.

"Sure you don't want out now?" Rep asked.

"Do I look like I want out?"

The Escalade lurched out of the parking lot and roared back up the road.

"I think I passed a boat-trail a quarter-mile or so back this way," Kuchinski said, gesturing at the windshield. "Keep your eye peeled for it."

Rep did, but Kuchinski still spotted it first and swung the Escalade violently onto it. The "trail" was scarcely more than a snow-covered gap between the birches, barely wide enough to accommodate a bass boat on a hitch and the car towing them. Down that path, though, Rep could see the lake and, in the distance across it, the cabin, glowing valiantly in the steadily diminishing light. All that lay between them and that cabin now, aside from a ten-foot incline and a wire-and-post fence, was twelve hundred yards of ice over at least five hundred feet of water.

"This was their third hard freeze this winter," Kuchinski shouted. "If that ice is six inches thick, it'll support this truck with no problem."

Or to put it another way, Rep thought, *if my theory about how Ken Stewart killed Vance Hayes is right, I can get to my wife easily. And if it's wrong, I'll freeze to death in the next five minutes.*

Kuchinski hit the gas. Pushed back against his seat, Rep braced himself as the Escalade effortlessly shredded the fence.

"Was that a NO TRESPASSING sign we just pulverized?"

"Under the Northwest Ordinance, all navigable waterways in the State of Wisconsin are owned by the public up to the mean high tide line," Kuchinski said. "And that's right where we're headed."

The improvised snack bought Melissa another ten to fifteen minutes. When it had run its course, she grabbed a dish cloth and began wiping sticky fruit drippings from the counter.

"Skip it," Leopold said. "Back to the front room. We still have some time to kill, and what I have in mind will only take about seven minutes."

Melissa's belly churned with revulsion, but she managed to keep the disgust off her face. She walked back into the main room and over toward the fireplace. She turned to face him. Whatever he did here he'd do with his back to the door and windows. He took the pistol out of his belt with his right hand and spread both arms away from his body in a gesture of grotesque invitation. His posture left no doubt about either what he wanted or what was going to happen if Melissa didn't provide it. *Stall or force the issue now?* For a terrible moment she thought she was going to vomit, but the nausea passed.

"Do you know why there's no such thing as rape?" Leopold asked.

"No."

"Because a girl can run faster with her skirt up than a boy can with his pants down. Zipper only. Get to work."

Stall. If I can kill a man to save my own life, I can do this to try to save someone else's.

She stepped forward and knelt down submissively in front of him. She glanced up at the pistol, well out of her reach but in perfect position to club her if she tried anything.

She was raising her hands to his belt buckle and zipper when it finally happened. The accumulated drain of lights, computer, stove, and open refrigerator finally consumed the last drop of gasoline in the generator. It coughed to a sputtering halt. The lights went out.

With a startled obscenity, Leopold snapped his head around, momentarily disoriented. Melissa rocked her head back and slammed it as hard as she could against his groin—well, approximately his groin—as if she were trying to head a soccer ball into the net from ten feet out. Leopold reflexively doubled over, bringing both arms down to cross defensively in front of him. With desperate ferocity Melissa sank her teeth into his right hand.

Leopold howled and his gun clattered to the rough-hewn floor. Melissa grabbed it. An enraged Leopold viciously backhanded her cheek with his right hand, which sent her sprawling toward the window. Raising herself as much as she could, Melissa hurled the gun through the window with all the limited strength her awkward position allowed. It shattered the lowest pane and disappeared outside.

"Nguyen, look out!" Melissa yelled at the blank whiteness that was all she could see. "He might have another gun!"

Leopold froze in an instant of terrible revelation. His guts had gone through the window with his gun. He could run out and get it in seconds, or he could stay here and beat Melissa silly, but Melissa's warning made him think he might be facing Nguyen either way. He'd had all he could do to overcome Nguyen this morning, with the advantage of surprise. He had no stomach for a rematch.

Leopold's face transformed in an eye-blink into a mask of fear and panic. Melissa rolled to her feet and headed for the front door. He could have caught her easily if he'd leaped at her at that moment, but he hesitated in desperate uncertainty. As Melissa slipped outside, Leopold began blundering toward the rear of the cabin.

Melissa found the gun in the snow just outside the window and picked it up with quiet conviction. No agony of doubt gnawed at her now. Technical incompetence might keep her from killing Roger Leopold in the next five minutes, but moral qualms certainly wouldn't.

When Kuchinski had all four of the Escalade's tires on the ice he gunned it again. The ice held. Rep felt the chain-girded tires bite into the surface as the Escalade lurched forward. Fifty feet out and moving steadily, Rep held his breath, waiting for a sharp CRACK! that would mean his life had entered its last ninety seconds. It didn't come. They rolled along, one heart-stopping tenth-of-a-mile after the other. The opposite shore and the cabin drew closer, steadily but with maddening slowness.

"What's that?" Kuchinski asked when they were still a good hundred yards away. He pointed at a figure scurrying down the cabin's sloping back yard, toward its dock.

"Stop him!" a piercing contralto yelled. Rep saw Melissa with a gun, standing in back of the cabin. "That's Leopold! Don't let him get away!"

Holding Leopold's gun with both hands, Melissa pointed it at the fleeing figure and squeezed the trigger. In many of the mysteries she had to read Melissa ran across plucky heroines whose boyfriends or brothers or fathers were ex-FBI agents or cops who'd dragged them to the range for firearms training. Melissa had nothing so convenient in her background. Hitting a moving target some eighty feet away going downhill in fading light would have been a good shot even for a trained marksman, and it would have been pure luck for her. She heard the bullet *ping!* off the chain holding the tarpaulined sailboat above the dock. She had missed by at least eight feet.

That's just ridiculous, Melissa thought disgustedly. *MAHATMA GANDHI could have made a better shot than that.*

Leopold reached the dock, clearly headed for the snowmobile stowed under it. It would take the Escalade at least another twenty seconds to get there. By that time, Leopold figured to have the snowmobile started and away, and they'd never catch him. Maybe the police would, but maybe not. Maybe he'd still be out there, a lingering threat.

"This crate won't go any faster on the ice," Kuchinski said, "but I've got something that will."

He slammed on the brakes. The Escalade skidded to a stop five seconds later. Kuchinski leaped out with his Wetherby, knelt on the ice, and shouldered the rifle. Rep jumped out on his side, with Kuchinski's Winchester.

Nguyen, leaning out the front passenger side window, had already fired a shot that ricocheted off the ice two feet from Leopold as Leopold ducked under the dock and hopped on the snowmobile buried deep in the dock's overhanging shadow and partially shielded by its pilings.

"Stop or we'll shoot!" Rep yelled across the ice.

"Congratulations on complying with the Geneva Convention," Kuchinski barked. "Why don't you read him his *Miranda* rights while you're at it?"

His first shot coincided with the last syllable. It splintered a piling.

Leopold jumped on the snowmobile. Rep fired. Worked the bolt. Fired again. Both bullets pocked the dock's facing, well above where Leopold had to be. They could barely see Leopold in the flitting shadows under the dock. They had a glimpse of the snowmobile's nose cone, but no more than that. The only thing clearly visible near the dock was the chain suspending the sailboat above it. The rays of the setting sun glinted brilliantly off the chain's metal, emphasized by the sailboat, which had begun spinning lazily when Melissa's first shot grazed the chain.

The engine on the snowmobile caught, then sputtered.

The top of the dock now hid Leopold completely from Melissa. She swore in frustration. The glimmering chain and spinning boat caught her attention.

What the hell. I hit it by accident, maybe I can hit it on purpose.

Melissa squeezed off two quick shots at the chain. She didn't come close. Nguyen, however, saw what she was doing.

"The chain!" he yelled. "Aim for the chain!"

Desperately, Leopold jumped up and down on the snowmobile's seat, putting all the weight of his body behind the effort to start it.

Nguyen fed a cartridge by hand into the M-14's chamber and closed the bolt. Kuchinski swung the Wetherby up and tried to put the scope's crosshairs on the chain. Rep took a deep breath and pulled his muzzle up as well, willing his shivering hands to steadiness as the bead at the end of the rifle barrel jumped maddeningly to one side of the chain and then the other.

The snowmobile engine caught and revved.

Rep, Kuchinski, and Nguyen fired at almost the same instant. They never found out how many of their bullets hit the chain, but at least one of them did. As the snowmobile engine sent a sustained roar echoing across the lake, the chain snapped and the sailboat fell, smashing through the top of the dock and sending splintering wood and fiberglass onto Leopold and the snowmobile.

"Hit the deck!" Kuchinski yelled. "Kiss that ice like it had tits!"

For two terrible seconds, as Rep, Nguyen, and Kuchinski flattened themselves and Melissa recoiled against the cabin wall, plumes of black smoke billowed from under the ruined dock. Then a thudding explosion split the twilight stillness and a bright orange fireball flecked with black burst upward. They watched in awed silence as the fire burned itself out on the ice.

Epilogue

December 2005
Milwaukee, Wisconsin

Rep didn't have much time. A Realtor in Indianapolis, where the Pennyworths' home was up for sale, needed a call back urgently. Then Rep had to get on the road to drive across the state and confer with Simeon David, who wanted to know about minimizing the risks of ever being involved in trademark litigation again.

Even so, he took half-a-minute to review the few boxed lines on page seven of section B of the *Indianapolis Star Tribune* that Melissa had just brought by his office:

```
IN MEMORIAM

To the memory of Vance Hayes, Esq., who
deserved well of his country. MacBeth,
I, iv, 6-10
```

He passed the folded paper back to Melissa.

"Do you think Gael will look up the reference?" he asked.

"She'll know it without looking it up. '…nothing in his life became him like the leaving it.' She'll get it, all right."

"It's not much."

"I guess not. They say there's no sense putting lipstick on a pig. But sometimes that's the best you can do."

To receive a free catalog of Poisoned Pen Press titles, please contact us in one of the following ways:

Phone: 1-800-421-3976
Facsimile: 1-480-949-1707
Email: info@poisonedpenpress.com
Website: www.poisonedpenpress.com

Poisoned Pen Press
6962 E. First Ave. Ste. 103
Scottsdale, AZ 85251